"You're a r

It was cute to see him blush. "I'm glad y...
Look, I don't suppose—"

Just then the office aide tapped Carli on the shoulder and pointed to the phone. "Sorry to interrupt, but you have a call, Carli."

"Oops, sorry, Shay. Looks like I'm needed. You were saying?"

"It can wait. Besides, I've taken up enough of your time."

"If you do get a dog, tell Luca I'll want to hear all about it."

"I will. Thanks again for helping me."

Then he left, leaving her staring at his back and wishing she knew what he'd been about to ask her before they were interrupted. Maybe it was for the best that she didn't, though, considering he'd already made it clear that he needed to focus all of his attention on Luca. Even so, it was really tempting to chase after him to see what he'd wanted to know.

Dear Reader,

I am so excited to be sharing another story in my Heroes of Dunbar Mountain series. I love the characters who live in Dunbar and am so grateful for another opportunity to hang out with them again. Both Shay and Carli have appeared briefly in the earlier books in the series.

Evidently neither of them liked that they'd been relegated to the role of being a secondary character, because they each insisted they deserved a story of their own. Carli Walsh originally appeared in the first book, *The Lawman's Promise*. She was the last one of the casserole brigade to try to catch Cade Peters's attention with a hot cooked meal. Sadly, that didn't go well for her. She played a much bigger role in the third book, *Second Chance Deputy*, where she was Moira's best friend and confidante as Moira dealt with her unexpected feelings about Titus Kondrat.

It was through them that Carli met Shay Barnaby, owner of the tavern in Dunbar. There was just a hint of an unexpected spark between the two of them at that first meeting. I hope you enjoy watching that small spark grow ever stronger as they overcome all of the obstacles that life (and me) throws in their way.

Happy reading!

Alexis

THE UNEXPECTED FAMILY MAN

ALEXIS MORGAN

Recycling programs for this product may not exist in your area.

ISBN-13: 978-1-335-05141-7

The Unexpected Family Man

For questions and comments about the quality of this book, please contact us at CustomerService@Harlequin.com.

Harlequin Enterprises ULC
22 Adelaide St. West, 41st Floor
Toronto, Ontario M5H 4E3, Canada
www.Harlequin.com

Printed in Lithuania

USA TODAY bestselling author **Alexis Morgan** has always loved reading and now spends her days creating worlds filled with strong heroes and gutsy heroines. She is the author of over fifty novels, novellas and short stories that span a wide variety of genres: American West historicals; paranormal and fantasy romances; cozy mysteries; and contemporary romances. More information about her books can be found on her website, alexismorgan.com.

Books by Alexis Morgan

Harlequin Heartwarming

Heroes of Dunbar Mountain

The Lawman's Promise
To Trust a Hero
Second Chance Deputy

Love Inspired Suspense

A Lethal Truth

Love Inspired The Protectors

The Reluctant Guardian

Visit the Author Profile page
at Harlequin.com for more titles.

I would like to dedicate this book to Liz, my longtime friend and fellow writer. I'm not sure at this point that either of us had even finished our first manuscripts when we originally met all those years ago. Certainly neither of us had sold a book at that point. I'll be forever grateful for Liz's support, all the laughter we've shared and her amazing friendship.

CHAPTER ONE

"WHAT DO YOU mean Shay Barnaby hasn't called you? I heard him promise he would at our wedding. That was over two weeks ago."

While Carli Walsh appreciated her best friend's anger on her behalf, she really wished Moira would keep her voice down. The two of them were sitting in the middle of the only café in town, which meant it was packed even at this early hour. And while Carli was disappointed that she hadn't heard from Shay, she'd just as soon not risk having someone overhear their conversation. The last thing Carli wanted was for Shay to learn that she'd been foolish enough to take him at his word.

After all, she had firsthand experience in how duplicitous a man could be and should've known better. Granted, failing to call was pretty minor—especially compared to when she'd learned her now ex-husband had already had a baby on the way before he divorced her to marry her replacement.

Struggling to sound calmer than she felt, Carli mustered up a small smile to reassure her companion. "Seriously, it's no big deal, Moira."

Her friend snorted in disbelief. Sadly, Moira was the one person who could read Carli like a book. The two of them had grown up together there in Dunbar, Washington, a small town tucked in close to the snowcapped Cascade Mountains. They had been best friends from the beginning. In good times and bad, they'd always had each other's backs. If Carli wasn't careful, Moira Fraser-Kondrat would personally hunt down Shay Barnaby and rip into him but good for leaving Carli hanging.

It was definitely time to change the subject, so she pointed at the shiny badge pinned to her friend's police uniform shirt. "I see they've already updated your name tag."

Moira glanced down and grinned. "Yeah, Chief Peters gave it to me. He and Shelby dropped by the house last night with pizza and a six-pack to welcome us back from our honeymoon."

"That was nice of them."

It was hard not to be a teensy-weensy bit jealous of her friend's happiness, but Carli knew that Moira and Titus had waited ten long years to find their happily-ever-after together. It had surprised almost everyone in town when by-the-book Officer Moira Fraser had suddenly married Titus Kondrat, the tattooed mystery man who owned the café.

Speaking of whom, he was headed their way. Titus tugged on his wife's ponytail, gave her a quick kiss and then asked, "Well, ladies, is there anything else I can get you?"

Carli shook her head as she looked at the time. "Just my check. I need to get to work."

Titus waved her off. "Breakfast is on me today."

She didn't even try to protest as she picked up her purse and prepared to leave. "Thanks, Titus."

Turning to her friend, she added, "I'll talk to you later."

Moira stood up as well. "I'll walk out with you. I'm not officially on duty for another hour, but I'm going in early to get caught up on a few things before I leave on patrol."

Titus looped his arm around Moira's shoulders as the three of them made their way through the crowded café toward the door. Carli kept her fingers crossed that Moira wouldn't bring up Shay's name before she could make her escape, but no such luck.

Moira gave Carli a sly look before turning her attention to her husband. "Any chance you've talked to Shay since we got back?"

Carli cringed while she waited for Titus to answer. It was no surprise that he seemed a bit confused by his wife's sudden interest in the other man. "Nope, I haven't. I've spent most of my time getting caught up on stuff here at the café."

As Titus spoke, he flexed his fists and gave Carli a questioning look. "Why? Does he need a talking-to?"

There was a time when Titus's mere presence had made Carli nervous. But ever since he and Moira had reconnected, he was a different man—one who smiled a lot more often. Knowing how close she and Moira were, he'd started treating Carli like family. She kind of enjoyed their new and improved connection, but that didn't mean she wanted him poking his nose in her personal business. Besides, she didn't want to put Titus in the awkward position of having to call out his friend over a nonexistent relationship between Shay and Carli.

When Moira started to answer, Carli held up her hand to cut her off. "No, he doesn't. Everything is fine."

Then she hugged her friend to let her know that everything was good between them. "I missed you. I'm glad you're back, but now I really have to go."

Carli had no doubt that Moira would eventually fill her new husband in on the situation, but she really hoped that would be the end of it. After all, she'd only met Shay once before the two of them had gotten caught up in the hubbub surrounding Moira and Titus's wedding. She'd been the maid of honor while Shay had offered the use of the banquet room in the basement of his bar for their reception. Since Titus's best man was married, Shay had somehow unofficially become Carli's escort for much of the event. They'd had a good time…or so she'd thought. He'd even driven her home afterward and walked her to her door like the Southern gentleman that he was.

Maybe it had been the wine they'd had or the slow dance they'd shared at the end of the reception, but kissing Shay good-night had been the perfect way to end the evening. He'd promised to call her and then walked away.

But her phone had remained stubbornly silent in the days since that night, a strong indication that she'd misread the situation. Disappointing, but it was what it was. If she ran into him again, she'd be polite but distant. Make that *when* she ran into Shay again. Living in a town of just over six hundred people meant it was impossible to avoid anyone forever, especially when they had friends in common.

For now, she needed to get to the local elementary school where she worked in the main office as the chief administrative assistant. Once the kids started arriving, things often got pretty hectic. Yeah, she had more to worry about than why the only man she'd been attracted to in ages couldn't be bothered to make good on his promise to call.

"HOW ARE YOU doing over there?"

Shay's question was met with complete silence, which was pretty much the status quo these days. One look at his small companion's grim expression had Shay considering if he should give in to the temptation to turn around and go back home. Waiting another day or even another week probably wouldn't mean much in the grand scheme of things. Right?

No, Shay's conscience wouldn't let him take the easy way out. Life had taught him that putting things off just because they were difficult or scary never made them any easier to deal with. The longer he delayed enrolling Luca in first grade, the harder it would be on the boy.

"Listen, kiddo, I know starting at a new school is a big deal, but I'll do everything I can to make sure it goes smoothly for you. I'm sure they're used to helping new students figure things out."

At least this time Luca briefly looked at Shay from the passenger seat, his dark eyes full of sadness and more than a touch of fear. "I don't want a new school. I wanna go home."

His words hurt Shay's heart. They both knew there was no going back home for Luca. Not since a deer had run out in front of his parents' car during a rainstorm. The resulting collision with a tree had turned their young son into an orphan. If that hadn't been traumatic enough for the boy, he was now eleven hundred miles from everything he'd ever known and living with a total stranger.

Before Luca had been born, his father had served alongside Shay in the Marine Corps. Over the course of multiple deployments, the two men had become closer than most brothers, which was why Luca's parents had named Shay as the boy's legal guardian. Neither Kevin nor his wife had any family, both having grown up in the foster system. Shay understood why they wouldn't risk having the same thing happen to their son.

Now the unimaginable had come to pass, and Shay wasn't sure who was more bewildered by the sudden change in their circumstances—him or Luca. The only thing Shay knew for sure was that parenting a grieving child wasn't for the faint of heart. The bottom line was that he knew his duty and would see it done. He owed that much to Kevin, who'd had Shay's back on too many occasions to count.

Right now, that duty meant doing his best to offer what comfort he could to a heartbroken six-year-old. "I know you would like to go back to your old school, Luca, but your home is now here in Dunbar with me. It's probably hard to believe, but I know you'll make new friends. And I'll make sure that the school assigns you the nicest teacher they have."

Not that he knew if he'd actually have any say in the matter, so he probably shouldn't make promises he might not be able to keep. He'd give it his best shot, though. Shay needed to do everything possible to smooth the way forward for the boy. Losing his parents, his home, his friends, and his school all at the same time was more than any child should have to deal with.

"Looks like we're here."

Shay slowed his truck down as they cruised past the front of the school to turn into the parking lot. He'd deliberately waited until midmorning to register Luca for his first day at his new school. Hopefully, things would be quieter in the office than it would've been earlier when the buses were still arriving.

He parked in a visitor's spot and stared at the front door of the building for several seconds before making any move to get out. "Luca, I know you don't know me very well—" or really at all "—but I want to do right by you. If there's any way I can make things easier for you, please tell me."

Nothing but silence again. Sighing, Shay got out of the truck and walked around to the other side to open Luca's door for him. "Do you want me to carry your stuff for you?"

"No."

He waited until the boy got his backpack situated before offering to hold his hand. He took it as a positive sign that Luca didn't hesitate to latch onto Shay. "Okay, let's head inside."

It took forever to walk the short distance from the parking lot to the entrance of the single-story brick building. It was almost funny to see how Luca's strides became shorter and shorter with each step he took. Seriously, the only way they could make less progress toward reaching their goal would be if they took an occasional step backward. Despite Luca's best efforts to delay the inevitable, they finally reached the entrance, where a security officer was standing guard.

When he spotted Shay, he stepped forward. "Can I help you, sir?"

"I'm here to register a new student."

The man smiled down at Luca. "Welcome to our school, young man."

Turning his attention back to Shay, he said, "You need to go straight to the main office. It's the first door on the left. Someone there will be able to help you."

"Thanks."

Shay led Luca inside, where they both stopped to look around. Each of them drew a calming breath before crossing the threshold into the office. As it turned out, that was a good thing, considering who was waiting at the counter to greet them. All it took was one glimpse of Carli Walsh for the air to rush out of Shay's lungs and leave him frozen just inside the doorway.

He hadn't seen Carli since the night he'd driven her home from Titus's wedding. That didn't mean he'd forgotten about her or the embrace they'd shared that night. It had felt so good to hold her soft curves close, tangling his fingers in her long dark hair as they kissed. In fact, he'd closed his eyes and relived their embrace whenever he had a few seconds to call his own, losing himself in the sweet memory. Those were the only moments of peace he'd had since the call had come in from Child Protective Services in California, changing his life forever.

He should've called her, but it had never seemed to be the right moment. Less than an hour after he'd dropped Carli off, he'd already been tearing down the interstate to the airport to catch a flight to Los Angeles. Once there, he'd operated on caffeine and adrenaline while he dealt with all of the legal issues involved in taking custody of his friends' son. Then there'd been the funeral, followed by packing up the apartment, and then signing what felt like a lifetime's worth of legal documents.

"Mr. Barnaby, can I help you?"

He blinked, trying to regain control of the confused thoughts ripping through his mind. From the look on Carli's face, she'd already asked the question at least once before. And why wasn't she using his first name? She hadn't called him Mr. Barnaby since the first time they'd met a couple of months back at his bar. Obviously they'd taken a step backward in their relationship, no doubt because he'd broken his promise to call her. Hopefully, she'd cut him some slack once he explained the situation.

He nudged Luca a little closer to the counter. "Luca, this is my friend, Ms. Walsh."

At least he hoped they were still friends. Figuring that remained to be seen, he finished making introductions. "Carli, I'd like you to meet Luca Nix. We're here to register him for school."

Carli kicked up her smile several notches for the boy. "It's nice to meet you, Luca. Welcome to Dunbar Elementary School. May I ask how old you are and what grade you're in?"

Luca had positioned himself slightly behind Shay, probably to avoid drawing any attention to himself. That's what he'd been doing every time he and Shay had had to meet with someone over the past couple of weeks, but even he was drawn to the warmth in Carli's voice and smile. He moved up to lean into Shay's side before answering her question. "First grade, and I'm almost seven."

She beamed at him as if he'd made her entire day. "Thank you, Luca. Now that you've given me all the important information, why don't you come around the counter and have a seat at that table in the corner? You'll find coloring sheets and crayons in the blue box. I think we have pictures of dinosaurs and maybe some fighter jets. Help yourself while Mr. Barnaby and I work on a bunch of boring paperwork."

Luca sidled around the end of the counter and headed for the table. He dropped his backpack on the floor and climbed up into the chair. In short order, he was hard at work coloring a stegosaurus. Shay couldn't help but smile. That had been his own favorite dinosaur back in the day. It was probably too much to hope that he could join Luca at the table and color a picture of his own. Sadly, one of them had to be the grown-up in their relationship. That job had fallen to Shay, no matter how unqualified he was for the position.

Finally, he set the folder of paperwork he'd brought with him on the counter. "I hope this has everything in it that we'll need to get him registered."

Carli clearly had questions, but for the moment she held back on asking them. He appreciated that. He wasn't much for sharing his private business with just anyone, and there was a steady stream of people passing through the office. Perhaps sensing his discomfort, Carli pointed toward a nearby door. "Come on around the counter, and we'll go in the conference room to work. It's more private, but you'll still be able to keep an eye on Luca."

He did as she suggested. Once they were seated across from each other at a small table, Shay figured he should explain the situation. The trouble was deciding where to start. "You know that I was in the marines up until a couple of years ago when my uncle passed away. My aunt needed me to take over the bar, so I moved back here to Dunbar as soon as my enlistment was up."

Realizing he was talking a mile a minute, he made a conscious effort to slow down the flood of information. "For most of the time I was in the Corps, I served with a guy named Kevin Nix. The two of us hit it off from the moment we met in basic training. We went through a lot of tough situations together over the years."

He raked his fingers through his hair in frustration. "But nothing like this."

They'd looked death in the eye more times than he could count, but they'd both made it back home relatively unscathed. That's what made it so hard to get his head around the idea that Kevin would lose his life so soon after leaving the military behind. A world without Kevin Nix in it was wrong on so many levels.

Hoping his eyes weren't filling up with tears again, Shay stared at a blank space on the wall. "Anyway, I got a call about half an hour after I dropped you off after the wedding. It was from a caseworker at CPS in Southern California telling me Kevin and his wife, Marlee, had been killed in an accident. She was pronounced at the scene. He made it to the hospital but died not long after. Since neither of them had any close family, Kevin and his wife had named me as the boy's guardian in their will right after he was born. Until the call came that night, I didn't know they'd done that."

Shay struggled to tamp down the stab of pain that threatened to overwhelm him as he remembered hearing the news of his friend's death. It had nearly knocked him to his knees. The caseworker had kept rattling on about all the legal details even though Shay understood only a fraction of what she was saying. He'd finally asked her to start over at the beginning. Hearing the news a second time did little to soften the blow, but at least he'd been able to start formulating a plan of action. Now he needed to get back to explaining the situation to Carli.

"A friend of Marlee's was babysitting Luca that night while they went out to celebrate their wedding anniversary. At least she was able to stay with Luca until I could get there. Otherwise, he would've been fostered with some stranger."

Not that Luca actually knew Shay all that well. Realizing he was rambling on and on, he tried to focus on the matter at hand. "Sorry, that's probably more than you needed to hear. It's all knocked me a bit sideways."

Carli met his gaze, her soft gray eyes filled with sympathy. "I'm so sorry, Shay. This must all be so hard for both you and Luca. At least his parents had the good sense to make their wishes clear. It says a lot about you that your friend trusted you with his son's welfare. You should be honored."

Shay didn't feel honored. Instead he felt overwhelmed, not to mention seriously underqualified for the job. His previous record when it came to riding herd on a kid hadn't gone well, but now wasn't the time to relive that disastrous time in his life. Doing his best to ignore those painful memories, he continued his explanation. "We finally flew back up here three days ago. Things are understandably still pretty unsettled, especially for Luca. Having said that, he's already missed two weeks of classes. I thought if I got him back into school, it might help him start settling into a routine."

"Well, let me show you what paperwork needs to be filled out. While you work on that, I can walk Luca down the hall and introduce him to his teacher and show him around the building. After we finish the tour, we can go over what comes next."

Shay stifled the urge to sigh when he got a look at all of the forms in his immediate future. "I'd appreciate anything you can do to help the kid, Carli. He could use a friend about now."

So could Shay, for that matter. He kept that fact to himself, though. No one liked a whiner, and he very much wanted Carli Walsh to like him. The truth was, he'd even hoped that eventually they could explore the possibility of being more than simply friends. However, right now it was all he could do to get through the day taking care of Luca. Then there was the bar and everything that entailed.

Meanwhile, Carli had quickly shuffled through the paperwork, marking everything that he needed to fill out. After pushing the stack across the table to Shay, she stood up. "Set aside anything you have questions about, and I'll help you figure it out when we get back."

Shay watched as she approached Luca. The two of them talked briefly while she admired his artwork. After putting the coloring sheet in his backpack, the boy took Carli's hand. At least he looked to Shay for approval before trudging out of the office at Carli's side. It was hard not to go charging after them, to throw himself between Luca and anything that might upset the boy. Not that it would do any good. There was no way to protect his adopted son from all of the scary things in life.

Besides, Luca had already lost his parents, his home and life as he'd known it. Meeting a new teacher and some kids couldn't hold a candle to all of that.

Finally, Shay picked a form at random from the pile in front of him and started filling in a whole bunch of empty spaces. Too bad the holes inside of him couldn't be filled in just as easily.

CHAPTER TWO

IT TOOK A little while, but Luca had gradually gone from totally silent to asking a few questions as Carli showed him around the school. They'd visited the gym, the cafeteria, the library, and even the playground so he could check out the new climber that had been installed a few weeks earlier. Their final stop was the first grade class to meet his new teacher, Ms. Varne. Carli thought it would be a good placement for Luca. Paige Varne was warm and really patient with her young charges. She'd even managed to coax a shy smile from Luca, a promising start to their relationship.

Finally, Carli let her get back to her class, telling Ms. Varne she'd have Luca's records ready for her by the end of the day. At least she hoped that Shay would have managed to wade through the stack of paperwork she'd given him.

"Do you have any questions for me, Luca? Or anything else you'd like to see before we return to the office?"

He looked up and down the long hallway. "No."

"Okay, let's head back and see how Mr. Barnaby is doing on the homework I gave him."

They walked in silence the rest of the way back to the office, but at least Luca grinned a little at the idea of a grown-up doing homework. As they approached the door, she asked, "Mr. Barnaby and I need to finish up a few more things. Would you like a juice box to drink while you wait?"

"I like grape."

"That's my favorite, too." She smiled down at him. "I think I have some left. Otherwise it might have to be apple. Would that be okay?"

Luca smiled back at her. "Yeah."

"Perfect."

It was nice to see the little guy looking happy about something. For most of their time together, he'd acted pretty subdued, barely responding when she'd introduced him to the school librarian and the PE teacher. No doubt it was all a bit overwhelming to a child whose whole life had veered off course so recently.

When they reached the office, Shay was still working on his paperwork. She got Luca the promised juice box and let him choose another dinosaur picture to color. When he was settled, she picked up a folder of information that she'd put together for families who were new to the area. When she joined Shay at the table, he was just signing his name at the bottom of the last form. He dropped the pen on the table and sat back with a sigh.

He frowned when he spotted the folder in her hand. "I'm begging you—please tell me that's not another bunch of papers for me to fill out."

She grinned as she slid the folder across the table to him. "Nope, it's not. It's a bunch of information that people new to Dunbar and the surrounding area often find helpful. I know you've lived here for a while, but I figure you might need some of the info anyway. Stuff like the closest pediatricians, pediatric dentists, sports teams for kids and local day cares."

"That will be a big help." Shay let out a slow breath. "I'm going to need all of those things, especially the day care part. Do you know if any of them are open evenings?"

She winced. "Sorry, I didn't even think about that. I'm not sure how late they're open."

He picked up the folder and browsed through it. "I'll read all of this when we get back home."

After nodding in Luca's direction, he gave Carli a resigned look. "I'm guessing he's not going to start school today."

"It's better for everyone if new students start the day after they register. That gives their new teacher a chance to prepare for a new pupil. Luca did get to meet Ms. Varne on our tour, so he knows where his class is. By tomorrow morning, she'll have his desk set up along with all of the books and things he'll need. That folder I just gave you also has the list of school supplies Luca should have. They're all available at the drugstore here in town."

"Thanks for everything, Carli. I can't tell you what a relief it was to see a familiar face when I walked in here this morning."

"If you have any questions, call me. You've got my number."

When he grimaced, she realized that had sounded as if she were reminding him that he'd asked for her number at the wedding reception. To clarify, she pointed to the school's contact information printed on the front of the folder she'd given him. "I'm usually the one who answers the school's main phone number. If I'm not available for some reason, anyone who works here in the office should be able to help you. If not, they'll take a message, and I'll get back to you. The principal's direct number is on there, too. I would introduce you to her, but she's at the district office for a meeting this morning."

Evidently her attempt to clarify that she'd been talking about her work number had failed, because Shay was looking pretty guilty at the moment. "Look, I'm sorry I didn't call like I promised. Like I said, I flew out of SeaTac later that night. The past two weeks have been surreal. It took forever to pack up the family's apartment while trying to decide what Luca might want someday and what to get rid of. I probably kept more than I should have, but I figured I'd err on the side of caution. No idea where I'll store everything, but I have a little time before it all lands on my doorstep. Seriously, I couldn't believe all the legal stuff we had to wade through."

He latched onto the edge of the table as if he needed to hold on to something to keep himself centered. "Then there was the funeral. They did a full-on military service with everything that involves."

It was so tempting to reach across the table to hold Shay's hand, but that would be unprofessional. If anyone saw them, it would raise all kinds of questions she didn't want to have to answer.

Before Carli could think of anything to say that might ease some of his pain, he lurched to his feet. "Well, we should get going. I need to pick up those school supplies you mentioned and then feed Luca some lunch. My aunt is coming over later this afternoon to stay with him while I go to work."

He paused and shook his head. "Sorry—you

didn't need to know my itinerary for the rest of the day. We've taken enough of your time."

"It's no problem."

No wonder Shay looked tired. It sounded as if he'd been moving at a dead run for the past two weeks. While she gathered up the paperwork he'd completed, he headed over to where Luca sat waiting. "Come on, kid. We've got crayons and other stuff to buy before you start school tomorrow. After that, we'll have lunch at the diner in town where you'll get to meet a friend of mine named Titus. He makes really good burgers and fries, not to mention the best pie in town. How's that for a plan?"

Luca looked marginally happier. "I like pie." Then he picked up his coloring sheet and brought it over to Carli. "This one is for you."

She ruffled his hair as she admired his artwork. "Thank you, Luca. I think I'll take this one home and hang it on my refrigerator. All those great colors you chose will brighten up my kitchen. Would that be okay?"

He nodded and then headed for the door. Shay followed him, stopping to look back at her. "Goodbye, Carli."

Maybe she was imagining things, but she thought there was a depressing note of finality laced through those two words. It was as if he wasn't simply saying goodbye to her for the moment, but for the long term. All things considered, she couldn't really say she was surprised. Luca wasn't the only one whose reality had been turned inside out and upside down. Shay was struggling to come to terms with the changes in his own life, not just Luca's. She knew he wasn't the kind of man who would shirk his responsibilities, no matter the cost to himself. His complete focus had to be on creating a stable home for his young charge here in Dunbar.

Carli nodded to show the message was received and understood. "Take care, Shay. And like I said, let me know if there's anything the school can do to help."

He offered her a sad excuse for a smile, and then he was gone.

AS SHAY SETTLED in at a table in the back corner at the café, he found himself rubbing his chest again. It had become a habit ever since a jagged ball of grief mixed with fear had taken up residence right next to his heart over two weeks ago. Nothing he'd done so far had eased the ache in the least. It was also a sad state of affairs when nothing on the menu sounded good. Considering the quality of food that Titus Kondrat produced, that was a real shame.

Hopefully, his companion was having better luck. "What sounds good today?"

Luca shrugged and reached for the cup of crayons that came with the children's menu. If all else failed, Shay would order for him, but he'd rather let Luca make his own decisions whenever possible. There was little enough the poor kid had control over these days. Shay leaned across the table to get a better look at the kid-friendly offerings before Luca colored all over the list. Pointing at the paper, he said, "Looks like you can have a cheeseburger, a hot dog, chicken fingers, or macaroni and cheese."

Before Luca could answer, someone walked up to their table. Luca's eyes opened wide as he got his first look at their host. Titus smiled down at him as Shay performed the necessary introductions. "Luca, this is Mr. Kondrat. He owns this café. Titus, this is Luca Nix. He lives with me now."

Luca's chin quivered. "My mom and dad got killed."

Titus winced. "I'm really sorry to hear that, Luca. That's got to be hard for you, but I know Shay will take good care of you."

Then he crouched down to Luca's eye level. After looking around as if to make sure no one else was listening, Titus whispered, "It's not on the menu, but I could also make you a grilled cheese sandwich. It comes with your choice of sweet potato fries, regular fries or applesauce.

Dessert is included, but you don't have to let me know whether you want pie or ice cream right away."

Luca sat up straighter at the mention of dessert. After a second, he whispered, "I want a grilled cheese sandwich. I like fries, but I really like applesauce, too."

"Not a problem." Titus winked at him. "Since it's you, I'll bring both."

Having settled that much, Titus turned his attention to Shay. After studying him for a few seconds, he said, "I'll bring you the Thursday special. As I recall, you've wanted to try my chicken and dumplings for a while now."

"That sounds really good." Then Shay blinked in surprise. "Today is Thursday?"

Titus stood up. "What day did you think it was?"

"To be honest, I'm not sure. The past couple of weeks have been pretty much a blur."

"Well, maybe a good meal will help."

Titus started to turn away and then groaned. "I swear that dog never learns. No matter how many times I tell Ned to stay in the kitchen, he insists on coming out here to greet special customers. Luca, don't let Ned's size worry you. He's well-behaved, especially if he thinks someone might slip him a French fry or two. He also likes small bites of crust from a grilled cheese sandwich."

Meanwhile, the huge dog shoved his way past Titus to sit down next to Luca. After giving the boy's arm a quick lick, he plopped his huge head on Luca's lap. Shay could only sit and stare in wonder as the pair quickly became friends. Luca was sporting a full-blown grin as he ran his fingers through Ned's thick black-and-tan fur, which hinted at the dog's parentage. Shay's best guess was that the dog had the coloring of a German shepherd and the fluffy coat of a golden retriever.

Titus finally pointed at his pet and said, "Okay, dog, you can keep Luca company while I go fix his lunch. Behave yourself."

Considering how happy Luca looked right now, Shay would have to thank Titus later for letting Ned hang out with them. "So, Luca, I'm guessing you must like dogs."

Luca nodded but kept his focus on his furry companion. "Yeah, but Mom said we couldn't have one. She's allergic."

Shay winced, hoping his question hadn't derailed the boy's good mood. "I like dogs, too. My family always had a couple when I was growing up."

Luca glanced at Shay with interest. "Were they big like Ned?"

"A couple were. We also had one little dog who thought he was the boss of everyone. I named him Rex, which means king. That's what he thought he was. Seriously, Rex was about fifty pounds of toughness stuffed into a ten-pound dog." Shay found himself smiling at the memory. "I still miss that little fur ball."

It was clear that Luca was drawing comfort from petting Ned. Maybe getting a dog might give the boy something to concentrate on other than the loss of his parents. Shay and his father had gone through some pretty rough times when Shay had been a kid. Having Rex to share his troubles with back then had been a real godsend.

It was something to consider. Getting a pet on impulse probably wasn't a good idea. However, the more he thought about it, the more it felt right. That didn't mean he would mention it to Luca quite yet. It was probably smarter to wait until the two of them settled into some kind of routine before adding a new member to their small family.

Meanwhile, Titus was headed their way with three plates heaped high with food. "I thought I'd join the two of you for lunch. I hope that's okay."

After distributing the food, he sat down and pointed at Luca. "The one rule here in the café is that you eat your lunch while it's hot. Also, Ned can eat only a couple of your fries."

Then he reached into his jeans pocket and brought out a few small biscuits shaped like paw prints. "These are his favorite treats, and they're better for him than people food. Put one in the palm of your hand and then hold it out for him."

Luca did as Titus suggested and giggled when Ned licked his palm after taking his treat. Then Luca picked up half of his cheese sandwich and dug right in. While Luca was occupied, Shay expected Titus would start asking questions about what was going on. Instead, Titus gave Shay's plate a pointed look. "That rule applies to you, too. Besides, Carli called to tell me what was going on. She knew you were going to bring Luca here for lunch and thought I might appreciate a heads-up. Sorry you and the munchkin are going through such a tough time."

Shay nodded. He knew Carli well enough that she wouldn't broadcast the news all over town, and he appreciated not having to answer a bunch of questions in front of Luca. "We're hanging in there. Mostly, anyway."

"Let us know if there's anything Moira and I can do to help."

"I will."

As he watched Luca dole out another doggy treat, Shay came to a decision he hoped he wouldn't regret. "Where did you get Ned?"

Titus's mouth quirked up in a little grin. "Actually, I have no idea where he came from. He was a stray who started turning up on my doorstep hoping for a handout. It didn't take him long to realize I was a soft touch and decide to take up permanent residence on my couch. Why? Are you thinking a certain someone needs his own four-legged companion?"

"Maybe."

"Let me know when you decide for sure and what preferences you might have. Better yet, ask Ryder Davis. He helps out at more of the no-kill shelters in the area than I do. He'd be glad to ask the people who run them to keep an eye out for a suitable candidate for you. Just let him know what features you want—age, size, gender and breed. Keep in mind, though, most will be a mix like Ned."

Then he arched an eyebrow and pointed at Shay's plate. "Now eat."

Shay grinned and offered Titus a mock salute before digging into his chicken and dumplings. He wasn't sure if it was the food or the company, but for the moment, he felt more centered than he had since his phone had rung two weeks ago.

CHAPTER THREE

IT WAS AFTER midnight when Shay finally got home from the bar. He wasn't surprised to see Aunt Meg watching for him from the front window as he pulled into the driveway. She was probably more than ready to go home and get some sleep. At least she didn't have far to go since her house was located less than a half mile away on the opposite side of the same property. As she'd pointed out more than once since Luca arrived, she didn't have the energy at her age to keep up with a six-year-old boy for long periods of time. Worse yet, from what she'd told him earlier, Luca had cried himself to sleep for a second time that night.

"I'm sorry I had to call you home from work earlier. Nothing I did seemed to help."

It had taken Shay the better part of an hour to calm the boy and get him tucked back into bed. Once he was sure Luca was down for the count, he'd dragged himself back to the bar to finish his shift.

"It must have been one heck of a bad dream. We're all doing our best, Aunt Meg, but there are bound to be hiccups along the way."

Shay wrapped his aunt in his arms, taking as much comfort from the embrace as she did. "I wish there was some magic wand I could wave to make it all better for him, but I guess it's just going to take time. On another note, I called several day cares today. Seems none of them are open this late."

She gave him another quick squeeze before stepping back, her expression serious. "I'm not convinced that would be the best choice for either of you. Not for the long term, anyway. Luca can't possibly stay up this late waiting for you to get off work and still be able to function at school in the morning. Even if he slept at the day care, you'd have to wake him up to bring him home and hope that he could go right back to sleep. And it's not just him I'm worried about. You can't keep burning the candle at both ends like this. I bet you haven't had a full night's sleep since this all started. Eventually you'll crash if you don't slow down."

She wasn't telling Shay anything he didn't already know. It was his problem, and he was doing the best he could to solve it. He just needed time—something that was in short supply these days. Yeah, he felt guilty asking Meg or anyone else to watch over Luca for him, but Shay also had a business to run. Unless he could magically be in two places at once, hiring a babysitter was the next best option. "I'm hoping to find someone local to stay with Luca while I'm at work. If that doesn't pan out, I'll look further afield. I'd hate to hire someone who would have a long commute once winter comes."

That was because Dunbar was located off a state highway that was sometimes closed for days at a time when it snowed. There was also the more immediate problem of paying for everything. After taking over the family bar, Shay had invested a lot of his savings to fix up the place starting with upgrades in the kitchen, plumbing and wiring. He'd also made some changes to the decor, plus there'd been the expense of adding an expanded menu and wine list. All of that had been aimed at attracting more customers. The plan was working, but it would be a while before he'd made back his investment.

There was an attorney in California working on settling Kevin and Marlee's estate with Luca as their sole heir. After much discussion, the attorney suggested that he set up a trust for Luca. Shay would be able to access only up to a certain amount each year for the boy's care without having to get approval from the court. Shay could cover the everyday expenses like food and keeping a roof over their head, but he'd need help with the day care costs for a while.

Aunt Meg bit her lower lip as if she had something she wanted to say but wasn't sure if Shay would want to hear it. "Tell me what you're thinking."

Finally, she nodded. "If you really think that's best for Luca, maybe someone would be interested in taking the job if it included free rent for your cabin. It's close by, so the commute wouldn't be a problem."

Actually, that wasn't a bad idea. Shay and Aunt Meg's late husband had built the cabin back when Shay needed a place to live after his life with his parents and sister had blown up. It had become his safe haven while he finished high school and whenever he came back on leave after joining the marines. It hadn't been until he'd decided not to reenlist that he'd built the house he lived in now.

"Thanks for the suggestion. I'll wait to see what kind of response I get to the ad and then sweeten the pot if I need to."

Meg picked up her purse. "I'd better go. By the way, I have a doctor appointment tomorrow morning. It's just a routine visit, so I should be back in plenty of time to stay with Luca."

Shay walked her out to her car. "Text me when you get home."

Meg laughed at him. "Shay, I've been getting myself home safely for longer than you'vc been alive."

"I worry."

"Save it for Luca, Shay. He's the one you need to look after now."

He grinned and kissed her cheek. "I've got enough room in my heart to worry about both of you."

"You definitely inherited a full dose of your uncle's stubbornness. Instead of worrying about me, you'd be better off finding a nice woman of your own to fuss over. You'd think there would be any number of possibilities right here in Dunbar who are smart enough to recognize what a catch you are."

Carli Walsh's pretty face immediately came to mind, but he couldn't go there. Not right now when it was all he could do to get through the day. Between Luca, managing the bar, and keeping both his customers and his employees happy, he had as much as he could handle. But rather than point that out, Shay kept his smile firmly in place and gave his aunt the same answer he always did when she brought up the subject of his love life—or actually, the lack of one. "I'm holding out for someone like you, Aunt Meg. Sadly, you've set the bar pretty high."

She rolled her eyes as she got into her car. "Go

get some sleep, Shay. You're so tired, you're delusional."

He watched and waited until her taillights disappeared in the night before going back inside and locking the door. He ate a quick snack as he waited to hear Meg had made it home. Ready to be done for the night, he turned off the lights and went down the hall to check on Luca. As usual, the boy had kicked his covers off. Shay pulled them back up and then gave Luca's shoulder a soft squeeze. "Sleep tight, big guy. We'll have to hit the floor running in the morning to get you to school on time."

Luca frowned in his sleep, mumbling something as he snuggled farther down to almost disappear under the covers. Shay grinned in response. Evidently he wasn't the only one who hated getting up early in the morning. He'd had to during his time in the military, but working evenings definitely suited him better. It was one of the many reasons Shay had been happy to take over running the bar.

But for Luca's sake, he'd drag himself out of bed early enough to make sure the boy ate a good breakfast and got to school on time. For the first few days, Shay would drive him and either he or Aunt Meg would pick him up. Once Luca had a chance to get his feet solidly beneath him, hopefully he could start riding the bus to and from school.

For now, it was well past time for Shay to seek out his own bed. He took a quick shower in the hope it would help him to relax enough to fall asleep. When he came out of the bathroom, Luca was waiting for him, his cheeks wet with tears.

"Another bad dream?"

The poor kid nodded as he wiped his dripping nose on the sleeve of his pajamas. Shay put his arms around the boy's shoulders and gathered him in close. "Want to talk about it?"

Luca shook his head and then burrowed into Shay's chest. Rather than stand there, Shay sank to the floor and lifted Luca onto his lap. It nearly killed him to hear the boy's gut-wrenching sobs, but maybe it would be better to let him cry himself out. Stroking the boy's back, he cupped Luca's head with his hand, hoping the physical contact would offer the comfort Luca so badly needed.

When that didn't seem to be enough, Shay started murmuring anything he could think of that might help. "I know all of this is hard, but I've got you, Luca. You're safe here with me."

Luca finally looked up at him, his tear-streaked face radiating nothing but anger. He curled his hand into a fist and pounded on Shay's chest as he screamed, "I want my mom and my dad to be here, not you."

His words stabbed Shay in the heart even though he didn't blame the boy for rejecting him as a substitute for his parents. He gently wrapped his hand around Luca's fist and pressed it against his chest, afraid Luca would hurt himself if he kept striking out at Shay.

"I miss your parents, too, and I really wish they were here with us. Your dad was my best friend—the brother I never had." He closed his eyes, trying to ignore the burn of tears. "I would do anything…anything at all…to change what happened, but that's not possible. All we can do is keep our memories of your parents alive and live every day in a way that would make them proud."

Picturing Kevin in his head, he said, "Your father had the goofiest smile, but he was also the best man I ever knew. The best marine, too, and everyone who served with him knew it. He was the guy we all wanted to be. He was strongest when the times were the hardest, which was a good thing. That's when people need to be able to depend on you the most. I know I'll never be able to replace him or your mom in your heart, and that's the way it should be. They loved you first, and they loved you the best."

He crooked his finger and gently tilted Luca's

face up. "But now I am going to try to be strong for you, Luca. Somehow the two of us need to become a family. It won't be the one you had, but I promise I will be here for you even if I'm only a poor substitute for your parents."

Luca's dark eyes stared up at him for the longest time. "But what if you die like they did?"

Shay wanted to believe the fates would never be so cruel, but stuff happened. "No matter what happens in the future, I will make sure that you will be taken care of just like your parents did. For starters, you can stay with Aunt Meg. She's my family, and that means she's yours as well. There are other adults, like Mr. Titus, who would step up to make sure you're okay."

He ruffled Luca's hair. "So, are we good?"

Luca nodded as the last bit of tension in his body slowly drained away. When he snuggled in close again, Shay wrapped his arms around him and let the silence settle around them. He gave it a couple of minutes to make sure the crisis had passed. Finally, he asked, "Want me to tuck you in bed and sit with you while you go back to sleep, or would you rather bunk in here with me?"

Luca drew a long, sniffly breath. "In here."

Shay gave him a squinty-eyed look. "Okay, but no stealing the covers. And if you snore really loud, all bets are off."

Looking happier now that he didn't have to sleep alone, the little rascal climbed into the bed and tugged the covers up to his neck. It was one more reason that had Shay thinking maybe getting a dog was a good idea. He'd always slept better as a kid with Rex curled up at his feet and another of the dogs sprawled on the rug beside his bed. He'd check in with Ryder tomorrow and go from there.

Happy with his plan, Shay turned over on his side and closed his eyes. A few seconds later, Luca faked a huge snore and then laughed.

So did Shay.

FRIDAY MORNING WAS always busy in the school office. The phone rang almost constantly with parents calling in to say their kids would be absent that day. There was always some virus making the rounds, which accounted for most of the calls. While Carli noted the names, she kept an eye on the people passing by the office. So far, there had been no sign of either Luca or Shay, and the first bell was due to ring in less than ten minutes.

Maybe they'd decided that next Monday would be a better day for Luca to start school. Personally, she thought that would only make it harder for Luca since he'd have all weekend to worry about it. It wasn't her decision to make, and Shay would make the best choice he could for his… ward? Adopted son? She wasn't sure what the right term was. Shay had given her copies of the legal papers, but she'd passed them on to the principal and school counselor to read first.

The phone rang again. As she answered, she finally spotted Shay walking by. There were a lot of people out in the hallway, but he was the kind of man who always stood out in a crowd. She guessed his height at a shade under six feet, and there was no shortage of well-defined muscle in his build. What really drew the eye, though, was his air of confidence and something in the way he moved that said no matter the situation, no matter the problem, he could and would handle it.

When she looked up after adding yet another sick kid's name to her list, Shay shot a quick glance in her direction. Carli felt the impact of those blue eyes, not that she allowed herself to respond other than with the same smile she would have offered any other passing parent. Good thing he was already out of sight when she went to hang up the phone and dropped the receiver on her desk instead of back in its cradle. She met with greater success on her second attempt.

"Did our new student arrive?"

Carli turned to face her boss. "Just now. Shay is walking Luca to his class."

Principal Britt stepped closer. "I finished reading through the boy's file earlier this morning and passed it onto Mr. Grimm. He said he'd wait a few days and then check in with Ms. Varne to see how he's doing in class. He'll also give Mr. Barnaby a call to see if there's anything the school can do to support him as well as Luca."

It didn't surprise Carli that both the principal and the school counselor would immediately step up to bat to help a new student succeed. "I'm sure Shay will appreciate that."

Kendra tilted her head and studied Carli for a second, looking a bit surprised. "So I take it you met Mr. Barnaby before he enrolled Luca here at the school."

That's what Carli got for calling him by his first name. "Actually we have friends in common. Moira Fraser and I grew up together here in Dunbar. Recently I was her maid of honor when she married Titus Kondrat, and the reception was held in the banquet hall under Shay's bar. From what he told me yesterday, he got the call about Luca's parents right after he got home from the wedding."

Her boss cringed. "Boy, that had to be tough for both him and Luca. At least the parents had plans in place. A lot of people don't think that far ahead."

The office door opened just then, and the man in question stepped inside. "Hey, Carli, got time for a quick question?"

"Of course."

She headed for the counter with the principal following right behind her. Before Carli could perform the introductions, her boss handled it herself. "Mr. Barnaby, we were just talking about you. I'm Kendra Britt, the principal here at Dunbar Elementary."

He gave Carli a questioning look as he reached across the counter to shake Kendra's hand. "Nice to meet you."

"The school counselor and I thought we'd wait until next week to check in with both you and Luca to see how he's doing. That said, please don't hesitate to reach out to us or his teacher if you have any questions or concerns."

"I will. This is all pretty new to me." His mouth quirked up in a small grin. "I don't think I've set foot in an elementary school since I was a kid myself."

Kendra smiled back at him. "I doubt it's changed all that much."

Then she checked the time. "Oops, I'm supposed to be observing one of the classes right now. Nice meeting you, and we'll talk soon."

Shay waited until her boss was out the door before speaking again. Looking a little suspicious, he asked, “So the two of you were talking about me.”

There was an odd note in his voice that had her feeling a bit defensive. “Principal Britt wanted to know if you brought Luca today, and I told her I’d just seen the two of you pass by the office. She let me know that she’d read Luca’s file and passed it onto the school counselor. Then she said the same thing that she just told you—that she or Mr. Grimm would touch base with you in a week or so to see how things are going.”

“And?”

“And because I referred to you as Shay rather than Mr. Barnaby, she asked me if I’d known you before you came into register Luca. I told her we had friends in common whose wedding reception had been held in your banquet room. That was all I told her.”

He arched an eyebrow as if doubting that. Seriously, did he think she went around telling everyone she knew that the two of them had spent a good part of the reception dancing together or that she’d kissed him? It was time to get back to business. “So what was your question?”

“I packed Luca a lunch this morning, so he’s good for today. But Ms. Varne said that some parents pay ahead for a few hot lunches in case their kid either forgets or loses his lunch. I thought that sounded like a good idea."

"Not a problem. You can buy as many lunches as you like. They'll be on his account in case he needs them or if he just wants to eat a hot lunch because they're serving something he really likes. We post a calendar every month on the school's website with the daily menus listed so you can plan ahead. Pizza and hot dogs are always popular with the kids."

She set a print copy of the calendar on the counter for Shay to take home. He gave it a quick glance as he reached for his wallet. "Looks like the food choices haven't changed since I was Luca's age. My favorite was always the mac and cheese."

"Mine was the hamburger and Tater Tots."

"Those were good, too." He handed her some cash. "I'll buy him ten lunches to start."

As she made change and wrote out a receipt, he leaned on the counter as if he didn't have the energy to stand erect. It was clear all of this was taking a toll on him. "You look tired."

He shrugged. "I normally don't get home from work until after midnight, so I'm not used to being up this early. I'll adjust to my new schedule eventually."

"Any luck finding a sitter for Luca?"

"That's still on my to-do list. Aunt Meg is willing to fill in for the short term."

When Shay didn't immediately move to leave, Carli asked, "So what do you and Luca have planned for the weekend?"

"I haven't told him, but I'm thinking about getting us a dog. I had one when I was his age, and I thought he might like having a furry friend. I know it will only be one more complication for me to deal with, but it will give him something positive to focus on rather than everything he's lost."

"You're a nice man, Shay Barnaby."

It was cute to see him blush. "I'm glad you think so. Look, I don't suppose—"

Just then the office aide tapped Carli on the shoulder and pointed to the phone. "Sorry to interrupt, but you have a call, Carli. They said it was important."

"Oops, sorry, Shay. Looks like I'm needed. You were saying?"

"It can wait. Besides, I've taken up enough of your time."

She scrambled for something to say. "If you do get a dog, tell Luca I'll want to hear all about it."

"I will." He stepped back from the counter. "Thanks again for helping me."

Then he left, leaving her staring at his back and wishing she knew what he'd been about to ask her before they were interrupted. Maybe it was for the best that she didn't, though, considering he'd already made it clear that he needed to focus all of his attention on Luca. Even so, it was really tempting to chase after him to see what he'd wanted to know.

Telling herself it was better to do the smart thing, she did her job instead. "Hello, this is Ms. Walsh. How can I help you?"

CHAPTER FOUR

LUCA FROWNED BIG-TIME as he climbed up into the truck and buckled in. "Where are we going?"

It wasn't surprising that Luca was feeling a bit crabby. He'd been watching his favorite Saturday morning cartoons when Shay had turned off the television and announced they had somewhere to go. "It's a surprise, but we have to stop by the fire station first."

At the mention of their immediate destination, Luca perked right up. "Can I look at the fire truck while we're there?"

Shay buckled his own seat belt. "The crew might be out on a call, so it could be gone. If so, I promise I'll bring you back another time. I'm a volunteer firefighter, so I can show you all around."

Luca's eyes lit up with interest. "You fight fires for real?"

At least there was one thing about Shay that Luca liked. "Yep, for real. Dunbar isn't big enough to afford its own professional fire department, so some folks here in town volunteer to do the job. I've had to cut back on my shifts lately, but I'm still a member. They know they can call me if they need extra help."

It was one more thing Shay felt guilty about. They'd been short on volunteers even before he'd taken off for California with no warning. He'd hated telling them that he could no longer handle his fair share of shifts, even though they understood why. Maybe eventually he would be able to work something out, but that was a problem for another day.

He pulled up behind the square two-story cinder block building that housed the town's emergency vehicles and parked next to Ryder Davis's white van. Good, he was hoping Ryder would be around and available to talk. Shay led Luca around to the front of the building. Before he could key in the security code, the huge garage door rumbled open, and Ryder stepped outside. "Hi, guys. I thought I heard someone pull up."

Ryder smiled at Luca and held out his hand. "I'm Shay's friend Ryder. And you are?"

After a brief hesitation, Luca put his hand in Ryder's. "Luca."

"Well, Luca, I have a couple of things I need to discuss with your buddy Shay. Mostly boring grown-up stuff. Would you like to check out the fire truck while we talk?"

The boy's face lit up. "Yeah!"

"Okay, come with me. There are a few rules you have to follow, but I know you'll be careful."

He opened the driver's door on the fire truck and let the boy climb up inside. "You can look at everything, but you can't take the truck out for a drive. If an emergency call comes in, I'll need it myself."

Ryder winked at Luca, letting him know he was teasing. Once Luca was busy looking around in the cab of the truck, Shay led Ryder a short distance away where the two of them could still keep an eye on Luca while they talked.

His friend kept his voice low. "Does he know where you're heading next?"

Shay shook his head. "No, I thought it was better to keep it a surprise in case you found out there weren't any good candidates today."

"Smart thinking. I called ahead and asked. As it turns out, your timing is perfect." He held out a small piece of paper containing an address and phone number. "Try this shelter first. They brought in a bunch of dogs from a shelter in another part of the state that had more than they could handle. If one of them is a fit for you and Luca, give me a call and let me know the details. I have beds in several sizes in the back of my van, as well as some chew toys and enough kibble to last you a few days."

That was way more than Shay had expected. "Look, I can buy all of that."

Ryder shrugged. "I call them starter kits, and I provide them to new owners all the time. There's also a gift certificate for a wellness checkup with a local vet. The idea is to let folks take their new family member home without having to rush back out the door to buy a bunch of stuff. The shelter will also provide you with a collar and leash. They're not the best, but they'll do until you can buy something better. Personally, I think most dogs do better with a harness."

"Good to know."

His friend studied him for a few seconds. "How are you doing otherwise? All of this has to be a bit overwhelming for both of you."

Shay watched as Luca turned around to check out the back of the truck's cab. "It hasn't been easy, but we're slowly getting things figured out."

"You do know that he's lucky to have you."

Shay wasn't so sure about that but changed the subject. "Is it okay if I fix myself a cup of coffee to take with me? I made some at home but managed to leave it sitting on the kitchen counter."

"Sure thing. I put on a fresh pot right before you arrived, so it should be ready. I'll keep an eye on Luca while you're gone."

"I'd appreciate it."

Luca was now sitting in the driver's seat with his hands on the wheel pretending to drive the truck while making siren noises. "I'm going to grab a cup of coffee to take with us. Ryder will be right here, though. He'll show you around the rest of the truck while I'm upstairs."

"Okay."

Shay helped Luca climb down out of the cab before heading upstairs to the kitchen on the second floor. He returned a few minutes later to find Luca wearing a child-sized fire helmet, the kind they kept around to give kids who toured the station. He was talking a mile a minute to Ryder, pointing at the various pieces of equipment on the truck and asking questions.

It was nice to see the boy so animated and excited. Hopefully his good mood would continue through their next stop. Shay rapped his knuckles lightly on Luca's plastic helmet. "This looks good on you, kid. Better thank Ryder for showing you around so we can head out. We have one more special place to go today."

Luca smiled at Ryder. "Thank you for my helmet and showing me the engine."

"Anytime, Luca. Next time we drive the truck in a parade, maybe Shay will let you ride with us and throw candy to other kids as we go through town."

Shay hadn't thought that far ahead, but it was

a great idea. "The next parade isn't for a couple of months, but we'll be sure to reserve a spot for you."

Ryder followed them around to where Shay had parked. "I'll be waiting for your call, Shay. Good luck. Ask for Trisha. I told her you'd be stopping by."

"Thanks, I will."

LUCA SAT WITH his red helmet in his lap and stared out of the passenger window. Shay thought about their next stop and decided maybe keeping their destination a complete surprise might not be the best approach. It would also probably be better to lay down some ground rules just in case.

"So, Luca. I've been thinking that maybe we should see about adding a new member to our family."

There was new tension in Luca's body language, and he remained silent with his gaze trained on the horizon. Maybe it was too soon for him to accept Shay as family. Hopefully, that would happen in time. For now, Shay hastened to clarify what he was trying to say.

"Anyway, here's the thing. Ryder helps out at local animal shelters. You know, one of those places where dogs and cats go to stay until they get a new home."

Okay, that got the boy's attention. Shay kept

going. "I've been talking to him about how these things work. Evidently it's really important that both the people looking to adopt a dog and the dog itself have a chance to check each other out. You know, to see if they're a good match."

He slowed to a stop at a red light and glanced at Luca. "Depending on what kind of place the people live in, some dogs might be too big or too small. An active dog needs someone who likes to run and play and can take the dog for long walks. All of these things have to be taken into consideration. What I'm trying to say is if the right dog for us isn't at the shelter today, we'll come back again and again until we find one that will be the perfect fit for us."

Deciding Luca should have some say in this decision, he asked, "So, do you think the two of us can take good care of a dog? You'd have to help, you know. Dogs need lots of pets and cuddles. They need to be brushed. Someone has to check to make sure they have fresh water and get fed on time. We'll also have to find time for those walks I mentioned. This will be a big responsibility for both of us. What do you think?"

He liked that the boy seemed to be giving the matter some serious thought before he finally nodded. "Can he sleep in my room?"

"That's what I was thinking. But just so you

know, we might decide we like a girl dog the best."

"That would be okay."

"Good, because we're here."

Ryder's friend Trisha was waiting for them in the lobby. She handed Shay a clipboard and a pen. "Before we go in back, I need you to fill out some information for me."

Shay made quick work of completing the forms. The only questions he left blank were on what kind of dog they were looking for. He didn't have any particular breeds in mind, just that the dog had to be kid friendly.

He handed back the clipboard. "Luca here has never had a dog, but I grew up always having two or more underfoot. The right kind of purebred would be okay, but a mixed breed would be fine for us. I'd also rather not have a really young puppy."

"We have a variety of candidates that might fit your criteria." Trisha paused to make some notes on her clipboard. "Let's head back to where the kennels are. I'll let the two of you walk through and see if any of our current residents catch your eye." She addressed her next remarks to Luca. "We have a fenced play area outside. If you want to check out a specific candidate, I'll bring the dog out there so you can spend time alone with him or her away from the others. Keep in mind, the dog will need to get to know you, too, so it's best not to rush things. I always recommend sitting on the bench and giving them a chance to come to you. Okay?"

Luca gave her a solemn nod. Having gotten their marching orders, Shay took Luca's hand and led him through the door to see if their new family member was waiting for them.

THE TWO OF them took their time and wandered up and down several aisles, stopping to say hello to each candidate they passed. Shay let Luca walk a little ahead as they turned up the last row. A few seconds later, Luca came to an abrupt halt in front of a pen. Judging from the huge smile on the boy's face, Luca was experiencing love at first sight. That was the good news. The problem was that there were two dogs staring back at Luca, their tails wagging a mile a minute and their eyes bright with interest.

Shay moved up beside Luca to read the description posted on the front of their pen. The pair were brothers and looked like some kind of hunting dog mix. The shelter's best guess was that they were about a year old, making them the right age for what Shay had in mind. They'd been returned to the shelter by their previous owner, who had decided they were too active for him to care for.

A second later, Luca looked up at Shay with a worried expression on his young face. Shay knew what he was going to ask before he even opened his mouth. "Do we have to pick just one?"

Studying the two dogs, Shay knew Luca wasn't the only one who couldn't stand the thought of separating them. "Wait here. I'll go get Trisha. If she says it's okay, we'll go wait in the play area outside and let her bring them out there so we can all get acquainted."

Fifteen minutes later, Shay watched as Luca sat on the ground with the two dogs vying for his attention. Finally, they laid down on either side of him with their heads in his lap. He chattered at them, telling his new best friends all about his room and how they'd all be sleeping together. Surrendering to the inevitable, Shay texted Ryder to let him know they were going to need two of his starter kits.

MONDAY MORNING, the door to the school office slammed open with a bang as a young voice called out, "Ms. Walsh, guess what happened!"

Carli looked up from her computer screen to see who had called her name. As soon as she recognized Luca, she smiled. Something definitely had the little guy all wound up. "Give me a second, and you can tell me all about it."

Carli saved the document she'd been proofreading before joining him at the office counter. While she'd seen Luca smile before, this was the first time she'd seen him this excited. "Whatever it was must be pretty spectacular to have you looking so happy."

"It is. Me and Shay added to our family on Saturday."

Ordinarily, Carli would have corrected his grammar, but she let it slide this time rather than risk dimming the glow of his good mood. Meanwhile, he slid a photo across the counter toward her. It was a picture of him kneeling on the ground with his arms around two dogs. No wonder he was excited.

He pointed at each of the dogs in turn. "The white one with brown ears is Beau. The brown one with white paws is Bruno. They're brothers, and they get to sleep in my room."

All of that came out in one excited breath. Then Luca rose up on his toes and leaned in closer. Keeping his voice low, he whispered, "Mr. Ryder gave us beds for them, but they've slept on mine instead. They needed cuddles 'cause they're still getting used to a new home. You know, just like me."

Then he bit his lip and looked around guiltily. "Don't tell Shay. He said they should get used to sleeping in their own beds."

It was hard not to laugh as she whispered back, "Don't worry. He won't hear it from me."

Besides, she bet Shay probably knew full well where Beau and Bruno were spending their nights. If sharing his bed with his furry family members helped Luca feel more connected to his new situation, Shay would be the last one to complain.

Luca was back to talking at normal volume. "Shay turned off my cartoons on Saturday morning so we could go to the fire station and talk to Mr. Ryder. I got to sit in the fire engine and got my own helmet just like the ones they wear. Afterward, we went to the shelter to meet the dogs waiting for a new home. They had a whole bunch, but I liked Beau and Bruno the best. We were supposed to pick one dog, but we couldn't separate brothers. You know, 'cause they wouldn't like that."

The boy definitely had a tender heart, but she suspected his guardian did as well. Not everyone would've been willing to take on the responsibility of caring for a heartbroken boy and two new dogs all at the same time.

"Well, I'm sure Beau and Bruno are really happy that they get to live with you and Shay. Did you bring the picture to share with your class today?"

He nodded as he picked up the picture. "Yeah,

Ms. Varne says we can always talk about good news."

She glanced at the clock. "Thanks for sharing the photo with me, Luca, but you'd better head down the hall to your class. The bell is about to ring."

He was out of the door like a shot, leaving her grinning. It was nice to see him looking so happy. She was about to return to her desk when the office door opened again. Expecting it to be another student, she turned back around only to find Shay standing there holding up a kid's backpack. "Luca forgot this in his hurry to show you his picture. I was hoping to catch up with him, but a couple of buses were blocking the drive, and it took me a while to park."

She grinned at him. "I'm not surprised he forgot it. He was bouncing with excitement from getting to adopt Beau and Bruno. That was a nice thing to do for him."

Shay looked a little uncomfortable. "I thought having a dog would give him something else to think about…you know, other than everything he's lost."

"I'm sure it will help." She pointed to the backpack. "Would you like me to take it down to him?"

"No, I can run it down to his class if that's okay."

"Sure, go ahead." When he didn't immediately leave, she asked, "Was there something else I could help you with?"

Before he could answer, another parent walked into the office. She ignored Shay as she pushed past him to reach the counter. "Excuse me, but I need to speak to the principal. Now, please."

Shay stiffened, clearly not liking the woman's tone. Carli acknowledged the woman with a small smile. "I'll be right with you, Mrs. Case."

Turning back to Shay, she offered him a bright smile. "Mr. Barnaby, Ms. Varne's class is down the hall to your left."

He didn't look any happier, but he accepted his dismissal. "Thank you for all of your help, Ms. Walsh."

"Anytime."

Turning her attention back to the other woman, she dimmed the wattage on her smile before speaking. "Did you have an appointment with Principal Britt?"

"No, I don't have an appointment, but I shouldn't need one. Just tell her I'm here."

This conversation wasn't going to get any easier. "I'm sorry, but Mrs. Britt is out of the building right now at the district office. I can let her know that you would like to speak with her. I'm sure she'll be glad to call you as soon as she gets back."

"And exactly when will that be?"

There was no way Carli was going to give her a specific time in case the meeting ran long. "My understanding is that she'd be back around lunchtime."

Mrs. Case sniffed in disapproval. "I would think she would keep you better informed of her plans. My tax dollars are paying her to be here, not hanging out with her buddies at the district office."

Only years of practice in dealing with difficult parents allowed Carli to keep her smile firmly in place. "Could someone else possibly help you? Mr. Grimm, the school counselor is here."

"If I wanted to talk to Mr. Grimm, I wouldn't be asking to see Mrs. Britt."

What did the woman expect Carli to do? It wasn't as if she could wave a magic wand and make the principal appear on demand. "I will tell Mrs. Britt that you would like to talk to her as soon as she's back in the office."

Still not placated, Mrs. Case tapped her forefinger on the message pad sitting on the counter by the phone. "Don't you think you should write that down? I wouldn't want it to accidently slip your mind."

Carli gritted her teeth when the woman actually did air quotes around the word *accidentally*. Did she think Carli was in the habit of ignoring a parent's request? Rather than respond in anger, she quickly filled out the message form, pausing only long enough to ask for Mrs. Case's phone number. After verifying all of the information was correct, Carli taped the note on Mrs. Britt's door where she'd see it as soon as she got back.

Her duty done, she returned to her desk. When Mrs. Case remained right where she was, Carli asked, "Was there something else I can help you with, Mrs. Case?"

"Just so you know, when I have dinner with the superintendent and his wife tomorrow night, I will be sure to let him know how completely unhelpful you've been."

Before Carli could even think of how to respond, someone else entered the conversation. "Ms. Walsh, I meant to tell you when I was in here a few minutes ago how much I appreciate everything you, Mrs. Britt and Mr. Grimm have done to make Luca feel welcome."

"Thank you, Mr. Barnaby."

He stepped up to the counter. "While I'm here, I'd like to see about prepaying some lunches."

Before Carli could point out that he'd only just done that, he turned his attention to Mrs. Case, who remained standing at the counter. "I'm sorry, ma'am, I didn't mean to interrupt. I assumed you were done abusing Ms. Walsh for simply doing her job."

Mrs. Case glared at Shay, her mouth tightening into something close to disdain as she shot a dark look in Carli's direction. Then without saying another word, she spun around and marched out of the office.

While relieved the woman was finally gone, Carli wasn't sure what to say to Shay about his heavy-handed attempt to defend her. Before she could figure it out, he offered her a sheepish grin. "Judging by your expression, Ms. Walsh, you probably would have preferred if I stayed out of your business. Having said that, I have no patience with bullies. That woman was spoiling for a fight, and she wasn't going to give up until she got one. At least now she's probably angrier with me than she is with you or Mrs. Britt."

He leaned his elbows on the counter and smiled. "So, do I need to apologize?"

How had she not noticed that Shay had been there long enough to overhear so much of her conversation with Mrs. Case? "To me or her?"

"You, of course. There's no way I'd apologize to her."

Meanwhile, he pulled out his wallet and held out a twenty-dollar bill. "This is for the lunches."

"You just bought some."

He shoved the money back in his wallet. "Oh, so I did. Must have slipped my mind. I guess I'll go now and let you get back to work."

When he turned to leave, Carli called after him, "Thanks for what you said, Shay."

After all, his words of appreciation had sounded sincere and had made up for Mrs. Case's jibes. Confrontations like that didn't happen often, and Carli generally loved her job. However, there was no denying that some people were easier to deal with than others.

Meanwhile, Shay winked at her and left.

Her good mood restored, she went back to work.

CHAPTER FIVE

LUCA CROSSED HIS arms over his chest and stuck his lower lip out in defiance. "But I don't want to go."

Shay prayed for patience and tried again. "I'm sorry, kiddo, but we have to. We have a parent-teacher conference with Ms. Varne, and the paper she sent home says students are supposed to attend. I know you've only been going to this school for about two weeks, but she wants to let us know how you're doing in class."

Luca knelt beside his furry friends. "But Bruno and Beau don't want me to go. They think we should stay home."

Truth be told, so did Shay. It wasn't as if he knew anything about conferencing with a teacher. He wasn't even sure if they'd had such things back when he was in school. If so, his parents must have handled it on their own.

He glanced at the other adult in the room in the vain hope she would offer up some sage advice. Instead, Aunt Meg maintained a stubborn silence as she positioned herself off to one side at an equal distance between the two combatants. Shay knew it wasn't that she was exactly neutral; she'd read the note and knew attending the conference wasn't optional. She was probably more worried that if she stood beside Shay, Luca would feel like the new adults in his life were ganging up on him. Conversely, if she took a position nearer to Luca, the boy might interpret that to mean she was buying into the argument that the dogs desperately needed the boy to stay home with them.

Shay hated to admit defeat, but right now he didn't have the energy to engage in a losing argument with a kid. He might regret what he was about to do, but he was quickly learning that when logic failed, bribery might get the job done.

"I thought the three of us might drive up to Leavenworth after the meeting and have pizza for dinner. When we get back, it will be about your bedtime. Then I have to go to work for a while. Don't you think it would be nice to give Aunt Meg a night off from cooking?"

She rolled her eyes and shook her head. "You two go enjoy your pizza. We were just going to have leftovers tonight, anyway. I'll have some for my dinner and the rest for lunch tomorrow.

I'd rather stay here and get caught up on a couple of my shows."

Shay knew all the late nights when she watched Luca for him while he worked at the tavern were taking a toll on Meg. At least he'd had a couple of responses to the ad he'd posted looking for a nanny, although neither one had gotten back to him as yet about whether they were willing to take the job.

"So, what about it, Luca? You come with me to the conference, and then we'll eat out. If pizza doesn't sound good, we can try the pancake place or go for burgers somewhere. There's a whole bunch of different restaurants out on the interstate about twenty miles from here."

"Can we have pepperoni pizza?"

"Sure, but I'll want a few vegetables on it, too." Knowing the boy's feelings about vegetables in general, he added, "I'll ask them to put them on just half of the pizza."

He stuck his hand out to Luca to seal the deal. As soon as the boy put his hand in Shay's, he swept the boy up in his arms and gave him a hug. After he set him back down, he said, "I'll grab my keys while you get your jacket. It's nice outside right now, but it gets chilly this close to the mountains after the sun goes down. Meet you at the truck in three minutes."

Luca hugged each of the dogs and then crossed

to Aunt Meg when she held out her arms. "I won't complain if you bring back a slice or two of pizza for me, even if they have icky vegetables on them."

Luca laughed and darted into his room to get his jacket while Shay went outside to start the truck. He was about to honk the horn when Luca came flying out of the house and climbed into the front seat. Once Shay got Luca buckled into his booster seat, he backed down the driveway and turned in the direction of town. He let the quiet settle around them for several minutes, but he had a couple of questions he wanted to ask before they reached the school.

"So, is there anything you want me to ask your teacher about? For example, is there anything you find confusing because she does things differently than your teacher down in California?"

He kept his eyes on the road, so he didn't know if Luca either nodded or shook his head. "I have to watch where we're going, so you'll need to use your words to answer me. So again, do you have any questions?"

"No."

The single word wasn't surprising and not exactly helpful. "So everything is going okay in class?"

This time he did glance in Luca's direction just in time to see the boy shrug. Shay figured that probably meant things were a bit bumpy at times. Great.

"Have you made any new friends you like? If so, maybe we can invite them over sometime."

When all he got was another shrug, Shay added that subject to the list of questions he had for Ms. Varne. Surely she would have noticed if Luca hung out with anyone in particular in her class. If not, maybe she could offer suggestions about how to help Luca start making friends. The more connections Luca had in town, the better. He needed those attachments to make Dunbar feel like home.

They'd reached the school where there was a smattering of vehicles in the parking lot. Shay pulled into a spot near the main entrance into the building and turned off the engine. Although they were cutting it pretty close to their scheduled time to meet with Ms. Varne, he once again found himself reluctant to leave the sanctuary of the truck.

Not that he was afraid of talking to the woman who'd been nothing but friendly in their previous brief encounters. No, it was more that he was worried what she had to tell him would only further cement his belief that he wasn't cut out to be a father to Luca and was failing the boy miserably. Not in everything, of course. He really believed getting Bruno and Beau would help the boy's emotional wounds heal over time.

"Well, I guess we should head inside."

Luca's eyes were huge in his young face when he looked at Shay. "Do we have to?"

It was tempting, so very tempting, to decide attending the conference was optional and head on down the road for pizza. However, that would only postpone the inevitable, not to mention it would be rude to back out now when Ms. Varne had reserved this time for the two of them.

"Yeah, we have to go talk to your teacher. It shouldn't take long, so we'll be ordering that pepperoni pizza before you know it."

Luca heaved a huge sigh and opened his door. It was hard not to laugh at the melodrama, but Shay couldn't help but sympathize with the boy. For his own part, he'd far rather be working at the tavern. Between being gone two weeks and everything else that had followed, he had a lot of catching up to do. He'd made sure his people were paid on time, but he'd had to let a lot of other stuff slide. Thank goodness for Jody, his head bartender, who had handled Shay's workload as well as her own while he'd been gone. He was lucky to have such a dependable staff and made sure they knew he felt that way. Although money was tight, he'd included a small bonus in everyone's last paycheck.

For now, he and Luca walked down the hall together. He found it amusing that both of them had paused outside of the office long enough to see if Carli was there. Sadly, she was nowhere in sight, probably because it was after her normal working hours. They continued down the hallway to Luca's classroom. The door was closed, and there was a sign posted on the wall above some chairs inviting visitors to be seated.

As Shay sat down, he noticed a folder on the student desk next to his seat that had Luca's name on it. Picking it up, he glanced at his companion. "I like how you decorated this folder. You did a great job drawing Beau and Bruno curled up on your bed. It looks just like them."

He leaned over and nudged Luca with his shoulder. "So tell me—if they sleep on your bed, where do you sleep? Because I'm guessing your twin bed gets pretty crowded with all three of you on it."

Luca looked guilty until he glanced up and realized Shay was smiling. "They mostly sleep by my feet. I like them there."

Shay understood how the boy felt. He'd drawn comfort from having Rex curled up next to him back when things weren't going well between Shay and his father. "It's hard to guess how big Bruno and Beau will get by the time they reach their full size, not to mention you're a growing boy yourself. If it ever gets to be a problem, let me know. We can always get you a bigger bed."

Before Luca could respond, the classroom door opened. A couple walked out followed by a small girl. She smiled as soon as she spotted Luca. "Hi, Luca."

Luca offered her a shy smile. "Hi, Marnie."

She looked up at her folks. "He's new."

Her parents smiled. "Nice to meet you, Luca."

He didn't respond until Shay gave him an encouraging nod. "Hi. Marnie sits in front of me."

By that point, Ms. Varne had joined them, ending any further conversation. As the other family walked back down the hall, Shay and Luca stood up. Ms. Varne's smile looked a bit strained as she said, "Please come in and have a seat. We have a lot to talk about."

A sense of dread washed over Shay as they followed her inside. It sounded as if he'd been right that whatever information she had to share wasn't going to be all sunshine and rainbows.

BY THE CLOCK, the meeting didn't last all that long, only about thirty minutes. In reality, it seemed like an eternity had passed by the time he and Luca walked back out of the building. Ms. Varne had Luca sit at his desk in the front row with some art supplies to keep him occupied while she and Shay had huddled up at a horseshoe table in the back corner of the classroom.

Ms. Varne had done her best to be encouraging, but her concern about how Luca was doing came through loud and clear. He was lagging behind in his homework in almost every subject, art being the sole exception. It was the one time that Luca showed any interest in putting much effort into his work.

Having said all of that, she offered some encouragement. She'd reviewed Luca's file from his previous school. Prior to the death of his parents, he'd been at or above grade level in both math and reading. She'd also had a long talk with the school counselor about Luca. It was Mr. Grimm's opinion that the boy was still processing the loss of his parents. It would take time, patience and a lot of support from the adults in his life to get him back on track.

None of it had come as much of a surprise to Shay, but that didn't mean he was happy about the situation. Luca would need help getting caught up on his assignments, and Shay was willing to do whatever it took. The problem was that Shay worked evenings and weekends, meaning he wasn't always home when Luca should be doing his homework. Aunt Meg would do her best to help, but Shay felt guilty asking her to take on even more responsibility. Something was going to have to change and soon.

Meanwhile, Luca trudged along beside him, his mood subdued. Shay hesitated to press him on what was wrong even though he couldn't help Luca if he didn't know what was going on in that little head of his. But before he came up with an opening salvo, the boy's whole demeanor changed between one second and the next. It was as if someone had flipped a switch, because Luca was now bouncing in excitement. He let go of Shay's hand and charged across the parking lot.

"Ms. Walsh! Ms. Walsh! We stopped to see if you were in the office, but you wasn't there."

Carli had been about to get into her car, but she closed the door and stepped away from the vehicle. "I'm sorry I missed you, Luca. I must've been in the back room when you came by."

Luca skidded to a stop right in front of her. "Shay and me had to meet with my teacher. It was boring and took *forever*, but she said we could leave now. We're going for pizza. Wanna come with us?"

Shay knew he should explain to Luca that Carli had probably put in an extra-long day at work considering she was just now leaving the building. She was undoubtedly more than ready to head home and relax. But instead of gently offering up an explanation about why she couldn't go with them, she glanced at Shay as if waiting to see his reaction to the boy's spontaneous invitation.

With both Carli and Luca staring at him, Shay didn't hesitate. "We'd love to have you join us. That is, if you've got time and would like to come."

Luca turned back to Carli. "We're going to order a pepperoni pizza. Shay wants some icky vegetables on his half, but you can share my side if you want."

Her laughter rang out over the parking lot, vanquishing the last bit of Shay's dark mood. He grinned in response. "If having veggies on the pizza is a deal-breaker, we can stick to plain pepperoni."

She held out her hand to Luca. "How can I resist an offer like that?"

CHAPTER SIX

CARLI HADN'T HAD the heart to turn down Luca's invitation to dinner. She'd actually been aware of them crossing the parking lot before they'd spotted her. The slump of Shay's shoulders and the way Luca had been shuffling along with his attention completely focused on the ground probably meant the news at the teacher conference hadn't been all good.

If it made the boy happy to share his pizza with her, she wasn't about to turn him down. The chance to spend more time with Shay Barnaby was just the icing on the cake. Not that she'd admit that to him. He'd made it clear that his focus going forward had to be on providing a stable home for his young charge. She understood that and even approved of his determination to do right by Luca. That didn't mean she wasn't a bit disappointed that she and Shay might never have a chance to further explore the attraction they'd felt for each other during the wedding festivities.

Rather than take two vehicles to the restaurant, he'd followed her home first to drop off her car. Meanwhile, Luca moved to the back seat so Carli could ride up front with Shay. He'd already explained that they were heading to a pizza place about twenty miles away rather than the local pizzeria, which only offered either takeout or delivery. It also had a more limited menu.

Once they were on the road, she turned at an angle so she could look back at Luca. "So how are Beau and Bruno doing? Are they settling into their new home?"

"Yeah. They don't like it when I leave for school in the morning, but they're really happy when I get back home. We play fetch in the backyard and watch TV together."

"Do they like their beds?" Carli asked with a wink to let the boy know she wouldn't spill his secret.

Shay answered that one. "Yeah, but evidently they like Luca's bed better."

So the secret was out already. She grinned. "Doesn't that get a bit crowded?" she asked, still looking at Luca.

He giggled a little. "Yeah, but Shay said we could get me a bigger bed if the dogs and I get too big for the one I have now."

"So who takes care of them?"

Luca hesitated. "I do, but not all by myself. I

fill their water bowl and brush their coats. Shay feeds them most of the time. I can give them dry food, but he has to open the cans to give them the other stuff."

"Sounds like a lot of work."

"It is, but it's our responsibility to take good care of them. They need us to do what they can't do for themselves to keep them healthy and happy. In return, they protect our house and love us back."

Luca's voice took on a different cadence when he said that last part. She suspected he was quoting what Shay had taught him. She liked how he was teaching Luca about responsibility while making him feel needed.

"I'd like to meet Beau and Bruno sometime. They sound pretty special."

"They're my best friends." His expression turned more serious. "I wish my mom and dad could meet them."

Carli felt so bad for him. "I bet they would have liked them a lot."

Luca wrinkled his nose. "Dad would've, but Mom had allergies."

Maybe it was time to change topics. She directed her next question to Shay. "How are you doing?"

"I'm fine."

She would have called him on the lie if it had

just been the two of them in the truck. Aware of the boy sitting behind them, she expressed her disbelief with an eye roll. Shay shot her an exasperated look before turning his attention back to the road ahead. "Fine. I'm behind on things at work, and evidently a certain someone hasn't been doing his homework. I haven't found a nanny, and I can't keep asking Aunt Meg to take on more. It's not fair to her, and she's not as young as she used to be."

"How many nights a week do you have to work?"

"Before things changed—" he paused to glance in the rearview mirror, probably checking to see how closely Luca was listening to their conversation "—I worked six nights a week. The tavern is closed on Sundays, so that was my one full day off."

She found herself reaching across to rest her hand on his arm, instinctively offering him the comfort of her touch. "I know it's a big adjustment for all of you, but I'm sure you'll get it figured out soon."

He glanced down at her hand as if surprised by her impulsive move. "I hope so."

By that point, they were almost to the restaurant. Time to lighten up the mood. "Hey, Luca. How do you feel about mushrooms or olives on your pizza."

"Gross."

"Okay, just checking. I'll have them on my salad instead."

Luca giggled. "Still gross."

"How about anchovies?"

That had the boy sounding suspicious. "What are those?"

Shay answered for her. "Creepy little fish that have no business anywhere near a pizza or any other kind of food, at least nothing I'd want to eat."

Carli pretended to be insulted by his assessment. "But I love anchovies on my pizza. If you get to have icky vegetables on your half of the pizza, I should get to have anchovies on it, too."

"I'll tell you what, woman. I'll buy you your own pizza. You can put whatever grossness on it that you want to, because there will be no anchovies on my half." He glanced at Luca in the mirror again. "Or maybe Luca will feel sorry for you and let you put a couple on his half. What do you say, kid?"

By that point Luca was giggling. "No grossness on my pizza, either."

Carli gave both of her male companions a snooty look. "Fine, gentlemen. No anchovies. But the next time we go out for dinner together, I get to choose what we eat."

She shook her finger at them. "And there will be no complaints. Got it?"

Luca grinned at her. "Got it."

It was Shay's response that puzzled her. His eyebrows rose high over his eyes as he gave her a look that was both confused and surprised at the same time. Then it hit her. She'd made it sound as if she assumed that she would be invited to join them for dinner again sometime in the future. "I'm sorry, I didn't mean to imply that us hanging out together was a done deal."

"No apologies necessary, Carli. Besides, I'd like that. Like you said, eventually things will fall into a routine. Once that happens, Luca and I will be able to make more plans."

This time, he was the one who reached out to give her hand a gentle squeeze. "For now, we're taking things one day at a time."

He released her hand before slowing to turn into the restaurant parking lot. "Now, let's go eat some pizza!"

TWO HOURS LATER Shay drove Carli home. It had been a long day, and she was more than ready for a little downtime. That didn't mean that she was in a huge hurry for the evening to end. She couldn't remember the last time she'd laughed so much. Other than the time she'd spent with Shay at Moira's wedding, this was the closest thing to an actual date she'd had in ages even if it had included a young chaperone. She wondered if it had felt like that to Shay as well, not that she was going to ask.

When Shay started to get out of the truck, she stopped him. "You don't have to walk me to the door."

He reached across the distance between them to brush a lock of her hair back from her face. "I know I don't have to. I *want* to."

The slightly husky note in his voice sent chills through her. Was he thinking back to the one time before when he'd escorted her to the door? She didn't know about him, but the memory of the kiss they'd shared that night remained vivid despite the passage of time. Had he also wondered if it had been a fluke or possibly the start of something more?

Before she was foolish enough to ask, he was out of the truck and standing at her door to help her down out of the cab. She noticed how careful he was not to slam the door, probably because Luca had fallen asleep in the back seat shortly after they'd left the restaurant. The poor kid had had a long day, too. Meanwhile, it felt perfectly natural for Shay to rest his hand on her lower back as they stepped onto her front porch. It spanned the width of the small, shotgun-style house that she'd bought when she moved back to town.

Since she'd forgotten to turn on the porch light when she'd dropped off her car, Shay provided light with his cellphone while she dug out her keys. Once she had the key in the lock, he stepped back but made no move to leave. Instead, he paused at the front edge of the porch and silently stared up at the night sky. Often the stars were obscured by a layer of clouds, but tonight that wasn't the case. The moon hovered above the horizon, nearly full and bathing the area with its soft, silvery light. The night air held the usual cool chill of an autumn night, making her glad she'd worn a warm jacket. When Shay didn't seem inclined to talk, she stood nearby and gave him the space and time he seemed to need.

"Luca's not doing well in school." He shoved his hands in his front pockets and rocked back on his heels. "I'm not worried so much about his academics. He's a bright kid, and we can get him caught up on that stuff. It's that he's not making any effort to interact with the other kids. Ms. Varne says he spends his recess sitting by himself even if the other kids invite him to join in whatever game they're playing. At lunch, he picks a spot at the end of the table, usually with an empty seat between him and his classmates. I hate that he's choosing to be alone so much."

He finally turned his gaze in her direction. "Sorry, I shouldn't dump all of this on you. It's not your problem."

No, she supposed it wasn't. He also wouldn't appreciate a litany of platitudes like that all he could do was his best, or that he needed to be patient and give Luca more time to adjust. She knew in her heart that Luca was lucky to have Shay in his life even if the boy didn't know it yet. Finally, she once again offered Shay the small comfort of her touch, briefly putting her hand on his broad shoulder. "Shay, always remember you're not alone in this. You have your aunt Meg at home. You have Mrs. Britt, Mr. Grimm, Ms. Varne and me at the school. You said that your employees are stepping up to bat to keep things running smoothly at the tavern. And you also have friends like Ryder, Moira and Titus. Even if all you need is to talk, any or all of those folks are just a phone call away."

The stubborn man lapsed into silence again. She waited a few seconds and then tried again. "Luca just needs time to process the new reality of his life. You've already given him some of the tools he needs to do that. You've shown him how important he is to you by taking him into your home. You got him the dogs to give him something to focus on besides what he's lost."

Shay drew a ragged breath. "And if all of that

isn't enough? Heck, he still cries almost every day. The smallest thing can set him off, and lately it's getting worse, especially at night. I've had to leave work and come running to get him settled down. It upsets Aunt Meg that she can't seem to get through to him by herself. Once he's asleep again, I go back to work and try to pick up the pieces there. It's like I'm running on a treadmill and not getting anywhere."

He ran his fingers through his hair in frustration. "It's not like I have any experience in being a father, and my own dad wasn't exactly the poster boy for good parenting. Drinking and a bad temper were never a good combination. When I hit my teens, it seemed as if all we did was fight, and not just with words. It all came to a head one night. It was my fault, too, because I screwed up big-time. My little sister paid the price."

Shay shuffled his feet, as if unable to remain still. "Mom was gone for the evening. She sold makeup at parties and had one scheduled for that evening. I know she told Dad he'd have to come straight home from work that night to stay with Julie, but he didn't. Knowing him, he either forgot or didn't care, and went out drinking with his buddies. Whenever the folks were gone, I was supposed to hang around and watch my younger sister. I was sixteen, and Julie was thirteen. The trouble was I had plans for that night. A buddy's parents were out of town, and we were going to have a big party at his house."

He finally turned to face Carli. "I snuck out, telling myself she'd be okay on her own for a while and that Dad would be back soon. Instead, Julie followed me to the party. The crowd was huge, and I didn't even know she was there until I heard her screaming for help. Some college guys had shown up uninvited, and one of them had cornered her in one of the bedrooms. I got to her just in time—barely."

He sighed, his expression bleak. "Instead of taking care of her, I went after the guy with both fists. They had to drag me off him. Long story short, by that point my mom apparently had had enough of both me and Dad. She took my sister and left town while I was at school and my father was at work."

When he went silent, Carli gave him a verbal nudge. "What happened then?"

"Dad blamed me for blowing up his marriage. My mom said we were two peas in a pod and didn't want to have anything to do with either of us. As far as my sister goes…well, we exchange cards on birthdays and at Christmas. That's about it. Without Mom and Julie to act as buffers, things only got worse between me and my old man. After another major blowup, he kicked me out.

"I had nowhere to go, but eventually a social worker called my dad's older brother to see if they might be willing to take me in. Uncle Ray caught a red-eye flight to Georgia and picked me up the next day. He got my dad to sign over custody to him and said I could live with him and Aunt Meg while I finished school. I joined the marines as soon as I graduated, the same as Ray had done when he was that age. He told me the Corps had straightened him out, and he hoped it would do the same for me. I haven't been back to my hometown since."

There was such pain in his voice. Trying to lighten the moment, she pretended to look shocked. "So Georgia, huh? I sort of figured that you didn't get that charming Southern drawl living here in Dunbar."

Shay's mouth finally quirked up in a quick grin. "No, I didn't. That's pure Georgia, although it's actually faded some over the years. You should've heard me when I first got here. A couple of guys made the mistake of making fun of how I talked. They only did it once."

"And what happened after that?"

His laugh sounded a little rough. "The principal turned the three of us over to the football coach to deal with. We won our division that year."

Back to the subject at hand. "So you do know what it's like to find yourself living somewhere new."

"I wasn't six years old, and at least I actually knew my aunt and uncle. Luca had only met me once before I showed up after the accident."

"But you did show up, Shay. And you're still showing up for him every day. He might not understand the incredible sacrifices you're making for him, but eventually he will. For now, all he needs to know is that you'll be there for him. That will give him the solid foundation he needs to rebuild his life here in Dunbar."

Shay still didn't look convinced, but his phone rang, derailing any further conversation. "Hi, Aunt Meg. What's up?"

Carli couldn't hear what she said, but it had him frowning as he checked his watch. "Sorry, I lost track of time. We'll be there in fifteen minutes."

After disconnecting the call, he stepped off the porch. "I don't know where my head is these days. Aunt Meg has been sitting at my place waiting for me to bring Luca home, not to mention I still need to check in at the bar."

Carli wasn't sure if she should apologize for monopolizing so much of his time. After all, he and Luca invited her to join them. “I’m sorry for keeping you so long.”

That had him stepping back up on the porch to stand right in front of her. “You have nothing to be sorry for. This is the first evening since the wedding that I’ve actually relaxed and enjoyed myself. It was good for Luca, too. He might be shy around other people, but he’s different with you.”

Still keeping it light, she said, “I had fun, too, even if I did have to eat a few icky vegetables on my pizza.”

She stepped toward the door, figuring one of them needed to make a move toward ending their time together. “Tell Luca I’ll see him at school tomorrow.”

“I will.”

Shay started back down the sidewalk, but stopped one last time. “Thanks for listening to me whine. I promise not to do it again.”

Carli shrugged. “Don’t worry about it. After all, what are friends for?”

He looked as if he wanted to say something more, but instead he shook his head and made his way to his truck. Carli waited and watched until he started the engine and drove away. She wasn’t sure what she’d been hoping for, but he didn’t even wave one last time. Feeling far more disappointed than she should have, she went inside and locked the door.

Carli couldn't help but notice how her cozy house felt too silent, too empty. As far back as she could remember, she'd dreamed of a home and family of her own—having a husband and kids who loved her as much as she loved them. It was as if her ex was living Carli's dream but with someone else.

The time she'd spent with Shay and Luca that evening had given her a brief taste of what her life could've been like if only things between her and Peter had turned out differently. But that was water under the bridge. Looking back with regret and dwelling on what might have been never did anyone any good. It was time to call it a day and go to bed.

Even so, she lingered by the door as she studied her surroundings. She'd personally chosen the furniture, the warm palette of colors, and everything else. All in all, she was quite proud of how her efforts had turned out. It was a far cry from the fancy house she'd shared with her ex-husband. Peter hadn't trusted her to decorate the place, saying it needed to be upscale in order to impress his friends and clients. He'd loved the austere, ultramodern style the interior decorator had chosen for them.

Carli had hated it from day one, not that she'd

ever admitted it to him. Looking back, her reluctance to be honest with him should've been a big clue that her marriage wasn't going to last. She had some regrets about how things had played out, but moving out of that house hadn't been one of them. Tonight, though, the walls of her new home closed in on her, leaving her prowling from the living room in the front of the house through the small dining room and kitchen to her bedroom all the way in the back. Once there, she immediately made the return trip to the living room, still not quite ready to retire for the night.

Too restless to read, she turned on the television and scrolled through the menu looking for anything that would hold her interest. Finally, she picked a marathon showing of an old sitcom. Maybe it was her mood, but she could have sworn the show had been funnier back in the day. Still, listening to the inane dialogue was better than getting lost in the mire of her own thoughts.

Halfway into the second episode, her phone chimed to signal a text message. Seeing who it was from had her frowning. What did Shay want now?

Thanks for being Luca's friend tonight—and mine. It meant a lot to both of us.

Okay, then. It took her a couple of minutes to decide on an answer. To me, too.

Her mood much improved, she found herself smiling as she finally turned off the lights and went to bed.

CHAPTER SEVEN

LAST NIGHT HAD been a mistake of monumental proportions. Shay hated knowing that, but it was nothing less than the truth. Luca woke up shortly after they'd left Carli's house, and his first words were to ask where Carli had gone. When Shay told him that he'd just dropped her off at her house, Luca's second question was when they'd be going to dinner with her again. It had been tempting to say as soon as possible.

After all, Luca wasn't the only one who'd basked in the warmth of her smiles. Thanks to her, both Shay and his young charge had been able to dispel the cloud of gloom that had followed them out of their meeting with Ms. Varne at the school. Shay knew it wasn't the teacher's fault that there wasn't a lot of good news to share about the short time Luca had been in her class or that it had only reinforced Shay's feelings of inadequacy.

He even understood that she'd done her best to be encouraging after giving him a list of assignments that Luca needed to get caught up on. Although the counselor hadn't been able to attend the conference, he had provided Shay with several brochures and articles on helping young children deal with major upheavals in their lives.

All of it was done with good intentions, but there hadn't been a brochure on how to incorporate even more responsibilities into Shay's already complicated schedule. It looked like the two of them would be spending Sunday doing homework and getting ahead on a week's worth of reading time. Then there were the bills he needed to pay and—

"Hey, boss! Got a minute?"

Shay waited until he finished unloading the rack of clean glasses before seeing what Jody wanted. The two of them had worked together long enough for him to interpret the degree of urgency in her voice. Right now, she wanted his attention, but it wasn't an emergency. He wiped his hands on a towel as he turned to face her.

"What's up?"

"There's a couple of rowdy guys in the back corner who want to talk to you. Something about you owing them some free burgers and drinks."

As far as Shay knew, he didn't owe anybody anything. Looking toward the back of the bar, he spotted Titus and Ryder sitting together and watching him with big grins on their faces.

Ryder held up an empty coffee cup in one hand and pointed at it with his other. When Titus held up an empty beer bottle, Shay tossed his towel on the back counter.

Surrendering to the inevitable, he picked up a carafe of coffee and got a beer out of the refrigerator. "Jody, order three burgers with all the fixings, onion rings and fries. My treat."

"Already did. The order should be up in a couple of minutes. I'll cover anything that comes up while you're on your break."

"Thanks, Jody."

He walked around the end of the bar and headed toward his unexpected dinner guests. After handing Titus his drink and pouring himself and Ryder each a cup of coffee, Shay took one of the other seats at the table. He added a packet of creamer and two sugars to his coffee before speaking. "Not sure why I owe you two anything, but the burgers should arrive shortly."

Ryder smiled and jerked his head in Titus's direction. "We were just yanking your chain. It'll be Titus's treat."

The other man gave Ryder a narrow-eyed look. "That hardly seems fair considering how many free meals you've managed to have at my place lately. Seems like you should be the one paying for all of our meals tonight. Besides, rumor has it that you're the one with the big bank account."

Shay had heard the same rumor but hadn't quite believed it. Ryder drove a rusty old van and lived in a rustic A-frame cabin in the woods outside of town. Not exactly the lifestyle of the rich and famous. But from the way his cheeks had just flushed red, maybe there was some truth to the story. Rather than say anything that would make the man even more uncomfortable, Shay shook his head. "No, dinner is on me. Ryder can feed us next time."

Then he offered his friend an evil grin. "I've been wanting to try that new steak house up on the interstate. I hear the prime rib is amazing. Bonus points for the fact it will cost a lot more than a couple of burgers."

Titus's rough laughter rang out. "It's a deal."

Ryder made a token effort at protesting. "That's hardly fair."

His pretend outrage didn't stop him from joining in on the laughter. "But, yeah, it's a deal."

One of the servers appeared beside Shay with a tray full of food. She lowered it to make it easier for Shay to pass the plates to his two companions before taking his own. She stayed long enough to ask, "Do you guys need any dipping sauces for your fries?"

When Ryder and Titus both shook their heads, Shay said, "I guess we're good, but bring Titus another beer whenever he wants one. Make it that new IPA we just got in."

"Will do."

After Tiffany walked away, all three of them got busy eating. Shay hadn't realized how hungry he was until he took the first bite of his burger. When he'd taken the edge off his appetite, he sat back and relaxed. "So what brought the pair of you to my fine establishment tonight?"

Pinning his attention on Titus in particular, he asked, "As a newlywed, shouldn't you be home with your lovely wife instead of hanging out with the likes of Ryder here? He's a pretty poor substitute for Moira."

"Hey! Since when did this become Pick-on-Ryder Night?"

Titus piled on. "It's always Pick-on-Ryder Night. That aside, Moira is working evenings this week. I left Ned snoring on the couch and figured I'd check in to see how you were doing. How's the kid?"

It was tempting to gloss over the situation, to pretend everything was rolling right along perfectly fine, but he trusted these two men to keep his and Luca's secrets. "We're both doing better."

Honesty had him adding, "Most of the time, anyway."

He met Ryder's gaze. "The dogs have made a

big difference. We did have to move their beds to the living room today."

The reason for that had him smiling. "Luca said they wanted a more comfortable place to curl up and watch TV with him. Personally, I wouldn't care if they joined him on the couch, but Aunt Meg put her foot down on that. Something about not wanting to get dog hair all over her slacks."

Ryder picked up an onion ring and dipped it in ketchup. "Do you need another set of beds for his room?"

"Thanks, but they wouldn't get used. Beau and Bruno evidently need lots of cuddles at night, so the three of them sleep in a pile on Luca's bed."

Titus smiled. "Sounds like it gets a bit crowded."

Shay huffed a small laugh. "All three of them seem to like it that way."

He wasn't surprised by Titus's next question. "How about school? A new building, a new teacher and a strange bunch of kids...has to be a big adjustment for him."

Sighing, Shay pushed his plate to the side, his appetite gone. "Yeah, he's struggling a bit there. In fact, we had a meeting with his teacher last night. He's a little behind in his classwork, such as it is for a first grader. I'm more worried by the fact he hasn't clicked with any of the other kids yet. I know he hasn't been here all that long, but I was hoping he might have started making some friends."

Ryder topped off his coffee again. "It's not like I have any experience with kids that age, but I'm guessing he'll figure it all out pretty soon."

"I hope so. He's been through a lot, and I want him to be happy."

It was time to change the subject. "How are things at the fire station? I'm really sorry I haven't been able to help out lately."

Ryder rapped his knuckles on the tabletop. "We're hanging in there. Knock on wood, but it's been quieter than usual the past couple of weeks. A fender bender out on the highway and a grease fire that caused some minor smoke damage at one of the cabin rentals by the river. I'm on call tonight."

He held up his mug. "Hence the coffee instead of beer."

It was nice to know that things were going smoothly in Shay's absence, but he still felt guilty knowing other people were having to cover for him. "I'm hoping that once I get Luca used to his new routine, I'll be able to help out again. Maybe not as many shifts as I used to take, but enough so that the rest of you don't get burned out."

"Don't worry about it, Shay. Other than my volunteer work for the shelter, it's not like I have anything else to do with my time. Well, besides practicing my fly-fishing skills. I figure the fish deserve a break from me beating the water to a froth. It's not like I ever catch any."

Ryder rarely spoke about his life before moving to Dunbar, but Shay didn't hold that against him. It wasn't as if he often talked about his own time in the marines. Some stories weren't meant to be shared. It was bad enough that he had to live with those images in his own head. As for Titus's mysterious past, apparently some folks in town remained convinced that he'd learned to cook while in prison.

If those people bothered to think things through, they'd know their theory didn't hold water. For starters, Titus's wife and his closest friend were both police officers who were well-known to be straight arrows. Shay suspected the truth was far more interesting, and he knew the man had worked in law enforcement himself in the past. Something major must have happened at some point, because Titus had changed career paths and gone to culinary school. Eventually, he'd moved to Dunbar and bought the only café in town.

Shay was about to ask if they wanted anything else to eat when Ryder's phone let out a series of incredibly loud beeps. Shay's own phone was programed with the same alarm which signaled that the volunteer firefighters needed to come running. He'd toggled it off when he'd stepped down because of Luca.

Ryder shoved back from the table. "Sounds like I spoke too soon about it being quiet. Titus, can you hitch a ride home from someone else?"

"Don't worry about me. I can walk. It's not far."

"Thanks for feeding me, Shay." Ryder put on his jacket and started for the door.

"You're welcome." Shay couldn't resist calling after him, "Watch yourself, Ryder. Wouldn't want something to happen to you before you buy us those prime rib dinners we were talking about."

Ryder waved to say he'd gotten the message. When he was out the door, Titus gave Shay a sympathetic look. "Don't feel guilty. They understand why you need to take time off."

Shay still felt like he was letting everybody down. "I know they do, but we were already shorthanded."

"You can't be everywhere at once, and beating yourself up over that won't help anyone, especially you."

Shay leaned back in his chair and studied the man across from him. He and Titus had only recently become friends, but he recognized a kindred spirit when he saw one. The man had the same dark shadows in his eyes that Shay sometimes saw in his own when he looked in the mirror.

"Do you regret walking away from wearing a badge?" He stopped and held up his hand. "Look, forget I even asked. It's none of my business."

Titus answered anyway. "No, at least not most of the time. I like to think I did some good work back then, but I'd never pick up where I left off. The price was too high. A job like that takes a toll, both mentally and physically."

As he spoke, Titus rubbed his knee. Glancing down at what he was doing, he shook his head and added, "Sometimes to the point it takes multiple surgeries to put you back together."

His voice held more than a hint of bitterness when he said that last bit, but he sounded happier as he continued. "I decided I wanted to do something positive for once. Feeding people fit the bill."

Titus paused to glance around the bar. "Serving in the marines carries similar risks, so I'm guessing you enjoy running this place for the same reasons I like my café—giving people a place where they can enjoy good food, good drinks and good company. Finding the right person to share my life with has helped, too."

His smile turned sly. "On that note, have you talked to Carli Walsh lately?"

That was something else Shay didn't want to talk about. Besides, he needed to get back to work. But considering Titus had answered Shay's intrusive question, he figured he ought to say something. "Luca and I ran into her at the school after our conference last night. He invited her to have pizza with us."

He braced himself for more questions, but Titus simply nodded as he abruptly stood up. "Thanks for dinner and the company. Bring the kid by for lunch or breakfast over the weekend. Ned misses him."

Shay laughed. "How will Ned react when he realizes Luca has been hanging around with other dogs?"

"Knowing him, a few treats will buy a lot of forgiveness."

"I'll tell Luca to fill his pockets before we leave the house."

"Sounds good. See you then."

Rather than heading back to work, Shay accompanied Titus outside and watched until the other man disappeared into the night. In no hurry to go back inside, Shay enjoyed the fresh air and quiet for a couple of minutes. His mood much improved, he finally went inside to finish restocking the supplies behind the bar. After that, he had a stack of bills to pay waiting for him in his office.

Still not ready to face them, he decided to procrastinate a little longer.

"Jody, take your break now if you want to. I'll cover until you get back."

She wiped her hands on a towel and tossed it aside. "Everything is caught up. See those guys over in the corner? They haven't caused any problems yet, but it might be about time to cut them off."

They were regulars and had been known to get rowdy a time or two. The mood Shay was in right now, he almost hoped they did cross the line again. He could use the chance to let off a little steam. No, that wouldn't be smart. He had Luca to think about now. "Thanks for the heads-up. I'll keep an eye on them."

He let himself get lost in the rhythm of pouring drinks and filling orders. All of his problems could wait until tomorrow. For now, he was going to enjoy making sure his customers were happy and well-fed. No sooner did that thought cross his mind than his phone rang. Shay groaned when he saw who was calling.

"Aunt Meg, what's happened now?"

Stupid question. He already knew. "Never mind. I'll be there in a few minutes."

He hung up, barely resisting the urge to throw the phone against the wall, but enough was enough. Rather than abuse innocent electronics, he went in search of Jody. She had just sat down at the small table tucked in the corner of the kitchen where his employees could kick back and relax a little while.

"I need to talk to you in my office. Now."

She knew him well enough to know he wouldn't interrupt her downtime for no reason. As soon as they entered his office, she asked, "What's up?"

"I've been trying, but I haven't had any luck finding someone to take over watching Luca while I'm working. But it's become obvious that while I am needed here, he needs me more."

Jody was frowning by that point as if struggling to figure out where he was going with this. It was time to quit dancing around the issue and get to the point. "I've just made an executive decision that is long overdue. Starting as soon as we can get all the details hashed out, I want you to take over as the evening manager here at the bar. It's going to mean more responsibility and a raise. I'll be shifting my hours to earlier in the day because I need to be home evenings. Any questions will have to wait because I have to cut out again. Are you in or are you out?"

That she didn't hesitate was a huge relief. "I'm in. I'll handle closing tonight. Go take care of your kid."

"Good. Let's meet here on Sunday when the

place is closed to figure out schedules and other stuff. Say around noon?"

"I'll be here."

Feeling better than he had in ages, Shay headed home.

CHAPTER EIGHT

CARLI WAS ONLY too glad to accept Moira's invitation to join her for a late breakfast at the café on Saturday morning. She had errands to run and laundry to do, but all of that could wait until after she spent some quality time with her friend. While she'd never admit it to Moira, she'd been secretly worried that the demands of Moira's job combined with her new marriage might severely limit how often they could hang out together.

Not that she could complain if it did. Back when she was the married one, it had always taken some serious juggling of schedules to set aside time for the two of them to get together. Moira's job kept her busy, especially since she often worked evenings or nights while Carli had a day job. At least Peter had never complained when she and Moira were able to make plans to have dinner or even get away for a spa weekend.

In turn, she'd done her best to be understanding when he spent so much time playing golf. He always claimed the connections he made at the golf course were important for his career, but also to the future the two of them were building together—one where they'd finally be in a position to start their family. He wanted to make sure they were financially stable before adding any children to the mix.

At the same time, he'd encouraged her to start taking evening classes because he knew she wanted to finish her degree. Before that, she'd often hosted dinner parties for his clients. But once she was busy with both school and work, Peter offered to start taking them out to fancy restaurants instead. He was also understanding of why she couldn't accompany him.

He'd been attentive and considerate, the perfect husband, right up until the night that he announced he was filing for an immediate divorce. Her whole life had shattered the moment he told her that he and his new love were expecting a child together and wanted to be married before the baby was born.

Darn it, she'd sworn she'd stop dwelling on everything she'd lost. There was no use in rehashing things better left in the past. After taking a calming breath, she opened the door and stepped inside the café. It didn't take long to spot Moira. Carli waved to let her know she'd seen her and started making her away across the crowded room. Along the way, she stopped several times to acknowledge greetings from friends and get hugs from kids who knew her from school.

Seeing so many familiar faces was one of the things she loved most about living in a small town. She hadn't realized how much she'd missed that until she'd moved back home after her divorce. She and Peter had only lived about sixty miles from Dunbar, but it might as well have been a world away. Even after living in the same house for eight years, they'd barely met their neighbors. She doubted any of them had noticed when Peter switched wives.

When she finally made it across the café, Moira stood up to give her a big hug. "I'm so glad you could make it."

"Me, too."

Titus stopped by seconds later to fill her coffee cup and take their order. "French toast is today's special. It comes with locally sourced blueberry syrup and your choice of bacon, sausage or ham. Today's omelet has fresh asparagus, bacon and Swiss cheese. It's served with a side of hash browns and fresh fruit."

Both offerings sounded really good. Too bad she couldn't have it all. Well, she could, but she'd never be able to eat that much. Titus was always overly generous when it came to the size of the portions.

"I'll have the French toast and bacon."

Moira smiled up at her husband. "Me, too."

"Good choice. It shouldn't take long."

Tracking her husband's progress back toward the kitchen, Moira rubbed her hands together with greedy glee. "Not to brag, but Titus makes the challah bread for the French toast himself. That's what makes it so good."

Carli couldn't help but laugh. It hadn't been all that long ago that Moira had been convinced that Titus couldn't be trusted, her cop instincts insisting that he was up to no good. "Brag all you want, my friend. Everybody admires that man's cooking skills."

Moira finally turned her attention back to Carli. "So, how have things been going in your part of the world lately?"

Something in her tone struck an off note. "You make it sound like we haven't spoken in weeks instead of just days."

"We used to talk on the phone or keep in touch by text almost daily. We haven't been doing that."

For a second, Moira looked as if her feelings were hurt, which made Carli cringe. She'd been trying to give her friend time to settle into her new life as a married woman only to find out she'd gone about it in the wrong way. Carli reached across the table to take Moira's hand in hers. "I'm sorry. I've missed you, too, but I thought you had enough going on right now. You're barely back from your honeymoon, you've moved out of your mom's house and in with your handsome husband, and now you're back at work. That's a lot for anyone to handle."

Moira gave Carli's hand a squeeze and then let go. "You're my best friend. I'll always have time for you."

Carli sighed. "I'm sorry, Moira. I'm not sure why, but lately I keep thinking about Peter and how things went off the rails. It always throws me off my stride. I'll never understand how I could have so completely misread the situation back then. If there were signs that he was unhappy, I sure didn't see them. As a result, I find myself overthinking my relationships with everyone else, even those I know I can trust."

Moira's mouth was set in a hard line. "There are some days I wish I wasn't a police officer. Even after all this time, I would love for the two of us to have a discussion with your ex—one that would leave him a bit battered and bruised. I might even let you have the first swing at him."

"I'd be glad to provide an alibi for the two of you if you ever decide to pay the man a visit. Just let me know."

Carli jumped at the sound of Titus's gravelly voice from right behind her. She twisted in her seat to look up at him. Even though he was grinning at his wife, Carli suspected he wasn't kidding, but it wouldn't be worth the energy to go after Peter like that. Nothing would change what had happened, and once she'd gotten past the initial hurt, she counted herself lucky to be shed of the man.

Titus set her breakfast in front of her and did the same for Moira. "Better yet, you could let me pay a visit to your ex."

He gave Carli a knowing look. "I'm betting a certain bar owner would happily lend me a helping hand."

She was still sputtering in protest when he walked away. One glance at Moira had her wishing she'd managed to hide her reaction to Titus's less-than-subtle taunt. Rather than waiting for the inquisition to begin, she asked a question of her own. "What does he know that I don't?"

Moira tracked her husband's progress across the café. "I had to work last night and couldn't be home for dinner. Instead of cooking for himself, Titus and Ryder stopped by Barnaby's last night for a burger. Ryder is another volunteer fireman and got called in about the time they finished eating. Rather than leave with him, Titus hung out with Shay for a while longer. From what I gather, your name came up…something about

Luca asking you to join them for pizza night before last."

Who knew men were such gossips?

"I was going to tell you. It wasn't a big deal. Shay and Luca had a conference with Luca's teacher at the school. They happened to walk out of the building right after I did. As soon as Luca spotted me, he came running and asked if I wanted to join them for pizza. Technically, I was Luca's guest, not Shay's. He was just our chauffer."

By that point, Moira's eyes gleamed with excitement. It was time to rein her in. "It was just a spur-of-the-moment outing, nothing more. The truth is that Luca put Shay on the spot by inviting me without asking him first. He probably only backed the kid's play because he wants the boy to know what he wants matters."

Her friend wasn't having it. "Are you listening to yourself? Shay could have just as easily pointed out to Luca that it was nice of him to want to include you, but that you probably already had plans for the evening. He knows you would've picked up on his reluctance to include you and would have let Luca down gently."

When Carli didn't respond, Moira kept going. "So, I have two questions for you. First, did Shay act like he didn't really want you there? And second, did you enjoy yourself? If so, was it because you like hanging out with a six-year-old kid or with an adult male in his prime?"

What was Carli supposed to say to that? Especially if she didn't really want to admit the truth. She pointed at the two plates on the table. "I'm going to eat now. I don't want to insult your husband's great cooking by letting it get cold."

Moira picked up her own fork and pointed it in Carli's direction. "Fine. Just know we will revisit this conversation."

When Moira happened to look toward the door a few seconds later, her eyes widened in surprised delight. "Um, don't look now, but you've been spotted."

Carli knew she'd regret turning to see what Moira was talking about, especially since she could already guess. Sure enough, Luca was headed straight for her with a huge grin on his face. Shay was trailing along behind him looking a lot less excited by the situation. When he realized she was watching, he mouthed, *Sorry*.

Meanwhile, Luca came to a screeching halt just short of where she was sitting. "Carli! Mr. Titus told Shay to bring me here for breakfast because Ned has been missing me. I brought him treats so he won't be mad that I have Beau and Bruno."

All of that exciting news left him breathless. He paused to draw in more air and picked up right where he'd left off. "I'm going to have French toast and hot chocolate. Shay said he'd make up his mind after he looked at the menu."

It took him that long to realize Carli wasn't alone at the table. When he took a step back, looking as if he was about to bolt back to Shay, Carli held out her hand and coaxed him closer. "Luca Nix, I'd like you to meet Moira. She's a police officer here in Dunbar, and she's married to Mr. Titus. More importantly, she's my best friend. We met each other back when we were about your age."

Luca bobbed his head. "Nice to meet you. I like Mr. Titus and Ned."

Moira offered him a friendly smile. "From what I hear, they like you, too."

She nodded in the direction of the kitchen. "Speaking of Ned, it looks like he heard you come in. He's headed this way."

That was all it took to have Luca off and running again. Two seconds later, he was down on his knees with his arms around Ned's neck. It was so cute to see him looking so earnest as he talked to the huge dog. When he held out a treat, Ned responded by giving the boy's cheek a quick lick before accepting the goody. It was such a sweet moment, making Carli wish she'd thought to whip out her phone and snap a picture or two.

Luckily, Moira had. She took a couple more

before setting her phone back down on the table. "I'll send you those after we're done with breakfast. Now, I need to make a quick trip to the restroom. Invite them to join us if you'd like."

Carli might have believed Moira needed the restroom if she'd actually headed in that direction. Instead, the sneaky traitor disappeared into the kitchen, probably to let Titus know Shay and Luca had arrived. No doubt the maneuver was meant to ensure that Carli would have to talk to Shay alone. Not that she wanted to. Much. Sighing, she pasted on what she hoped looked like a genuine smile as she waited for him to reach the table.

SHAY GROANED AS soon as he stepped into the diner. He didn't know if Carli being there was just happenstance or if Titus had decided to play matchmaker. If that turned out to be the case, he and the man would be having a long talk, one that might end up with bruised fists and a bloody nose. Maybe even two considering he figured they'd be pretty evenly matched. It would serve Titus right if his new bride ended up tossing the pair of them in the slammer. She wouldn't be amused, but Shay would be.

Some of what he was thinking must have showed on his face when Titus poked his head out of the kitchen. The coward took one look at

Shay and immediately ducked back out of sight. If he thought hiding would save him, he was in for a rude awakening. For now, Shay would let it slide. He needed to corral Luca and sit down at a table before the little rascal decided to invite himself to sit with Carli and Moira. Well, if he hadn't already done so. Right now, he was making peace with Ned, so maybe Shay still had time to head the situation off at the pass.

He'd only gone a couple of steps when Moira abruptly left the table to join her husband in the kitchen. Despite his good intentions, Shay found himself drifting to a stop where Carli was now sitting by herself. "Hi, long time no see."

And if that didn't sound totally awkward.

Carli laughed and made a show of looking at the time on her phone. "I know! Gosh, it's been almost two days."

"Look, don't take this the wrong way, but I didn't ask Titus to…you know—"

He stopped talking, not sure how to finish that sentence. Surprisingly, Carli's smile didn't falter. Instead, she jerked her thumb in the direction of the kitchen. "And I didn't ask his wife to…you know. This was all on them, not us."

"And yet, here we are. Any suggestions on how we should handle the situation?"

"Well, that all depends. If you want to disappoint them, you and Luca could pick a table on the other side of the café. Or I could pitch a hissy fit, as my grandmother used to say, and storm out, nose in the air. That might be pretty effective."

"I'd actually like to see that." He crossed his arms over his chest and tilted his head to the side as if giving the matter some serious consideration. "On the other hand, I could move Moira's breakfast to that empty table, so Luca and I could join you. It would drive her crazy not being able to listen in on our conversation."

"Tempting, but I'm not actually convinced she knew you'd be here. Moira isn't all that good at subterfuge. We've only seen each other once since they got back to town, so she invited me to meet her so we could get caught up. Her surprise at seeing you and Luca come through the door seemed genuine."

That was disappointing. "Well, then, I guess Luca and I should sit over there, so the two of you can visit."

He looked around to check on his young charge. "That is, if I can pry him away from Ned."

Carli bit her lower lip as if pondering a hard decision. Finally, she shook her head. "No, sit with us. We've got the room, and that will give you someone to talk to while Luca and Ned hang out together."

"You sure?"

She answered by tugging the chair next to her away from the table in invitation. Okay, then. "I'll grab Luca and be right back."

As soon as he reached Luca, Titus stepped out of the kitchen. "For the record, I didn't know until this morning that Carli was meeting Moira for breakfast. I don't play games with my friends' lives. I might give you a hard time once in a while, but I wouldn't..."

When it looked like Titus was struggling to find the right words, Shay finished the sentence for him. "Are you saying that you're not starting a new career as a dating service?"

The other man didn't take that suggestion very well. "Very funny. Once you get Luca seated, I'll come take your order myself."

"Sounds good. Tell Moira it's safe to come back out."

"And you tell Carli I'll bring her a fresh order of French toast when I bring your food. Hers is probably cold by now."

"Will do."

In the end, Titus pulled up a chair and sat next to his wife while the rest of them demolished their breakfasts and then lingered over coffee and conversation. Shay half expected Luca to get restless once he polished off his French toast and hot chocolate. Instead, he seemed content to let the adults talk while he lavished all of his attention on Ned.

It would be interesting to see how Beau and Bruno would respond to Ned's scent on Luca when they got back home. No doubt it would involve more treats and extra cuddles.

Carli directed her next question to Shay. "So what are your and Luca's plans for the rest of the day?"

"We're going to work on some assignments he needs to get done for Ms. Varne. Mostly practicing his handwriting and doing some math. After that, he also needs to read aloud to me for thirty minutes before I leave for work around four. I have to help man the bar on Saturdays. It's the busiest night of the week."

"That makes sense."

"How about you? Anything fun planned?"

Carli laughed. "Depends on whether grocery shopping and cleaning house counts as fun."

Shay gave a low whistle. "We're a couple of wild ones, aren't we? Pouring drinks and folding socks—you can't get more exciting than that."

Moira joined in. "Well, unless you count driving in endless circles around town on patrol for eight hours straight. That's always a lot of fun… or a snooze-fest. I'm never sure which."

Titus clearly wasn't buying it. "You love your job, and you know it."

Her expression softened. "Yeah, I do. A police officer is all I've ever wanted to be."

Shay turned to Carli. "How about you? Did you always want to work at an elementary school?"

"Yeah, I did, although I'd originally planned to become a teacher. But I never finished college."

"How come?"

He knew he'd touched on a sore subject when both Carli and Moira grimaced. "Sorry, forget I asked."

"That's okay," Carli said as she waved off his apology. "My ex-husband, Peter, and I were both in college when we decided to get married. The original plan was that I would work until he graduated, and then it would be my turn to go back to school. He eventually graduated with his MBA and got his dream job. I had to keep working to help pay the mortgage on the house we bought. It was our dream home. He encouraged me to start taking evening classes, saying once his career took off, I could quit and go full-time."

Moira gave a disgusted snort. "He just wanted to keep you too busy to wonder what he was really doing with all of his time when you weren't home with him."

Shay figured Moira had it right considering Carli didn't dispute her assertion. Her ex sounded like a real piece of work. How could he have had someone like her in his life and treat her so poorly? Another good question would be why Shay was getting so mad about something that had happened years ago to a woman he hadn't even known at the time.

He forced himself to relax and let it go. Unfortunately, not before Titus noticed. His friend was giving him a considering look. At least he didn't say anything. Still, maybe it was time to get moving.

"Luca, tell Ned goodbye and thank Titus for feeding you. We need to go home and walk the dogs before you do your homework."

"But I don't want to do homework."

Titus reached over to ruffle the boy's hair. "No one ever wants to do homework, Luca. But that's your job like cooking for people is mine and protecting the people of Dunbar is Moira's."

Luca frowned. "And Carli working at the school?"

Shay nodded. "Yep, and me running the bar. We all had to do homework when we were your age. Now it's your turn. The thing is, if you work hard and get your homework done, then you can have more time with Beau and Bruno."

Still not looking all that thrilled with the idea, Luca patted Ned one last time and stood up. "Fine. Thanks for the French toast, Mr. Titus."

Shay was about to steer him toward the door when his phone rang. "Hey, Aunt Meg. What's up?"

Her voice was so faint, he could barely hear her. "I'm really sorry, Shay, but I've got one of my bad headaches, and the pills aren't helping at all. Do you think you can find someone else to stay with Luca tonight? If not, I'll still come."

That was sure not good news. "No, that's okay. Stay home and take care of yourself. Don't worry about us. I'll figure something out. If all else fails, I can always take him to work with me."

"If you're sure."

It wouldn't be Shay's first choice. A tavern was no place for a kid to hang out, but he might not have any other option. "It will be fine, Aunt Meg. I hope you feel better soon."

"Me, too."

She hung up, leaving him staring at the screen in frustration. It wasn't her fault, but what was he supposed to do now? It was no surprise that it was Carli who asked, "What's wrong?"

"Aunt Meg can't stay with Luca tonight. She's not feeling well."

"I hope it's nothing serious."

"She gets migraines now and then. Her medicine helps some, but she usually ends up going to bed early and sleeping it off." He looked around the café as if he'd somehow find an answer to his conundrum there. "I've been trying to find someone who can stay with Luca occasionally while I work, but so far I haven't had any luck."

Moira studied Luca with what looked like regret. "I'd offer, but I have to work again tonight."

Her husband didn't look much happier. "And I have to be here at the café."

Carli reached up to tug on Shay's sleeve. "How about me? The groceries can wait, and my house won't get much dustier if I don't clean until tomorrow. What time would you like me?"

Actually, he pretty much liked her around the clock, but that wasn't what she was asking him. "If you're sure, I should leave home around three thirty or so, but I can be flexible about that."

She nodded and then smiled at Luca. "So, what do you think, kiddo? Would I be an acceptable substitute for your aunt Meg? I hope so because it means I can hang out with you for the evening."

By that point, Luca was bouncing up and down in excitement. "And you can meet Beau and Bruno. They'll like that."

Shay listened while Luca began telling Carli all the rules the dogs were expected to follow, his words practically tripping over each other as he tried to tell her everything at once. It was nice to know the boy was so happy about getting to spend some unexpected time with Carli. And if he was more than a little jealous of Luca right now, he did his best to ignore it.

CHAPTER NINE

AROUND ELEVEN, Carli decided she should check on Luca again. Getting him to go to bed and stay there hadn't been easy. He'd really wanted to hang out with her until Shay got home. She wouldn't have minded his company, but that was a slippery slope. If she let him bend the rules, he might think he could do the same on weeknights when he'd have school the next day. She smiled when she crept into his room. He was sleeping peacefully curled up on his side with his arm around Beau. Bruno was sprawled across the end of the bed at Luca's feet. The dog lifted his head and then thumped his tail a couple of times in greeting before settling back into sleep.

Knowing all was well, she returned to the living room and sat down on the couch to channel surf while she waited for Shay to come home. He'd texted several times to check on how things were going over the course of the evening and then called to check in with Luca right before the boy's scheduled bedtime. Luca had filled him in on what the dogs had done and told him about the animated movie Carli had brought to watch with him. From what Luca told her, Shay called him every night, which she thought was really sweet of him. The man definitely took his new role as a surrogate father seriously. She truly believed that with Shay's help, Luca would weather the storm of losing his parents at such a young age.

After considering the available options on TV, she finally settled on one of her favorite movies, an old black-and-white classic that she never grew tired of watching. About an hour into the film, a vehicle pulled into the driveway. She twisted around to look out the window and was relieved but also surprised to recognize Shay's truck. Why was he back so early? She hadn't expected him for another hour at least.

He was already out of the truck and heading for the door. She turned off the television and waited for him to come inside. "Hey, there. You're getting home kind of early, aren't you?"

"A little. I've promoted Jody to evening manager, so she's handling closing tonight so I could get back to Luca." Then he smiled. "And let you go home a little earlier."

"I wouldn't have minded staying until your usual time."

He dropped down on the other end of the couch

from where she was sitting. Now that he was closer, she could see the lines of exhaustion on his handsome face. She shouldn't have been surprised. From what she could tell, he usually didn't get home from work until well after midnight, which wouldn't have been a problem back when he could sleep late in the morning.

"Did you have any trouble getting him to go to bed?"

"Nothing I couldn't handle. He wanted to watch the movie again, but I told him I'd loan it to him for a while. After that, he didn't argue, especially when I promised to read him an extra book. When I peeked in on him a little while ago, he was curled up with his buddies, sound asleep."

Shay looked relieved to hear that. "He's been sleeping a little better since Bruno and Beau moved in with us, but he still wakes up crying for his mom and dad. It happened again last night, and I feel so bad for him. I'm a pretty poor substitute for them."

His assessment of the situation made her inexplicably mad. "Don't say things like that, Shay Barnaby! You've done everything you can think of to make Luca feel safe and cared for. Without you being willing to step up to bat, he could've easily ended up in foster care and bounced around from one place to another, living with strangers until he turns eighteen and ages out of the system. Instead, you dropped everything to go get him. You brought him into your home and have bent over backward to help him settle in. You even let him adopt not just one dog but two, so he didn't have to choose which brother to bring home."

She let that much sink in before continuing. "At least you knew his parents. Even if he'd been adopted by a nice couple at some point, they would never be able to share real memories about his parents with him the way you can. He'll always be grateful to you for helping him to remember them. You might not have expected to end up raising Luca, but you are the perfect man for the job."

He blinked as if her tirade had surprised him. Then his mouth curved up in a hint of a smile. "Thank you. I wish I had that on a recording so I can replay it whenever I feel like I'm screwing up."

Her cheeks heated. Maybe she'd gone a bit overboard with the lecture. "I might not have any children of my own, but I've met an awful lot of kids and parents over the years. You're not the first parent to feel overwhelmed at times. But from what I've seen, kids are pretty forgiving. All they really care about is knowing they can depend on you and that you care. You've got those two things covered in spades."

He reached across the small distance between them to take her hand long enough to give it a quick squeeze. She found the warmth of the brief connection comforting and hoped it was the same for him. Deciding she'd made her point, she changed topics. "How was work tonight?"

"The usual Saturday night traffic. A lot of the regulars stop by for a cold brew and a burger. A few others are out to get loud and rowdy. There were also the usual nitwits who insisted on drinking a few too many. I called Moira to let her know I'd taken their keys so they couldn't drive. Cade Peters recently established a policy that his officers will offer people a lift home when that happens. As long as they cooperate and don't raise too big of a ruckus along the way, there are no charges. If it happens too often with the same culprits, he has a long talk with them. So far, it's reduced the number of arrests for DUI significantly."

"Sounds like a smart move."

"Yeah, Cade's done a good job since becoming the new chief of police."

As he spoke, Shay stretched his arms over his head and then yawned so wide that his jaw cracked. He immediately covered his mouth with his hand. "Whoops, sorry about that. It's been a long day."

As much as she enjoyed hanging out with Shay,

it was definitely time to call it an evening. "No apology necessary, but it's a reminder I should be going."

Shay frowned. "It's kind of late for you to be driving home alone. Let me get Luca up, and we'll follow you home."

Seriously? The man could hardly keep his eyes open. "There's no need to do that. I don't live all that far."

"Still..."

"Do you follow your aunt home every night?"

He heaved a big sigh. "No, but she only lives a half a mile farther down the same driveway on the back side of the family property."

She got up off the couch and picked up her purse. "I'll be fine, Shay."

With her keys in hand, she opened the front door. "Get some sleep while you can."

The stubborn man insisted on following her out to her car. "Thanks again for offering to stay with Luca on such short notice. I'm still hoping to find a few teenagers as backup. There has to be someone in town who could use some extra money."

Carli had a thought. "I don't know why I didn't think of this sooner. Do you know Elizabeth and Jimmy Glines? He runs a fishing and hunting guide business here in town."

When he nodded, she continued, "Liza, their

oldest daughter, has started babysitting for a few people. I know she helps out when Shelby Peters hosts a movie night for kids to give their parents a break, and I think she also occasionally babysits Rikki Volkov's son, who is around Luca's age. Shelby should be able to give you her number."

"Thanks! I'll give her a call."

When he yawned again, Carli gave him a gentle shove. "Worry about all of that tomorrow. You need to go to bed before you fall asleep out here."

"Thanks again, Carli." He opened her car door for her. "Text me when you get home."

The man was a protector through and through. Telling him not to worry would be like telling the stars to stop shining. "I will."

He was still watching as she drove out of sight.

BACK INSIDE, Shay turned off the lights in the living room and checked on Luca on his way to his own room. Once there, he took the world's fastest shower and practically dove under the covers to wait to hear from Carli. His head hit the pillow only seconds before his phone pinged.

I'm home. You can go to sleep now, worrywart.

He laughed. That's Mr. Worrywart to you, lady.

You think you're funny, don't you? she responded.

I am funny. Also charming and handsome.

I notice you didn't say you were humble.

I didn't want to brag. :) Shay grinned to himself.

Ha, ha. Get some sleep while you can, funny man.

Fine. Thanks again for helping out with Luca.

You're welcome.

Tempted to add one last thing, he typed, I wish I had kissed you before you left.

Still, he hesitated before hitting Send. Finally, he erred on the side of cowardice and deleted the message and ended the conversation with something far safer—and a lot lonelier.

Good night, Carli.

He sent the message and set his phone on the bedside table. After turning off the light, he went to sleep wondering how Carli would have responded if he hadn't chickened out.

SUNDAY MORNING CAME way too soon. One second Shay was sleeping peacefully, and the next his bed had somehow turned into a trampoline for one excited six-year-old. Luca bounced up and down while his two four-legged fans barked their enthusiastic encouragement, leaving Shay the only one who was growling.

He pulled his pillow over his head and did his best to ignore the happy antics. It didn't help. Not one bit. Finally, he surrendered to the inevitable.

Blinking grumpily at the trio, he mumbled, "Okay, I'm awake. Was there something you wanted?"

Luca put a momentary hold on the jumping to answer. "Pancakes."

"Fine. While I drag myself out of bed, why don't you let the dogs out?"

That might buy him another minute or two to get his brain jump-started for the day. Unfortunately, his crafty plan was an immediate failure. Luca went back to bouncing as he announced, "Already did that. I also gave them fresh water, but the three of us are real hungry."

"Go watch cartoons. I'll be along in a few minutes to make breakfast and measure out their kibble."

Luca and the dogs took off running for the television while Shay mustered up enough energy to sit up on the side of the bed. His eyes felt like sandpaper, and his brain was stuck in Neutral. He'd give anything to curl back up under the covers for another hour or two. Heck, he'd settle for fifteen minutes, but even that was wishful thinking.

Who knew what mayhem Luca and the dogs would cause if left to their own devices for much longer? Shay pushed himself up off the bed and staggered into the bathroom. He felt marginally better after splashing his face with cold water. By the time he reached the living room, Luca was sprawled next to the dogs on the floor watching television. Shay paused long enough to turn the volume down a notch before continuing to the kitchen.

For the sake of his own sanity, he put the coffee on to brew before gathering up the necessary ingredients for homemade pancakes. Next, he put several strips of bacon in a skillet to fry. By the time he had the pancake batter mixed up, the coffee was ready. That first sip of dark roast caffeine brightened his mood. He made quick work of setting the table while the cast-iron griddle heated on the stove. After getting out the maple syrup and butter, he ladled the first four pancakes onto the griddle.

When he flipped them to the second side, he poked his head into the living room. "Turn off the television, Luca. Your breakfast is almost ready."

"Can't I eat in here?"

"Nope. I like it better if we eat together when

we can. Once you've finished your pancakes and cleared your spot, you can watch your shows for an hour. After that, we have chores to do."

That earned him a major eye roll, but Shay didn't take it personally. He hadn't liked doing weekend chores when he was Luca's age, and the truth was he didn't make the boy work all that hard. Right after he'd brought Luca home, Shay had asked his aunt for advice about what expectations he should have for Luca when it came to such things. She'd said it was important for kids to have responsibilities that were suitable to their age and abilities when it came to keeping the house clean and tidy. It was part of being a family.

So far, he expected Luca to bring his dirty clothes to the laundry room and put the clean ones away once Shay finished the laundry. He also had to pick up his toys, make his bed and help clear the table after meals. Eventually Shay would add to the list, but he figured that was enough for the present.

Once they finished the indoor chores, they'd move onto working outside. In reality, that meant Shay mowed the front yard while Luca and the dogs played out back. They'd switch locations while he did the back. After that, he and Luca would head over to the bar to meet up with Jody. Luca could work on his homework while Shay and Jody figured out the details of their new working arrangement. No doubt they'd have to tweak things for a while until they got all of the kinks worked out, but starting on Monday Shay had every intention of being home no later than six o'clock, cutting way back on the number of hours he'd need someone to stay with Luca. He planned to see if the day care at the school had a space open. If not, he was pretty sure Aunt Meg would continue to help out until they did.

He'd tell her the good news when he saw her that evening. She'd texted earlier to say she was feeling better and wanted to invite them over for dinner. Even if she wasn't such a great cook, he would have happily accepted the invitation. When he only had to cook for himself, he'd often make a big pot of soup or a casserole and live off of it for several days. Failing that, he'd grab something to eat at the bar.

Now that he had Luca to think about, he was trying to do a better job of keeping things like fresh fruit and vegetables on hand. Aunt Meg cooked for herself and Luca when she was there, but Shay was responsible for the remaining meals and packing Luca's lunch for school. He'd had no idea how easy he had it before Luca moved in. Not that he was complaining. Much, anyway. Raising a kid took a lot of work, but he was determined to do it right. For now, he'd start by pouring Luca a glass of orange juice and feeding him some whole wheat pancakes.

"Come on, Luca. Pancakes aren't nearly as good when they're cold."

Luca appeared a few seconds later with the dogs hot on his heels. When he was seated at the table, Bruno and Beau parked themselves on either side of him, ready to clean up any bits and pieces of pancakes or bacon that happened to land on the floor.

After all, dogs should have chores, too.

CHAPTER TEN

LATE THURSDAY AFTERNOON, Carli carried the three dresses she'd picked out to the fitting room in the back of the shop. "Tell me why we're doing this again?"

Moira hung the slacks and blouses she'd chosen on the hook inside the first cubicle before turning to face Carli, her expression puzzled. "Because we agreed that you needed to update your wardrobe…you know, in case by some miracle you actually go on a date someday."

Carli stared at the three dresses she'd chosen off the rack. "But now that I think about it, what are the chances of that happening? Especially since I'm not at all that interested in that idea in the first place."

Her friend scoffed. "A few weeks ago, I might have believed that, but then I saw how you acted around Shay at the wedding. You have to admit you had a great time hanging out with him. Seriously, I can't remember the last time I've seen you laugh that much, and I'm guessing you were happy when he promised to call you afterward."

"That's just it, Moira. Shay didn't call. Still hasn't unless he's needed help with Luca."

Moira hesitated briefly before responding. "I understand why you were upset, but it wasn't like he meant to hurt you. I'm sure he regrets that he didn't at least text to let you know what was going on. He also knows you understand why Luca has to come first right now."

Of course Carli understood. That didn't change the fact that she'd spent two long weeks hurt and disappointed, each day wondering why Shay had broken his promise to call. The experience had served as a reminder of why she'd lost all interest in dating in the first place. Yeah, she really liked Shay and even admired his determination to do right by his new son. But when—or even if—she ever decided to date someone again, she didn't want to have to wonder if he was interested in her for her own sake or if he only needed a convenient babysitter who was available on short notice.

Unfortunately, stubborn woman that she was, Moira just wouldn't let it go. "Fine. Things didn't work out with him, but you never know when you might meet someone new. I also don't believe you actually enjoy sitting home alone every

Saturday night. Been there, done that myself, and I know how lonely it can be."

Desperate to derail the conversation, Carli held out one of the price tags for Moira's inspection. "Even you have to admit that staying home on Saturday night is a whole lot cheaper than this. And for your information, I'm going to the movies with two women from work Saturday evening."

Moira rolled her eyes as she stepped inside her cubicle and pulled the curtain shut. "That's not the same as dating."

"True, but it does prove that I haven't put my entire life on hold waiting for some man to sweep me off my feet."

"You're right, and I'm glad you're doing something fun this weekend."

There was a rustle of clothing as Moira tried on the outfits she'd picked out. "I like this red shirt. Sometimes I wish I didn't have to wear the same old uniforms day in and day out. You're lucky that way. At least you can wear pretty dresses to work if you want."

Carli wrinkled her nose as she studied the dresses again. "Don't you think these are a bit too dressy for where I work?"

"Even if they are, get them anyway. When was the last time you splurged simply because you wanted to wear something new and pretty?"

Too long, but that was beside the point. Carli liked nice clothes as much as the next woman. Besides, all three dresses were on sale 25 percent off. But even if they weren't, her misgivings had nothing to do with money. She lived well within her means and could easily afford a new outfit or two without totally blowing the budget. To avoid admitting what the real problem was, she gave up and stepped into the cubicle next to Moira's. "Fine, I'll try them on. That doesn't mean I have to buy anything."

She'd barely had time to hang them up when Moira yanked Carli's curtain back open. "Look, maybe this was a mistake. Do you want to call it a day and go home?"

Not really. Not that she'd admit it to Moira, but more and more lately the walls had been closing in on her. "No, I don't. We've always enjoyed shopping together, and the dresses are fine. If nothing else, I can wear them to church, so it's not like they'll go to waste. It's the whole idea of dating that's the problem. Even if I was interested, where would I meet someone? Most of the men I see at work already have families. The same is true at church."

"There's always online dating. We both know people who've found someone special that way."

Carli settled on a version of the truth. "Yeah, but it's not for me. I don't want to go out with someone I don't really know at all. Even if he's the nicest guy ever, I can't relax and enjoy myself when it feels more like a job interview than a date."

Moira looked sympathetic. "Look, I know putting yourself out there isn't easy."

"No, it's not. All things considered, I can't help but think that I'm better off playing it safe."

This wasn't the first time they'd had this conversation. In the past, it was Moira who'd gone through a few rough patches when it came to dating. The worst was when the man she'd fallen in love with had been arrested for drug trafficking. Carli had been there to help her friend patch her broken heart back together. Luckily for Moira, that story had ultimately had a surprisingly happy ending when that same guy had come looking for her and explained what really happened.

As it turned out, Titus had been working on an undercover operation to bring down a drug cartel, and he'd been "arrested" to maintain his cover. It had definitely taken some fancy talking on Titus's part to convince Moira to give him another chance, but the pair couldn't be happier these days.

In return, Moira had come running when Carli's husband had filed for divorce. Everything that had happened with Peter was enough to make a woman understandably gun-shy about dipping her toes in the water of the dating pool. If Carli couldn't trust a man she'd known so well, how could she risk her bruised and battered heart with a total stranger? It had been almost two years since the divorce, and she was still picking up the pieces of her life.

She suddenly realized that she'd remained silent too long. Considering Moira knew her better than anyone else did and had the well-honed instincts of a good cop, she was putting two and two together and coming up with an uncomfortable conclusion. "I wouldn't push you to give dating another chance if I thought you were truly happy on your own. Seeing you with Shay gave me hope that you were finally moving on from Peter, but here's the thing."

Carli held up one of the dresses and studied it rather than look her friend in the eye. "What?"

"I think Shay is the reason you're not really interested in dating anyone else."

It wasn't worth the energy it would take to deny the truth. "Maybe, but he's been pretty clear that he's not looking to date anyone."

Moira crossed her arms and leaned against the thin wooden wall that separated Carli's cubicle from the next one. "That doesn't mean he won't eventually. Did you tell him he could call you once he gets Luca settled into a routine?"

"No, although I did tell him he could call me if he needed someone to stay with Luca."

Moira closed her eyes and dropped her chin as if Carli's admission was a huge disappointment to her. "So, you've offered to babysit Luca whenever Shay happens to have plans for an evening? That's so generous of you."

Why did Moira make that sound as if what Carli had done was more foolish than nice?

"Seriously, I'm just backup if all else fails. I'd do the same for anybody."

"Yeah, you would, which is what makes you such a good friend." Moira straightened up and stepped back. "Do you want to hear my final take on the situation?"

While she considered how she wanted to answer that question, Carli unzipped the first dress. Might as well try it on since she'd come this far. Finally, she asked, "Would it stop you from telling me if I said no?"

"Probably not."

"Then lay it on me."

"Shay Barnaby is nothing like the men you've dated in the past. That's not necessarily a bad thing, but I have to wonder if that is part of the appeal. I don't know much about his past, but that both Chief Peters and Titus respect him is a point in his favor. Another is his willingness to take on the responsibility of raising Luca.

Having said all of that, don't let his easy charm fool you. The man has no trouble handling the rougher customers who hang out at his bar. He'll never be the suit-and-tie kind of guy you always said you wanted."

Carli pulled the dress off its hanger. "So you're saying that Shay is all wrong for me."

"No, what I'm saying is that you need to figure out what kind of guy will make you happy in the long run. If that means a guy more along the lines of your ex-husband, fine. Ditto if you want someone a little rougher around the edges. We both know outside appearances don't really matter. I always figured I'd end up with a spit-and-polish cop. Granted, Titus used to be a cop, but now he's a tattooed diner owner. The bottom line is that it's what's on the inside that matters. You want someone who treats you right."

"Trust me. I know better than to choose someone just because he looks good in expensive suits or even in faded jeans and a T-shirt." She'd learned that lesson the hard way. "There is one thing I really want, though. If I'm ever lucky enough to fall in love again, I'd like him to look at me the way Titus looks at you."

"And how is that?"

"Like he can't figure out what he ever did to deserve someone like you in his life, but he's not about to question his good luck."

Moira smiled, her happiness with her husband sparkling in her eyes. "I want that for you, too, my friend. Dating isn't easy, but you're never going to find that special guy if you don't put yourself out there."

Then she pointed at the dresses. "Back to why we're here. Which dress do you like best? I'm betting it's the burgundy one."

Having already come to that conclusion herself, Carli tugged her curtain closed. "You're just saying that because you're the one who picked it out."

Moira laughed as she returned to her own cubicle. "What can I say? I have perfect taste in both fashion and friends."

IT HAD BEEN a long week, but at least Shay hadn't run into any more glitches when it came to having someone stay with Luca. He'd been able to enroll Luca in the day care at the school, and Carli's suggestion that he reach out to Liza Glines had paid off. Not having to worry constantly about finding day care for his young charge was a real godsend at this point.

Having said that, there were definitely times Shay wished he had a legitimate excuse to ask Carli if she would mind taking the occasional shift. It had been a week since she'd been the one waiting for him when he'd gotten home from work. Shay could get used to being greeted by her sweet smile and having someone to unwind with at the end of a busy day. He still had their text conversation saved on his phone and had read through it far more times than he'd care to admit.

The truth was that he missed her way more than he probably should, especially considering they'd never actually been out on a real date. His biggest worry was that some other guy might have already staked a claim on her by the time Shay had his life back under control and had time for a serious relationship.

"Hey, boss. Can you take over for a second? I need to grab another couple of bottles of wine from downstairs. We've had a run on both of those new ones you've been thinking about permanently adding to our wine list."

He circled around to take Jody's place behind the bar. "I'll add more of them to Monday's order."

"Good idea. I'll be right back."

Working on filling the latest drink orders, Shay paused to scan the crowd and gauge the mood in the room. There hadn't been any problems so far, but he preferred to keep an eye on things before they had a chance to get out of hand. He happened to be looking toward the front of the bar when the door opened and a very welcome visitor stepped inside. His mood improved as soon as he spotted Carli. She wasn't alone, but he was relieved that her companions were both women.

He offered her a welcoming wave when she briefly met his gaze from across the room. She smiled and then followed her friends toward a table in the corner. He was debating whether he should abandon his post to wait on the group himself when Jody reappeared, wine bottles in hand. "I'm back. Who were you waving at?"

"A friend who just came in."

Jody tracked where he'd been looking. "Isn't that Carli Walsh? I don't recognize the others."

"Yeah, that's her. I don't recognize the others, either. Maybe they work with her at the school."

He tried to sound nonchalant, as if seeing her again was no big deal. From the smug look on Jody's face, he was pretty sure he wasn't successful. Time to make a strategic retreat. "I'll be in my office. It's time for my nightly call to Luca. Yell if it gets busy."

"Will do."

As soon as he reached his office, he dialed Aunt Meg's number. She picked up on the first ring. "Sorry, Shay, but Luca's already asleep. Do you want me to wake him up so the two of you can talk?"

"No, that's okay. How has he been this evening?"

"Good. He and the dogs played outside for a long time, so I think all three of them were more tired than usual. He conked out before I finished reading the first book to him."

While Shay rather enjoyed his nightly chats with Luca, it was a relief to know Meg was having an easy time of it. There had been a lot more peaceful nights lately, but some were still pretty rocky. "If he wakes up on his own and wants to talk, call me. Otherwise, I'll see you when I get back home."

"Sounds good."

Shay disconnected the call and considered his options. There was always paperwork to take care of, but right now he was too restless to stay shut up in his office. He didn't even have to guess why the room felt too small tonight, not with Carli sitting out there with her friends. Rather than second-guess himself, he headed back out to the bar to help Jody fill drink orders. When there was a break in the rush, he allowed himself a quick glance toward Carli's table in case they were ready for another round. Their glasses were empty, all right, but she was alone and talking to some guy at the next table.

Shay wiped his hands on a towel as he glanced around the bar to see where all of his servers were. "It looks like everyone else is busy, so I'll go see if Carli and her friends need anything."

Jody stepped in front of him, cutting off his escape. "I can do it. You said earlier that you've got paperwork to do, and I'm caught up right now."

"That's okay. I want to get her take on the new Riesling. She likes white wines."

"You keep telling yourself that's all you want, boss man." Jody poured a glass and set it on the counter. "There you go. Good luck."

Shay stopped and looked back at her. "What's that supposed to mean?"

She stepped closer, lowering her voice. "It means I saw how you looked at her at Titus's wedding."

That was the problem with letting employees cross the line to being friends. While Jody didn't hesitate to express her opinions, she wasn't given to gossiping about his personal business. Speaking slowly and clearly, he repeated his excuse for approaching Carli himself. "Like I said, I just want her take on the wine."

Jody fought to hide a smile as she picked up a towel and began wiping down the counter. "Message received and understood. I hope she likes it."

Shay picked up the glass of wine and started across the room. As a crow flies, the distance wasn't all that far, but his misgivings on whether he should be doing this grew with each step he took. He'd made it clear to Carli that he'd put his own personal life on hold for the time being, which meant she was free to talk to, or even date, anyone she wanted. Her companion even looked like a nice guy.

Shay hated him on sight.

If she hadn't already seen him coming, he might have given in to the temptation to veer off course and deliver the wine to someone else. Sadly, there wasn't anyone seated anywhere near her who was drinking wine. If he tried to hand it off to one of his other guests, it would only result in a discussion about why he was giving away free wine to one random person.

Having backed himself into an awkward corner, he had no choice but to tough it out. It was time to crank up some of the Southern charm he could turn on when the occasion called for it. "Carli, I'm glad to see you here tonight."

Her companion frowned as soon as Shay set the glass of wine down on her table. The guy took that opportunity to move his chair closer to hers, looking a little possessive. "Are you in the habit of choosing your customers' drinks for them?" the guy asked.

"No, actually I'm not." Shay met the other man's gaze head-on. "But I was hoping Carli would give me her opinion on this particular Riesling. It's one I'm thinking about adding to the wine list."

"I'll be glad to try it."

Carli offered introductions as she reached for the wineglass. "Dustin and his friends are in town on a fishing trip and staying at Rikki's bed-and-breakfast. This is Shay Barnaby. He owns this place, and he's a friend of mine."

It was hard not to smirk at the other man's flinch when Carli added that last part. Both men watched her take a small sip and then a second, larger one. Her smile was everything Shay could've hoped for. "This is really nice. Is it a local wine?"

"Yeah, the winery is in eastern Washington near Yakima. I'll definitely add more to the order tomorrow. Let me know if you'd like a refill."

He rubbed his hands together and shifted his attention back to Dustin. "What else can I get for the two of you? It will be on the house. That will include any appetizer you might like."

Dustin picked up the drink menu off the table, frowning as he made a pretense of studying the list of beers, wines and other drinks the bar offered. "I guess I'll have to settle on a Scotch on the rocks."

Carli gave the man a puzzled look at the way he'd phrased his order. "I won't need anything else," she said. "As soon as my friends come back from dancing with the two guys Dustin is with, I'll be heading home."

"Let me know if that changes." Turning to Dustin, he added, "I'll send your drink over."

Jody was waiting for him when he returned to the bar. Shay keyed in the order, trying his best to ignore Jody's reaction as she read it over his shoulder. If he had to guess, she was disappointed in him for some reason.

"What?"

She crossed her arms over her chest and stared up at him. "Did he actually order the cheapest stuff we carry?"

"No, not specifically. He just said 'Scotch on the rocks' when I told him his next drink was on the house."

Embarrassed about getting caught being a jerk, Shay voided the order. Figuring he was going to regret it, Shay got down the most expensive brand he carried. It wasn't that he cared about what Dustin thought about Barnaby's. He was doing it for Carli. If she wanted to spend some time with the guy, Shay wasn't going to spoil it for her.

No matter how much he wanted to.

He poured Carli a second glass of wine. "I'll be right back after I deliver these."

Jody nodded in approval. "For what it's worth,

he came in with two other guys. Her friends are dancing with them right now. I'm pretty sure she turned him down when he asked her to dance as well."

He wasn't about to admit how relieved he was to hear that.

CHAPTER ELEVEN

"SO, DO YOU come here often?"

Dustin's question wasn't much of a surprise, but the hint of snark laced through every word was. It took some effort, but Carli kept her own tone pleasantly friendly. "No, actually I don't. My friends and I went to a movie earlier and decided at the last minute we weren't quite ready to call it an evening. A few weeks ago, a friend rented the banquet room on the lower floor for her wedding reception, and I was here for that. I grew up here in Dunbar, but I've only been to Barnaby's one other time before that."

Dustin stared across to where Shay was working behind the bar. "And yet the owner knows you well enough to single you out to do an impromptu wine tasting for him?"

Carli didn't particularly appreciate the inquisition, but she made a determined effort to keep the conversation civil. "Shay has been expanding the selection of wines he offers. A while back, my friends and I stopped in after a local baseball game. When I ordered a glass of wine, Shay asked if I'd mind trying one he'd just started carrying."

She didn't feel the need to admit that she and Shay had spent time together on several occasions outside of the bar. It was none of Dustin's business, especially since she had no intentions of seeing him again after they parted ways tonight. From the questions he'd been asking before Shay brought her the wine, she suspected he was considering asking her out.

The current song on the jukebox ended. Hopefully Kim and Amy would be on their way back, and she could leave. Dustin scooted his chair closer. "Looks like my friends and yours aren't done dancing. Are you sure you don't want to join them?"

"I'd really rather not. I have a bit of a headache, and the music is pretty loud."

Besides, she'd already told him no twice. Even if she sometimes enjoyed dancing, she hadn't expected to end up at Barnaby's, hanging out with a man she didn't know at all instead of with her friends. She wasn't particularly happy with them for leaving her sitting at the table alone for so long.

She and Dustin had already pretty much exhausted most of the usual topics of discussion like movies, music and books. And she was struggling to come up with anything else to talk about. Finally, Dustin broke the silence. "I'm actually surprised that a woman like you would choose to live in such a small town."

What did he mean by that? "Like I said, I grew up in Dunbar."

"That doesn't mean you had to stay here." He made a point of looking around the room before adding, "You clearly have sophisticated tastes in food, movies and entertainment. Why not live closer to Seattle where those things are more readily available?"

She wasn't sure how to respond. "Dunbar is home to me. Besides, Seattle isn't that far of a drive."

It was none of his business that she had originally come back to Dunbar to lick her wounds after her marriage fell apart. Her intent had been to figure out what came next for her, but she'd forgotten how much she'd loved small-town life. Yeah, sometimes it got old having everyone all up in her business, but those same people would come running if Carlie needed them. She'd do the same for them, no questions asked.

"Do you live alone?"

Okay, she wasn't about to admit that there was no one waiting for her to come home. It was time to call it an evening even if her friends weren't ready to leave. To be on the safe side, she'd drive to Moira's house instead of her own. "I have a roommate. Which reminds me, I need to let her know why I'm running so late. She worries."

That didn't go over well. "Seriously? She likes to keep close track of you?"

Carli offered him a small smile. "Yeah, but that's probably because she's a cop. It's part of their nature to be overly protective."

She quickly sent Moira a text to give her a heads-up just in case. If Moira was working, she'd let Titus know that Carli might show up on their doorstep at some point. Dustin tried again. "I'm only in town for a couple more days. Maybe the two of us could have dinner tomorrow night."

It was time to put an end to this. "I'm sorry, Dustin, but I'm not really looking to date anyone right now."

He looked incredulous. "Why not? It's just one dinner. You could even pick the place."

Couldn't he take a hint? "I also already have other plans."

He didn't have to know those plans included doing the laundry and paying some bills. By that point, something else had caught his attention. "Well, it's about time."

When Carli looked around to see what Dustin was referring to, she spotted Shay headed their way with Dustin's drink and another glass of wine for her. She probably shouldn't drink anything else alcoholic since she was driving. On the other hand, it might help take the edge off her increasingly bad mood. She could always take advantage of Chief Peters's new program and ask his officers for a ride home. She could only imagine what Moira would have to say about that.

Shay set their drinks on the table. "A glass of wine for the lady."

She smiled. "Thanks, Shay."

He nodded and turned his attention to Dustin. "Here's your Scotch on the rocks."

After setting the glass down, he said, "Let me know if you want anything else."

Then he walked away without waiting for a response. She suspected he would have kept going until he reached the bar, but a customer at the next table asked him a question. Dustin took a sip of his drink and grimaced. "I should have known this place wouldn't offer a Scotch worth drinking."

Carli was pretty sure Shay had heard every word Dustin had just said. She'd had enough. "Maybe you're not happy that I'm not interested in having dinner with you, but that's no excuse for you to insult Shay or his bar."

She stood up, purse in hand. "Now, if you'll excuse me, I'm going to go tell my friends that I'm leaving."

He lurched to his feet, trying to block her way. "Look, I'm really sorry. Please stay. I'll even spring for a whole bottle of that wine if you like it so much."

Well aware they were drawing unwanted attention, she fought to sound calm and to keep her voice low. "Sorry, but I'm just not interested."

He looked insulted, as if no one had ever dared turn him down before. "I guess I was wrong. You do belong in a dump like this after all. I'm out of here. Tell my friends I walked back to the B and B."

Prolonging the conversation wouldn't accomplish anything other than to provide more grist for the local gossip mill. Right now, all she wanted was to head home, close her door and lock the world outside. She offered him her back and started toward the dance floor.

Unfortunately, Shay had a different opinion on the subject. He blocked Dustin's path to the door. "Apologize to the lady."

Dustin was smart enough to look around the bar before speaking. Maybe he hoped to find someone who would back his play, but he should've known better. He was an outsider there, and Shay's customers didn't like seeing one of their own come under attack.

"Sorry."

With that, Dustin turned on his heel and stalked

out the door. The one-word apology didn't seem to satisfy Shay, but Carli caught his arm when he started after Dustin. "Let him go. He's not worth bothering with."

"You deserved better."

"This might surprise you, but I'd already figured that out for myself. He didn't much like it when I turned him down flat when he asked me out. Now if you'll excuse me, I'm going to tell my friends it's time to go."

When Shay didn't immediately back off, she tried once again to stall him long enough for Dustin to make his escape. "Please, Shay."

The room had gone silent as if everyone sat holding their breath. Even the old-fashioned jukebox had suddenly stopped playing midsong. Shay remained motionless for the longest time before he finally took a step back from the door. Instead of returning to his position behind the bar, he dropped into the chair that Dustin had just abandoned. As soon as he did, the bar came back to life. Carli reversed course and returned to her own seat. She didn't know about Shay, but it was a huge relief to no longer feel the weight of all those eyes watching the drama that had just played out in front of them.

Shay held up his hand and signaled something to the woman tending bar. When she nodded and turned her back to the room, Carli wondered what mysterious orders Shay had issued without uttering a word. He didn't look like he was in the mood to explain, so she sat quietly and waited for him to calm down. It was only a couple of minutes later when the bartender appeared at their table and set down two coffees and walked away.

Carli wrapped her hands around the mug, letting its warmth seep into her bones. When she made no move to drink it, Shay finally spoke. "It's decaf, in case you're worried about the caffeine."

"Thanks."

She took a cautious sip and set the cup back down. "That thanks wasn't just for the coffee but for everything else. I didn't mean to stir up a hornet's nest by coming here tonight."

He leaned back in his chair, his arms crossed over his chest. "So how did you and your friends end up here? We both know this isn't the kind of place you normally hang out."

That was true. The problem was she didn't hang out much of anywhere. It had been a long time since she'd gone somewhere other than work and church. And considering how the evening turned out, maybe she should have stuck to her normal activities. After that sad conclusion, she realized Shay was still waiting for her answer.

"We went to a movie and weren't ready to go home. The plan was to have a quick burger and then leave, but then Dustin's two friends convinced Amy and Kim to dance with them. I should've left then, but Dustin seemed like a nice enough guy. I figured I could manage to carry on a conversation for the length of a song or two. I didn't expect Kim and Amy to leave me alone this long." She sighed and glanced toward the dance floor. "As you have probably already guessed, I don't date much…or really, at all. I'm not always comfortable around men I don't know, especially when they start asking if I live alone."

Shay sat up straighter and all but growled, "If you're worried that guy might be waiting to follow you home, I'll escort you there myself."

"Actually, I told him my roommate is a cop." She held up her phone. "I also texted Moira earlier and told her why I might stop by her place before going home."

For the first time, Shay grinned. "Sneaky woman. I can just imagine Dustin's reaction if he ran into Titus, not that Moira isn't scary in her own right."

"My thinking exactly." Carli took another sip of her coffee and then nodded toward the dance floor. "It looks like my friends are finally on their way back. They came in one car since they live on the other side of town, but I drove myself. If they're not ready to leave, that's okay. It should be safe for me to go home now. I also need to let Moira know I won't be coming over."

Before Carli could finish sending the message, Shay was up and moving. "I've got to check in with Jody. Talk to your friends, and then I'll walk you out."

"Why?"

He didn't answer her question, but the incredulous look he shot back at her was all the response she needed. One way or another, apparently, she was going to have an escort to her car. Fine.

At least her friends were alone when they reached the table. Kim dropped into her chair. "I'm sorry, Carli, we didn't mean to abandon you. We were having fun with Trevor and Bryan and lost track of time. They headed for the men's room and then are coming back here."

She looked around. "Where's their friend?"

Now wasn't the time for that conversation. "Let the guys know he decided to walk back to Rikki's place. I was about to come find you. I've got a headache and want to head on home."

Amy winced. "Are you sure?"

Carli managed a smile. "Yes. No use in you two cutting your evening short because of me."

Kim looked as if she wanted to protest, but her eyes widened in surprise. Carli knew without looking that Shay was back. It was time to go. "Have fun. I'll see you at work on Monday."

Shay didn't say anything as they walked outside together, once again drawing more attention from the others in the bar than she liked. At least he didn't crowd too close to her. Hopefully people would remember his well-deserved reputation for being protective of the women who worked for him as well as his female customers. This wasn't even the first time he'd escorted Carli to her car, claiming that he had a policy of ensuring women reached their cars without being hassled along the way.

When they reached her car, he said, "I'm sorry how things turned out tonight."

She leaned back against the driver's door and looked up at the stars overhead. "I figure I caught a lucky break. If he hadn't insulted your Scotch, I wouldn't have found out nearly as quickly what he was really like."

Shay leaned back next to her. "Maybe he was trying too hard to impress you."

Carli chuckled. "If that's true, he sure went about it in the wrong way."

"Yeah, he did. Even if his original intentions were good, he let his ego get in the way of common sense." Shay nudged her shoulder with his. "I think I know the answer to what I'm about to ask you, but I'm curious. If he'd actually meant that apology, would you have given him a second chance?"

Rather than answer immediately, Carli took a few seconds to think it over. In the end, she sighed. "Probably not. Besides, he and his buddies will be gone in a couple of days."

It was time to get moving. That's when she noticed Shay had his car keys in his hand and gave them a pointed look. "I can see myself home, you know."

"Yeah, I do. And ordinarily I would watch until you drove out of the parking lot safely and then go back inside." His expression turned grim as he stepped away from the car. "But once in a while, something manages to trigger my inner caveman into coming out to play. This is one of those times."

She would have laughed at his explanation, but something in his voice made her think that he hadn't meant it as a joke. Rather than fight a losing battle, she hit the button on her key fob to unlock her door. "Fine, but understand it's just this one time."

He stepped back out of her way. "I don't make promises I can't keep. Don't leave without me."

Without waiting for her to answer, he walked away, his caveman swagger on full display. Carli wouldn't have accepted such high-handed behavior from anyone else, but evidently the rules didn't apply when it came to Shay Barnaby. Instead, she found it cute.

Not that she'd ever admit it to him.

CHAPTER TWELVE

SHAY MAINTAINED A fair distance behind Carli as he followed her home. He figured she'd already had more than enough of the male population crowding her personal space for one night. He would also only hang around in front of her house long enough to know she made it inside safely. Yeah, he'd prefer to check out the house himself to make sure she was safe, but he suspected that would be one step too far for her to accept.

Law-abiding citizen that she was, Carli turned on her right turn signal as she slowed to pull into her driveway. He didn't know why he found that so amusing. Maybe because theirs were the only two vehicles anywhere in sight, no surprise at this late hour. He slowed to a stop and watched as she locked her car and then walked the short distance to her front door. He was glad to see she'd left the porch light on when she'd left earlier.

As the door swung open, she reached in and turned on the living room lights. He waited to drive away until after she closed the door and then waved at him from the front window. Her porch light went dark before he'd reached the end of the block. Lucky her, she'd probably be in bed and asleep soon while he still had another couple of hours to work before he could head home. It made him tired to even think about everything he had left to do before he could call it a night.

At the end of the block, it was all he could do to turn in the direction of the tavern instead of circling back around to Carli's house. Maybe she'd take pity on him and offer to make some coffee or tea. Heck, he'd settle for a glass of water if it meant spending a few more minutes in her company. There was something so soothing about her bright smiles and laughter. He also liked the way she called him on his sometimes overbearing need to protect the women in his life but put up with it anyway.

And Carli Walsh was definitely in his life. It had started even before she'd danced with him at Titus's wedding and then helped him get Luca settled in school. He also owed her for staying with Luca when Aunt Meg wasn't feeling well. All of those things were part of the big picture, but mainly there was something about her sweet nature that drew him like no other woman ever had.

Too bad the timing was all wrong.

Flashing blue lights in his rearview mirror finally jarred Shay out of his reverie. Great, he'd drawn the attention of one of Dunbar's finest. He drove through the intersection before pulling over to the side of the street. As he waited to see who was going to get out of the police cruiser, he wondered how long he had been sitting there staring into the darkness.

It was a mix of relief and embarrassment when he realized it was Moira headed his way. He dutifully rolled down his window and waited to see what she wanted. When she stopped beside his door, he tried to muster up a smile. "Hey, Moira. What's up?"

"Took you long enough to realize I was behind you, Shay. I thought maybe you'd fallen asleep at the wheel."

"Nope, just got lost in my thoughts for a minute there."

At least she looked more worried than mad. "Sorry to break it to you, but it was a lot longer than a minute. Everything okay?"

"Yeah, but thanks for asking."

She didn't look completely convinced, but at least she changed the subject. "Carli texted to let me know that she might need to stop by our house rather than go straight home from your bar. That was worrisome enough, but then she texted again to say you were following her home instead. Care to explain how you got tangled up in whatever was going on?"

How much should he tell her? No doubt Carli would eventually tell her best friend everything that had happened in excruciating detail. That didn't mean she'd appreciate him opening his big mouth about the evening's events.

"Actually, I think she'd prefer to tell you herself, so all I'll say is that she's fine." When Moira looked skeptical about his assessment, he added, "Mostly, anyway."

Moira looked down the street toward Carli's house. "She said she was going to a movie with two friends from work tonight, but her plans must have changed if she ended up at your place. I'm guessing if you felt the need to escort her home that something must have involved a guy."

Again, he was going to leave it up to Carli how much she wanted to share with her friend. "Like I said, she's fine. If that's everything, I need to get back to work."

Moira studied him for several seconds before stepping back from his truck. "Okay, I'll pry the details out of her. But, Shay, for what it's worth, thanks for watching out for her."

"Anytime."

He turned the key in the ignition but waited until she made it back to her own vehicle before driving off. Moira was another one who wouldn't appreciate knowing she brought out Shay's protective instincts. Too bad. Besides, he bet Titus would understand and would even like knowing someone else was keeping an eye on her. Moira probably wouldn't believe him, but it wasn't a reflection on Moira's ability to do her job. It was more of a compulsion on his part born out of his rocky family past.

But like he'd told her, it was past time for him to get back to work. People probably wondered why Shay had felt compelled to provide Carli with a personal escort home. The longer he stayed gone, the worse the gossip might be. While people could say whatever they wanted about him, he didn't want them bandying Carli's name around.

When he got back to the bar, he came in through the back door that led directly into the kitchen. After washing his hands, he picked up a couple of orders and delivered them himself. Maybe people would assume he'd been working in back. His office was off the back hall, and he often spent time working in there.

Jody looked over as he came around the corner. She raised one eyebrow, asking a ton of questions without speaking a single word. He didn't even slow down, knowing the inquisition would start as soon as he stopped moving. After delivering the burgers, he cleared a couple of tables and circled the room with a fresh pot of coffee to offer seconds to those who had switched beverages before driving home.

When that was done, he finally retreated to his office, glad to have a few minutes to himself. Unfortunately, his solitude didn't last long. Rather than growl about it, he leaned back in his desk chair as soon as Jody appeared in the doorway. "What's up?"

"I assume Carli made it back to her house safely."

Aiming for nonchalance, he said, "As far as I know."

That earned him an eye roll that would've done a teenager proud. "Shay Barnaby, we both know you waited around until she got inside before leaving. Especially after the way that guy she'd been talking to stormed out of here."

If it had been anyone else, he might have tried to bluff his way out of the discussion, but this was Jody. The woman was nothing if not stubborn. What was more, she had a bad habit of poking her cute freckled nose in his business whenever she thought the situation called for it. If he complained, she pointed out that was what friends were for. Evidently this was one of those times.

"Fine, but I didn't get out of the truck, and I drove away as soon as she walked in her front door. I would've done the same for any other woman. If you have more questions, make it quick. I still need to finish payroll before closing."

"I just have one." Jody's expression softened with something that looked like a mix of concern and exasperation. "When are you going to admit that Carli Walsh isn't just some other woman?"

"She's a friend, nothing more. I don't have time for anything else." He shot her a hard look. "Look it's late, and I'm tired. Can we please drop the subject? Besides, if we're both in here, who is tending the bar?"

Jody had been leaning against the doorframe, but she straightened up. "Fine, I'll go. But before I do, I have one more thing to say."

He'd started shuffling through the stack of papers on his desk, hoping she'd take the hint and leave. Instead, Jody went silent until he finally surrendered to the inevitable and looked up. "Which is?"

"I'm not in the habit of beating my head against brick walls, so I won't bother pointing out that I'm not wrong about how you feel about Carli."

After a brief pause, probably to make sure he was still listening, she continued. "It's taken a while, but it looks like Carli is finally starting to date. Tonight might have been a bust, but that won't keep her from trying again eventually.

One of these days, a woman like her is bound to get lucky and find a great guy."

The solid lump of tension in his throat made it difficult to speak normally, but he gave it his best shot. "Isn't that the whole idea?"

Jody nodded as she focused her attention on the death grip he had on the edge of his desk before speaking again. "So when that happens, how are you going to like dancing at her wedding?"

Then she walked out, closing the door behind her. Good thing she did because it muffled the sound of his stapler hitting the wall. The childish fit of temper did nothing to take the edge off his frustration, but that was all the time he had to devote to his tantrum. As much as he sometimes hated the busywork that came from running his own business, at least there was always a right answer when it came to dealing with numbers.

Too bad the same couldn't be said for dealing with people.

THE FRONT DOORBELL chimed twice in quick order. Carli had a very good idea who had come calling and didn't particularly want to answer the summons. She'd barely crawled out of bed and was in no mood to rehash the previous evening with anyone, not even her best friend. But even if she could convince Moira of that, it would only serve to postpone the conversation. Might as well get it over with, but not until the coffee finished brewing.

She unlocked the front door and opened it a few inches. "Come on in."

It wasn't the friendliest of greetings, but that's what the woman got for showing up without calling first. At least Moira came bearing gifts—a box from the local bakery, no doubt filled with some of Bea O'Malley's best doughnuts. If Carli was really lucky, Moira might have scored some fresh-from-the-fryer apple fritters. Sadly, the only thing Bea was better at than making doughnuts was spreading gossip. Titus had been known to refer to the woman as Dunbar's town crier, and Carli couldn't help but wonder if her name had been featured in today's headlines.

After Moria came inside, Carli closed the door and then shuffled back through her living room toward the kitchen. She waved a hand in the direction of the small drop-leaf table in the corner. "Sit. No talking until the coffee is ready."

Moira did as instructed while Carli stared impatiently at the coffee maker as the level of the heavenly elixir slowly rose in the carafe. If she'd been alone, she would've been chanting, *Faster, faster, faster.*

But that wasn't the case, so she remained silent. As the brew cycle neared completion, she put a mug and a plate in front of Moira and set another in front of her own spot. Next, she tore a couple of paper towels off the roll for napkins, picked up the sugar bowl and the special vanilla bean creamer she knew Moira liked, and carried them over to the table.

Thank goodness the coffee was finally ready. Figuring they were both going to need a lot of caffeine to get through the upcoming discussion, she filled both mugs and set the carafe within easy reach on the table. Considering how sluggish she felt, the coffee wouldn't have time to get cold before she finished off the pot.

As soon as Carli sat down, Moira opened the lid of the box. Carli leaned closer and drew in a deep breath of cinnamon and yeast. She picked one of the fritters and mumbled "Bless you" right before she took a huge bite and then washed it down with a sip of coffee.

She met Moira's gaze over the rim of her coffee mug. "Look, I know you have questions, but I'm begging you to give me time to get my brain function up to full speed."

"Fine, but only because you look as if you haven't slept at all. I worked all night, and I'm in better shape than you are. I'm dressed. I've also combed my hair and brushed my teeth. Showered, even."

"Quit bragging, woman."

Ignoring her friend's laughter, Carli glanced down at her moose print pajamas and winced. They might be faded and worn, but they were oh so comfortable. It wasn't as if anyone ever saw them. Besides, she'd only been up and about a few minutes when Moira showed up. If she'd taken the time to make herself more presentable, Moira would've simply kept ringing the doorbell.

Carli finished the fritter and then eyed the choices of cake doughnuts. It wasn't a matter of if she should eat another one, but of which one she should start with. Most days she tried to watch her carb intake, but today wasn't going to be one of those days. Settling on the blueberry one, she put it on her plate and then topped off her coffee. After stirring in a little more sugar and creamer, she considered what to say next. With anyone else, she would try to gloss over the events of the past evening, but this was Moira. Even if she didn't know that her friend would poke and prod until she got all of the nitty-gritty details, it might help to share everything with the one person who really understood her.

If she laid it all out there, maybe she could make sense of an evening that had had so many ups and downs that she'd gone to bed feeling as if she'd been on some kind of emotional roller coaster. The result was that what little sleep she'd gotten hadn't been particularly restful, which accounted for how stiff and achy she felt.

Moira reached across the small table to rest her hand on Carli's arm. "Look, the main reason I came by was to make sure you were okay. You don't have to tell me anything about what happened last night if you don't want to. That said, I'm willing to listen if it would help."

Carli had been reaching for her doughnut, but she decided maybe she should slow down on her sugar consumption for a moment. "There might be rumors flying around this morning, and I'd rather you heard it all from me. Knowing Bea, she's already gotten wind of the story. What she lacks in actual facts, she will no doubt embellish with her overactive imagination."

"I can't swear she hasn't heard anything, but your name never came up while I was in her shop."

"No matter." Carli pushed her hair back behind her ears and did her best to organize her thoughts. Finally, she launched into an abbreviated version of last night's events. When she ran out of words, Moira looked genuinely shocked.

"Sounds like this Dustin turned out to be some kind of Jekyll-and-Hyde guy. No wonder Shay insisted on following you home."

That still rankled. "What is it about me that makes men think I'm not capable of driving myself home without an official male escort? Do I act that helpless?"

"No, you don't, and neither do I. But if you'll recall, that didn't stop Titus from watching over me from the shadows when my boss put me in charge of the police department while he was on his honeymoon."

Carli couldn't help but grin at that memory. "That's true—he did do that, didn't he? As I recall, you didn't much appreciate him acting like you couldn't handle yourself."

Moira reached for another doughnut. "True, but I also know he respects my ability to do my job. He's protective because he cares, and he's never once asked me to change careers."

Which reminded Carli of something Shay had said last night. "Shay admitted that normally he would've only made sure I reached my car safely and then gone back inside the bar. You know, like he did the first time he walked me out to the parking lot."

"And what excuse did he give for going the extra step to follow you all the way home?"

"He said occasionally something sets off his inner caveman."

Moira started to snicker but stopped when Carli didn't laugh. "It wasn't a joke?"

"He wasn't smiling when he said it, so I'm not sure. That's the reason I didn't argue more than

I did. For some reason he really needed to make sure I got home okay."

"Maybe he was worried that guy was still lurking around."

"Could be."

Carli finished her blueberry doughnut and then started to reach for another one. At the last moment, common sense kicked in, and she closed the lid instead. "Those look delicious, but I'm not sure the events of last night justify having three doughnuts for breakfast."

Moira finished off the last bite of her second one and pushed her plate to the side. "Fine, if you're going to insist on setting a good example. Next time I'll only buy two for each of us."

"Now, wait a minute. I wouldn't go to that extreme." Carli held up her thumb and forefinger to indicate a very small space. "It would have only taken this much more badness to push me over the brink into three-doughnut territory. It's always better to be prepared. I would have felt awful if you'd had to make a second trip to Bea's."

After wiping her sugary fingers on the paper towel, Moira held up her right hand as if taking a solemn vow. "I would've done it, though. That's what good friends do for each other."

Then she topped off their coffee again. "So do you have any fun plans for today?"

"Nothing special." Carli checked the time. "Normally, I would've gone to church, but I couldn't drag myself out of bed in time for the early service, and now it's too late to make the later one. I'll probably spend most of the day doing grown-up things like paying bills. If I have enough energy, I might work out in the yard a little. I've been meaning to pick up some more fall mums for my planters out front. How about you?"

"I'll probably take Ned to the park. I could use the exercise after sitting in my cruiser for hours on end and walking him will help work out the kinks." Moira stretched her arms and twisted from side to side. "Afterward, I'll hang out at the café with Titus for a while since I'm on the night shift again tonight. I don't mind working late hours, but it does make it harder to spend time with my handsome husband. The good news is that Cade is hoping the town council will let him hire at least one more officer soon. If so, I might be able to work days more often."

"I'll keep my fingers crossed for you."

"Do that."

Moira picked up her keys as if getting ready to leave, but then she set them back down. "I really wish last night had turned out better for you."

Carli waved off her concern. "Don't worry about it. Maybe next time it will."

She immediately wished she hadn't added that last part considering the spark of excitement that appeared in her friend's eyes.

"So there will definitely be a next time?" Moira leaned forward, elbows on the table. "Not with Dustin, of course, but with someone else?"

Right now, the very thought made Carli tired. Sighing, she said, "Eventually, I suppose. Honestly, it seems like a lot of effort for very little return. We both know I've never been comfortable in social situations and especially around strangers. It's nerve-racking trying to sound a lot more interesting than I really am."

At least Moria didn't try to convince her she was wrong about that. Instead, she said, "I've been there, done that, too. I could always ask Titus if he knows of someone you might like. If so, maybe the four of us could do something together."

"Like who?"

"Well, he's friends with Ryder Davis. I don't know him all that well, but he seems nice enough. You must have seen him at our wedding. He's about six feet tall, brown hair and bright blue eyes. Drives a white van."

After a moment's thought, Carli was pretty sure she knew who Moira was talking about. "He's pretty new to the area. Doesn't he live outside of town in one of those A-frame cabins?"

Moira nodded. "Yeah, that's him. He helps out at the animal shelters like Titus does. He's also a volunteer firefighter here in town."

"What does he do for a living?"

Moira sat back in her chair and frowned. "Honestly, I don't know. I could ask Titus if you're interested."

"No, not right now."

"Why not?"

"Mainly because he's a stranger to me, and I'd have to jump through those same hoops to get to know him." She closed her eyes and let out a slow breath. "I really need to let the dust settle after last night's debacle before I can work up that much energy again."

She hoped that would put an end to the discussion, but her friend obviously didn't get the message, because she moved right onto another possibility. "I get why you don't want to go out with a stranger, but you already know Shay."

Where was she going with this? "So?"

"So maybe you, me and Titus could casually drop by Barnaby's next weekend for a burger and to listen to some music. We both know Shay's a great dancer. It would be fun."

"He's not looking to get serious with anyone."

Moira's eyebrows shot up in surprise. "Neither are you, so there would be no pressure. However, it is interesting that the prospect of getting serious was the first thing that popped into your head."

"I just don't want anyone to get the idea that he and I are more than friends. He's been up front that between his responsibilities at the bar and trying to help Luca adapt, he has all he can handle."

Moira clearly wasn't ready to give up on the idea. "All of that might be true, but I wasn't talking about the two of you going out on a date. I was saying that if we went to his place for dinner on Saturday night, he might ask you to dance. Don't tell me you wouldn't enjoy that."

It was time to put a stop to this discussion. "I'm not going to agree to anything right now."

Never one to be easily discouraged, Moira gave her what could only be described as a smug smile. "Fine, I'll check back with you tomorrow."

She stood up, once again picking up her keys. "And the day after that, and the one after that. Eventually you'll give in if only to get me to stop nagging. To summarize the plan—it will be the three of us next Saturday evening at Barnaby's for burgers and dancing. No pressure. No expectations."

While Moira let herself out, Carli remained behind at the table trying to make sense of their conversation. She was quite sure she hadn't actually agreed to the nondate outing with Moira and Titus. That said, she surrendered to the inevitable on two fronts. First, that come next weekend, she would somehow end up at Barnaby's and probably dance with the man himself. At the moment, she wasn't sure how she felt about that. And second—with a heavy sigh, she lifted the lid on the box from Bea's shop and reached inside—seemed it was a three-doughnut day after all.

CHAPTER THIRTEEN

"I'LL FIND A WAY. Don't worry about it, Ryder."

Shay ended the call and dropped his head down onto his desktop. He would've thrown his stapler against the wall again, but he'd broken it the last time and hadn't had a chance to buy a new one.

After wallowing in frustration for a few more seconds, he sat up straight and looked around the office as if he'd find an answer hidden somewhere in the piles of clutter. What was he going to do? He wasn't in the habit of making promises he might not be able to keep, but that's exactly what he'd just done.

First up, he needed to let Jody know he was going to have to leave her completely on her own to set up for the evening crowd. Luckily it was Thursday and not a busy weekend night. He sent her a text and was relieved when she responded seconds later to say she'd come in earlier than usual to get on top of things. That was one job done.

Next, he had to check in with Aunt Meg to see if she'd mind staying overnight at his place since he was going to have to bunk at the fire station to cover Ryder's shift. She'd also have to stay long enough to get Luca off to school in the morning. Crossing his fingers, he made the call. Five minutes later, he hung up and sat staring at his phone.

How could he have forgotten school was going to be closed tomorrow because of an all-day teachers' in-service? He checked the calendar on his phone and realized that he'd messed up and entered it in the wrong week. He'd also promised his aunt he'd take Friday off work to stay with Luca himself. Her favorite cousin was coming through town for just two days and was arriving that evening. The two women rarely got to see each other, and he wouldn't ask Aunt Meg to change her plans because of his screwup.

At least not if he could help it.

But now what was he going to do? Who else could he call? Liza Glines was too young to be responsible for Luca overnight. No, he needed a responsible adult for that.

One other name leaped to mind—Carli.

Would it be fair to call her? Ryder coming down with some kind of flu bug was hardly her problem. Technically, it wasn't Shay's, either, but all of the other volunteers had been taking extra shifts at the firehouse since the night Shay had gotten the call about Luca. Being able to fill in for Ryder one night would go a long way toward assuaging his conscience.

Again, that wasn't Carli's problem. Besides, she might have to attend the same training session as the teachers. There was only one way to find out. He punched in the number for the school and hoped she'd be the one to pick up.

"Dunbar Elementary School. How can I help you?"

At least one thing was going his way. "Carli, it's Shay. I have a question for you. Please feel free to say no. I mean that. I have a favor to ask, but don't hesitate to turn me down. It's not your problem. It's mine. In fact, forget I called. Bye."

His phone rang five seconds after he hung up. Should he answer it? Stupid question. What choice did he have? "Sorry, Carli. That was rude of me. I should have at least let you speak before I hung up."

"Shay, take a deep breath and relax. I know you wouldn't have called me unless something important came up. What's happened?"

"I don't know if you're aware that I'm a volunteer firefighter here in town or at least I was. I had to drop out of the regular schedule when Luca came to stay with me. And that's the problem right now."

"I see."

Although her tone made it clear she really didn't. "Sorry, I'm not explaining this very well. Evidently the flu has hit several of the other volunteers at the same time. The latest victim is Ryder Davis, and he was supposed to be the one on duty at the station tonight. He asked if I could cover his shift this one time. Ordinarily Aunt Meg could spend the night at my house and get Luca off to school in the morning."

"But there's no school, and I'm guessing your aunt can't stay with Luca."

"Got it on the first try."

There was a long silence. "I'll call you back in a few minutes."

Before he could tell her not to bother, she'd already hung up.

He sat staring at the phone, not sure if he should hope she'd be able to come through for him or relieved if she couldn't. Before he could decide, the phone lit up, and he swiped his finger across the screen. "That was quick."

"I won't get off work until four o'clock today, and I'll have to go home to pack a few things before I can head for your place. Will that be okay?"

"Yeah, but don't you have to work tomorrow?"

There was a brief hesitation before she answered. "Not anymore. I told my boss I need to take a personal day. She's okay with the short notice since the building will be closed, and she'll be at meetings all day at the district office. One of the other aides who helps out in the office can watch the phones."

As grateful as he was, he still felt bad for having to ask for help. "I hate inconveniencing everybody like this."

Carli laughed softly and whispered, "To be honest, I'm glad to have an excuse not to come in. Trust me, I'll have a lot more fun hanging out with Luca and the dogs."

"The kid will be thrilled to hear that. He and I'll have you over to the house for a steak dinner for this."

"I'd say that's not necessary, but I'll jump at any chance to not have to cook for myself."

The amusement in her voice vanquished the last bit of guilt he had about calling her. "I really appreciate this."

"Don't worry about it. It makes up for that kerfuffle I caused at the bar the other night."

Now she had him laughing, something he wouldn't have thought possible fifteen minutes ago. "Seriously? A kerfuffle? Is that what it was?"

"Yeah, but it could also have been a small brouhaha or maybe a minor hullabaloo. It's hard to tell. I'm not sure what the differences are."

He could hear the rustle of pages turning in a book coming from her end of the call. "Wait a minute. Are you flipping through a thesaurus right now?"

Her answering giggle had him grinning. "I'll never tell. I'm just glad it didn't turn into a great big old ballyhoo."

He hadn't known wordplay could be this much fun. "Let me know when you make up your mind. Otherwise, I'll see you at my place."

"Okay, I'll be there."

"I can't wait to tell Luca he's going to get to hang out with you this evening."

Too bad that wasn't true for Shay as well.

"I should be there a little after five o'clock."

"See you then."

Feeling much better about everything, Shay texted Ryder he could cover at the fire station and then called Aunt Meg to let her know he'd made other arrangements for Luca.

After finishing up a few more things at the bar, he'd pick up Luca and head home to make sure the place was presentable. Thanks to his time in the marines, keeping things neat and tidy had become second nature for him. However, now he had three new roommates who made keeping up with chores harder. If he hustled, he'd have time to vacuum and put fresh sheets on the bed in the guest room. Hopefully, there was something Carli could fix for dinner that wouldn't be a huge hassle. He also didn't know what the food situation was at the fire station. He wasn't picky, but he'd just as soon not have to make do with ramen or cereal.

Once again he had more chores than he had time for. It made him tired just thinking about it. With luck, he'd have a quiet night at the station and be able to get some sleep. If so, he might just dream about a certain kindhearted brunette.

WHEN CARLI MADE it home from work, she practically ran through the house to grab the few things she'd need to spend the night at Shay's house. The hardest decision was which set of pajamas to take. She normally bought ones that made her smile, and her newest set was covered with all kinds of cats wearing top hats and bow ties. It was doubtful Shay would see them, but she suspected Luca would think they were funny. His dogs might have a different opinion on the subject.

After exchanging her work clothes for jeans and a Henley shirt, she headed out the door. She made it to Shay's house in what seemed like record time. He hadn't said when he had to be at the station, but she didn't want to make him late if she could help it.

Luca and the dogs came charging across the

yard, reaching her car before she'd even had time to turn off the engine. As soon as she got out, Luca flung himself into her arms and gave her a huge hug while Bruno and Beau danced around her feet. As much as she loved their enthusiasm, it was hard to maintain her balance with all of that going on.

Luca leaned back enough to look up at her. "Carli! There's no school tomorrow, and Shay says I can stay up late enough to watch two movies tonight if it's okay with you."

It would have taken a much harder heart than Carli had to deny the little charmer the special treat. "Then I guess it's a good thing I brought two movies with me."

"Yay! We can have popcorn, too."

She winced as Luca practically shouted the words next to her ear. Before she could ask him to lower the volume, Shay intervened. "Settle down, all three of you. Give the woman some space."

Both the boy and the dogs recognized a serious command when they heard one. Beau and Bruno immediately sat down and awaited further instructions while Luca struggled to break free of Carli's grasp. She made sure he was steady on his feet before setting him free.

Shay stepped closer, his expression concerned. "Are you okay?"

She laughed. "Yeah, I'm just glad everyone is so happy to see me."

"That was never in doubt." He eyed their companions. "Luca, take Carli's bag and put it in the guest room. We'll join you in a minute."

"Okay."

Carli surrendered her small duffel and watched as Luca led the charge back into the house. "I wish I had even a tenth of that energy."

"Me, too." Shay sounded a little exasperated. "I swear he picks up speed about the time I'm ready to crash."

"It's the same at school. I've heard teachers theorize there's some mystical power that lets the munchkins steal every drop of energy the adults have by the end of the day."

"I believe that."

When Shay made no immediate move to go inside, she assumed he wanted to talk to her about something without Luca hearing the discussion. "What's up?"

He stuck his hands in his back pockets and shifted from foot to foot, making her think he wasn't comfortable with whatever he needed to tell her. "Just spit it out, Shay. What's wrong?"

"Nothing. At least nothing serious. I ran out of time to do any grocery shopping, so it's pretty slim pickings when it comes to dinner for you and Luca. I'd order in for you, but we're outside of the city limits. The pizza joint doesn't deliver out this far."

There was an easy fix as long as he didn't object. "How about Luca and I either have dinner at the café or call in an order and bring it back here to eat?"

He reached for his wallet and pulled out several bills. "Either of those options is fine with me."

She took the money only because she knew he was already feeling guilty about having to ask her for help again. "What about you? Do they keep food at the station?"

"It all depends on who has been on duty. Some are better about keeping some fresh stuff around. There are usually a few frozen dinners in the freezer or canned soup and chili in the cabinet."

"None of that sounds very appetizing."

He waved off her concern. "I won't starve. Besides, if it's a busy night, I won't have time to cook anything more complicated than that."

"It's nice of you to cover the shift for them. Do you miss helping out as much as you were before Luca came?"

He shrugged. "Yeah, I do. The one thing I really miss about being in the military was being part of a team with a common goal. Volunteering for the fire department sort of filled that niche for me. I also feel guilty for leaving them shorthanded."

"I'd tell you that was silly, but you can't help

how you feel. We both know your friends understand that your life situation has changed drastically. It's not like you quit because you got bored."

"Thanks, I think I needed to hear that."

They started toward the house. "Do you have any questions before I leave for the station?"

"Not that I can think of off the top of my head. I'm pretty sure Luca and I can figure things out."

He followed her inside. "You have my number if anything comes up. If I don't answer, it's because I'm out on a call."

"We'll be fine."

When they reached the living room, Luca was waiting with a package of microwave popcorn and two juice boxes in his hands. "I've got our snacks for the movie."

"Good to know we're all prepared, but those will have to wait until after dinner. I promise we'll have them, though."

Luca's shoulders drooped. "Okay."

Carli knelt in front of him to meet him at eye level. "I just want to make sure that you're not too full to have dinner at Mr. Titus's café."

That perked him back up. "For reals?"

"For reals."

He started to smile but it faded as he briefly glanced in Shay's direction and then back to her.

"What about him? He's going to be by himself at the fire station because Mr. Ryder is sick."

She leaned closer to whisper, "I thought we might surprise him with a dinner from the café. What do you think he'd like?"

Luca gave the matter some serious thought before finally answering. "Meat loaf and pie."

"Perfect. Now, why don't you go run around the backyard with Bruno and Beau for a little while. That way they'll be tired enough to nap while we're gone and won't miss you so much. I'll join you in a couple of minutes."

He immediately started for the door, but Shay called him back. "Wait a second, big guy. I need a hug before I leave. I won't see you until late tomorrow."

Luca came running back. "But we're gonna bring you—"

He stopped talking midsentence and looked panicky as he slapped his hand over his mouth. "Never mind. It's a secret."

Shay pretended to not know what was going on. Instead, he gathered Luca up in his arms and gave him a quick squeeze. "I'll see you when I see you. Be good for Carli. Don't argue when she says it's bedtime, don't beg her to read too many extra books and don't snore so loud she won't be able to sleep."

Luca grinned at that last instruction. When

Shay set him back down, he headed for the back door where the dogs were waiting for him. Before going outside, he faked a loud snore then dashed out the door with his buddies, giggling up a storm.

Carli's heart positively melted while watching the interaction between Shay and Luca. "You're so good with him. You're a natural at parenting."

Shay didn't look convinced. "I might get some things right, but there are times I feel as if I'm floundering in the deep end. When I think about all of the decisions I'm faced with every day that could make or break his future, I can hardly breathe."

Acting on instinct, Carli stepped closer and put her arms around him. "All you can do is your best. That's the same for every parent. If you could go back in time and talk to Luca's father, I bet he would admit he was just as scared about raising his son as you are."

She leaned back to look Shay directly in the eyes. "And you're not alone. If you need help, don't be too stubborn to ask for it. Again, you have your aunt, his teacher, the principal, the counselor, his pediatrician when you find one. The list goes on."

He tightened his hold on her, his voice getting deeper when he said, "And then there's you."

She didn't know which one of them decided

the moment called for something more than a hug, but suddenly his lips found hers. Her pulse jumped and her breath caught in her chest as he kissed her, gently at first and then with more intensity. It would've been so easy to get lost in that moment, to forget that Shay had somewhere he needed to be and that she was there for Luca, not him.

Unfortunately there was a third party there to remind them as the back door slammed open, and Luca came running back in. "Carli, where are you? We're waiting to show you a new trick."

She and Shay each jumped a step back. If not for his quick reflexes, she might have fallen when she backed into the coffee table. His hold was gentle as he asked, "You okay?"

His hands dropped away as soon as she nodded. "I'm sorry, Carli. I don't know what I was thinking."

By that point, Luca had come closer, a puzzled expression on his face as he looked first at Shay and then at her. She drew a shaky breath and hoped that her face wasn't as bright red as she feared it was. "I'll be right out, Luca."

"Is something wrong?"

Shay answered for them both. "Nope, everything is fine. I was just leaving."

Before Carli could even say goodbye, he'd walked out the door without a backward glance.

It was amazing how much that hurt. But rather than dwell on what had obviously been a monumental lapse in judgment on both their parts, she held out her hand to Luca. "Okay, let's go see that trick you mentioned."

CHAPTER FOURTEEN

It was just Carli's luck that Moira was standing at the front counter when she and Luca arrived at the café to pick up their order. The only question was if it was purely happenstance or if Titus had given her a heads-up exactly when Carli would be stopping by.

One look at Moira's face answered that question. Given a chance, the inquisition would begin even if Carli would rather not answer a bunch of questions in front of Luca. Fortunately, he tugged his hand free of hers and took off for the far side of the room as soon as he spotted Ned sitting near the door to the kitchen.

They couldn't hang around the café for long. But as soon as he was out of hearing, she launched into a quick abbreviated explanation of why she was spending the night at Shay's house while he was at the fire station. "Since all of this was a last-minute deal, neither Shay nor I had made any plans for dinner tonight. When I suggested we eat here, Luca got worried that Shay would go hungry. I told him we could order a meal to go and drop it off at the station on our way home. Luca thought that was a good idea, but he didn't like knowing Shay would have to eat alone."

She pointed toward the insulated bag sitting on the counter with her name on it. "Hence, three meat-loaf dinners complete with desserts to go."

"So you're spending the night at Shay's."

"I am. Like I said, that's because he has to be at the fire station for twenty-four hours. I'm staying with Luca until Shay's shift ends."

Moira frowned. "Tomorrow is Friday. Don't you have to work?"

"It's an in-service for the teachers, so I took the day off."

"That's not something you'd do for just anyone."

No it wasn't, but she also didn't want Moira to blow the whole thing out of proportion. "I'm helping out a friend, that's all. The same as Shay is doing—he's filling in because Ryder is sick. Evidently no one else was available at the last minute to take his shift. Shay's aunt couldn't stay with Luca, and I'm the only one who Luca knows well enough to feel comfortable with for that long."

Moira shook her head. "You keep telling yourself that, Carli, but I would point out that Shay could have called us. We would've been glad to watch Luca."

"You're right, but you have to be on patrol, and Titus has a business to run. Luca is just now getting used to living with Shay. There's no telling how he would've reacted to having to sleep over at your house, and then there are his dogs to consider."

She let that much sink in before adding, "Besides, tomorrow happened to be one of the few days during the school year that I could take off without having to call in a sub to cover for me. If it had been a regular school day, I might not have been able to stay with Luca."

That wasn't true, either. She could've spent the night at Shay's and then taken Luca to school with her in the morning. He could have hung out at the day care until she got off. Rather than prolong the discussion, she reached for her wallet. "We should get going before the food gets cold."

Moira took the bills and rang up the order. "I'm sorry. I didn't mean to upset you."

"Don't worry about it. I just don't want you to think that this is any more than a friend helping a friend. It's no different than him making sure I got home safely the other night."

"Okay, I believe you. Now I'll go send Luca back your way." She came around to Carli's side of the counter and gave her a quick hug. "And don't forget our plans for Saturday night. We'll pick you up at seven thirty."

Surrendering to the inevitable, she agreed. "I'll be ready."

It was a huge relief that Moira didn't ask any more questions. Maybe she finally accepted that Shay and Carli were simply friends. At least Moira didn't know about the kiss Carli and Shay had shared right before he'd bolted out the door, and Carli wasn't about to tell her. As soon as Luca came running back with Moira following close behind, Carli took his hand and smiled at her friend. "We'll talk tomorrow."

Moira gave her a narrow-eyed look and said, "We will, indeed."

Okay, so maybe she hadn't believed Carli's story after all. That made two of them.

SHAY WAS STRETCHED out dozing on one of the bunks upstairs at the fire station when his phone signaled a new text message. Checking the screen, he rolled to his feet and hustled down the stairs to open the door for Carli and Luca. He had mixed feelings about letting them in, mostly because he wasn't sure what, if anything, he should say to her about what had happened right before he'd left home.

Should he pretend the kiss never happened? That didn't seem right and might very well hurt her feelings. A simple apology was another option, but there was one problem with that—he wasn't sorry he'd kissed her. Besides, with Luca there, it wouldn't be the right time for a a serious discussion.

He still hadn't come to any kind of decision when he opened the door and Luca yelled, "Surprise! We brought a picnic for all three of us! We didn't like you eating alone."

Carli hung back a little, letting Luca take the lead. It was a smart move on her part since it bought the two adults a little extra time to get their bearings. Shay swung Luca up in his arms. "What a great surprise, little man. I was going to have to make do with canned beans and stale crackers."

"Yuck!" Luca wrinkled his nose before adding, "What we brought is way better. It's Mr. Titus's meat loaf and pie."

"Sounds delicious, and we'd better get to eating. An emergency call could come in at any time, and I'll have to drop everything to get the truck ready to go before the rest of the crew gets here. If that happens, you two will have to pack up the food in a hurry and take yours home to eat."

He set Luca back down and took his hand. "With luck, that won't happen. Let's head upstairs to the kitchen."

It was hard to miss how quiet Carli was being. Was it because she was angry or because, like him, she was unsure of how to act? It was uncharted territory for both of them. He led the way up to the second floor. Luca poked his head into each door they passed. To satisfy the boy's curiosity, Shay described each room. "We sleep on those bunks when we're on duty here. We used to have two people on-site around the clock, but right now we don't have enough volunteers for that."

Pointing toward the next door, he said, "That's the restroom and showers. The next one is a tiny gym, so we can work out if we want to while we're here."

He paused to let Luca and Carli catch up. "This is the office where we have computers and stuff like that. Across the hall is a lounge where we can listen to music or watch television and movies. Finally, we have the kitchen."

Carli set the bag from the café on the table. "I've never been in a fire station before. It's really interesting."

Luca climbed into one of the chairs at the table. "I got to sit in the fire truck when we came here before. It was fun. You should do that, too."

She ruffled Luca's hair and smiled. "Maybe I will."

A brief surge of jealousy flashed through Shay,

not that he resented Luca's easy relationship with Carli. Instead, it was because he wished his own feelings for her were that uncomplicated. Doing his best to ignore the growing urge to touch her again, he turned his attention to setting the table for the three of them. Carli unpacked their dinners and reheated everything in the microwave.

Finally, she set out four of Titus's mini pies. "Luca and I each picked one of the pies, but we thought you'd like two. If you don't eat them both now, you can keep the other one for a late-night snack."

"I appreciate it. There's pretty slim pickings on hand right now."

As soon as the food was divvied up, all three of them dug right in. Carli held up a forkful of the meat loaf and frowned. "I've been trying to figure out what Titus's secret ingredient is that makes his meat loaf so much better than mine. I wonder where he got the recipe."

Shay added more potatoes to his plate. "After Titus went to culinary school, he worked at several different high-end restaurants back East before deciding to open his own place. My guess is he picked up a few tricks from other chefs along the way or else learned how to make it from his grandmother. I know she's the one who taught him how to make his famous chicken and dumplings."

Carli finished the bite of meat loaf before speaking again. "Wow, I knew he had training, but I didn't realize he'd worked at such fancy places before coming here. Transitioning from working in five-star restaurants to running a small-town diner had to have been almost culture shock."

"You'd think that, wouldn't you? But you don't have to spend more than a few minutes in Titus's company to realize he's happy with his current lot in life. It took guts to set up business in that diner on the off chance living in Dunbar would bring Moira back into his life."

Carli looked up in shock. "He told you about what happened back in the day?"

He wasn't surprised that Carli knew all about the couple's troubled past. "No, other than they'd crossed paths in the past. He didn't offer details, and I didn't ask. Most of us have secrets we'd just as soon not become public knowledge."

"True enough." She served herself another small slice of the meat loaf. "All I'll say is that it's amazing that things worked out for them, and I'm glad they did. It's enough to reaffirm my faith that miracles can and do happen."

Luca held up his plate. "Can I have more potatoes?"

Shay used his fork to point at the pile of green beans on the boy's plate. "You know the rule,

Luca. Eat half of your green beans, and then you can have more potatoes."

Carli looked at Luca and then at Shay. "What rule is that?"

Sounding much put upon, Luca answered before Shay could. "I have to eat vegetables, not just the good stuff."

She bit her lower lip as if trying not to smile as the boy stabbed half a dozen green beans with his fork and shoved them all into his mouth. "That's a wise rule. Eating a balanced diet is important if you want to grow up big and strong like Shay."

Her cheeks immediately flushed rosy as if she regretted saying that last part. Rather than comment on it, he flexed his right arm to show off his muscles for Luca. Well, mostly for him anyway. "You don't get guns like these eating nothing but pie and potatoes."

Luca studied Shay's muscles for a few seconds and then devoured his few remaining green beans. As soon as he swallowed them, he held up his plate again. "More potatoes…and green beans, please."

"You got it, kiddo."

THEY FINISHED THEIR meal in good order and then made quick work of the cleanup. After wiping down the counter and table, Carli folded the dish towel and hung it up to dry. Looking around, she said, "Why don't you keep the leftovers? You can have them for lunch tomorrow."

Shay wasn't going to argue. "Thanks, that keeps things simple for me."

Just that quickly, the moment turned awkward. It was as if they'd run out of chores to do and things to talk about at the same time. "Well, you and Luca are probably in a hurry to get back to the house to watch those movies you promised him."

She huffed a quiet laugh. "Yeah, we need to get started on that. Otherwise, we'll be up till all hours."

Luca came back from using the restroom. "We also have to make the popcorn."

Carli picked up her purse and headed toward the staircase. "We might need to hold off on that a while. I'm pretty full from dinner."

"Okay, we can wait until the second movie starts."

Clever kid. He was doing his best to ensure Carli was seriously committed to her promise about the extra movie. Shay waited until Luca started down the steps after her before joining their small parade. "Sorry I'm going to miss the party."

Luca called back over his shoulder, "I can save you some popcorn."

Shay loved the boy's generous heart. He smiled and said, "I appreciate the offer, but that's okay."

When they reached the ground level, Luca stopped by the fire truck. "Carli didn't get a chance to check out the truck."

Carli shook her head. "Maybe some other time, Luca. We need to get back to the house, and Shay probably has work he needs to do around the station."

"But I wanted to show you my favorite parts."

She met Shay's gaze and raised her eyebrows, leaving the decision up to him. "Okay, but make it quick."

He opened the driver's door and boosted Luca up into the cab. Once he'd scooted over to the passenger side, Shay stood back and let Carli haul herself up into the driver's seat where her mouth widened into a big grin. "Wow, we're really high off the ground, and this thing is huge. My feet don't even reach the floor."

When she latched onto the steering wheel and pretended to be driving, he couldn't help but grin. Nothing like a fire truck to bring out the kid in everybody. He stood back and let Luca take charge of explaining everything he'd learned about the vehicle from Ryder. Shay stood ready to answer any other questions Carli might have, but Luca had obviously sucked up all of the information like a sponge. His range of knowledge was pretty impressive.

Carli looked suitably impressed as well. "Thank you for sharing all of that with me, Luca. I think I'll have to see if the school library has any good books on fire trucks, so I can learn more about them. If I find one, I'll let you know in case you want to check it out after I'm done with it."

Shay didn't want to be left out of the discussion. He waited until the pair climbed down out of the truck. "Wait here a second. I'll be right back."

He charged upstairs to the office to retrieve two copies of a coloring book that they handed out to kids who toured the station. Carli and Luca stood waiting by the door when he returned. "I thought you each might like one of these. I'm sure you can find more detailed books about fire trucks, but these should get you started."

It was no surprise that Luca was excited by the unexpected gift, but Carli seemed pleased as well. The coloring books weren't anything fancy, but they didn't seem to care. She quickly flipped through the pages before tucking the book inside her purse. "Thanks, Shay. We can get started coloring in them while we watch the movies tonight."

Luca handed her his book to keep for him.

"I've got a whole bunch of markers and crayons we can use."

"Sounds perfect. We can sit on the floor and do our coloring on the coffee table while we watch the movies." Carli glanced at Shay. "We'll be careful not to mark the wood."

He waved off her concern. "It's not fragile, so don't worry about it. Besides, I put my feet up on the coffee table, boots and all."

Before she walked away, she looked past him toward the fire truck. "I hope you have a quiet night, Shay. But if you do get called out, stay safe."

"I'll do my best."

She didn't look happy with his response, but she didn't say anything else on the subject. Funny, but he wasn't used to having someone waiting for him to come home. While he hated that she might worry, it felt oddly satisfying knowing she would.

Finally, she said, "We'll see you tomorrow."

"I'll text you when I know when I'm getting off. The time might vary if I'm in the middle of a call."

Shay helped Luca get buckled into Carli's car and then stood in the doorway waving as they drove away and wishing he could go with them. When a call came in ten minutes later, he was almost glad for the distraction. He opened the garage door, got on his gear, and waited for the other volunteers to come pouring in.

They'd been asked to respond to a report of a grass fire along the highway about five miles outside of town. The county was also sending a crew and had asked Dunbar to assist in fighting the blaze. With luck and a lot of effort, they hoped to get it under control while the fire was still manageable. It had been a dry summer, and the usual fall rains hadn't been heavy enough to make up for it. Wildfires could destroy thousands of acres in no time, putting lives and homes at risk.

The smoke rising high into the evening sky was visible long before the fire itself came into view. The men and women in the crew immediately put on their game faces even though their body language remained calm. As their truck pulled to the side of the road, the crew chief called out, "Everybody, you know your assignments. I'll coordinate with the county fire chief and let you know if there are any changes. Do Dunbar proud, be careful and stay safe! Got that?"

"Yes, sir!"

The familiar routine served as a reminder that it was time for Shay to get his head in the game. For a brief second, he let himself think about the woman and boy who were waiting for him to come back home and then turned his complete attention toward the fire. Like he'd told Carli, it felt good to be part of a team that served a higher purpose. He wasn't facing enemy forces in the same way he had when he'd been in the marines, but the principle was the same. The situation was deadly, and carelessness could cost lives. It took every ounce of strength and every bit of concentration to make sure everyone would return home safely.

It was his duty, and he'd see it done.

CHAPTER FIFTEEN

FRIDAY MORNING, Carli woke up tired and wishing that she could stay in bed for another hour or two, but she couldn't leave Luca on his own indefinitely. It also wasn't his fault that she'd been up for hours after he'd gone to bed.

Last evening, they'd watched both movies while eating popcorn and coloring pictures of fire trucks and firefighters. After that, she'd helped him get ready for bed and then read him three of his favorite picture books. She'd found it funny that Beau and Bruno had stayed awake the whole time as if listening to the stories, too.

After turning out his light, she'd washed the few dishes they'd used as she waited to make sure Luca fell asleep and stayed that way. The only mistake she'd made was in watching the local news. In the opening story, they'd talked at length about a wildfire burning near Dunbar. There was a news crew on-site showing the efforts to contain the blaze. As their camera crew panned the area, one firefighter stood out—Shay

Barnaby. He happened to be in the shot while the reporter described the efforts to put out the flames. The main worry was that a new weather front was due to move through the area and was expected to bring high winds.

Rather than go to bed, Carli had curled up on the couch to monitor the developing situation. She'd been unable to relax enough to even think about sleeping until she caught one last update that said the fire was almost out. Even better news was the fact that there were no reported injuries related to the incident. She waited another hour and then gave in to the temptation to send Shay a quick text. Heard about the fire on the news. Are you okay?

When he didn't immediately answer, she reluctantly turned off the television. After brushing her teeth, she put on her pajamas and crawled into bed. A short time later, her phone finally pinged.

I'm fine. On our way back to the station. See you tomorrow. Or I guess later today since it's after midnight. Was the munchkin good for you?

He was. You must be tired. I hope you can get some rest.

Me, too. Night

With that, she'd finally relaxed enough to sleep. Unfortunately time and six-year-old boys wait for no woman. The sounds of cartoons and dogs romping through the house had dragged her out of a deep sleep. She took a quick shower, hoping that would help clear out the cobwebs enough for her to function. After getting dressed, she put her hair up in a ponytail before joining Luca in the living room.

"Hey, kiddo, did you sleep well?"

He nodded but kept his eyes focused on the kids' show he was watching.

"Have the dogs been outside?"

"Yeah."

"I'll feed them and then fix our breakfast. I'm thinking scrambled eggs and toast. Is that okay?"

That earned her another nod which was fine with her. Right now, she wasn't sure she was up to a more involved conversation. She made quick work of giving the dogs fresh water in case Luca hadn't gotten around to it yet and then fed them. Both dogs came running at the sound of their kibble hitting their bowls. To her surprise, they both came to an abrupt halt and sat down just shy of their goal and watched her with hopeful expressions. It finally dawned on her that they were waiting for permission to eat.

She stepped back out of their way and smiled.

"What nice manners you two have. Go ahead and eat."

It took her slightly longer to put together a quick meal for the two humans in the house. Luca dragged his feet a bit when she called him to the table, but he finally came. "I hope you like cheese in your eggs."

He reached for his glass of apple juice. "That's how my mom makes them because Dad likes them that way. We eat them every Saturday. On Sunday, Dad makes pancakes."

Then he frowned and corrected himself, his dark eyes filling with tears and looking so sad. "I mean that's how we used to do things but not now."

As if sensing his distress, Bruno and Beau whined softly and licked Luca's hands when he reached down to pet them. Carli wasn't sure what to say that would ease the little boy's pain. She settled for, "It's nice that you have such good memories."

He shrugged. "It hurts when I think about them."

Carli gathered him in close for a hug. "I know it doesn't seem like it now, but I promise eventually it won't hurt so much. It's never easy to lose someone you love, but I've found thinking about the happy moments we shared helps a lot."

Luca sniffled as he rubbed his eyes with his fists. “Did you lose your mom and dad, too?”

She nodded. “I was a little older than you are when my father died, and I lost my mom about five years ago. It’s not easy, no matter how old you are. I do my best to think about how much they loved me and how much I loved them. They wouldn’t want me to be sad all the time. I’m sure your parents would feel the same way.”

He mulled that over for a little bit before nodding. After that, they ate in companionable silence. When he finished his last bite of toast, he cleared his spot at the table. “Can I watch my shows now?”

“Go ahead. I’ll finish cleaning up in here. You need to get dressed soon so we can take the dogs for a walk.”

“Okay.”

Twenty minutes later, she sat down at the kitchen table with a heavy sigh. Starting off the day tired was never a good thing. At least Luca had finally turned off the television and headed to his room to get dressed. She figured that would give her time to finish a second cup of coffee before the two of them took Beau and Bruno for their morning walk. It would do all four of them good to get some fresh air and exercise.

That left the rest of the day to figure out.

Maybe she should've asked Shay if there were any chores that needed doing. Considering she had to be there anyway, being useful would be better than simply sitting around all day watching cartoons with Luca. She considered sending Shay a text but decided against it. It had been hard enough for him to ask for help, and she didn't want him to think that his housekeeping wasn't up to her standards.

Luca was back with the dogs following right behind him. He sat down on the kitchen floor to put on his shoes. "Can we go to the park to walk? The dogs love sniffing around the woods there."

That would mean getting dog hair in her car, which made it tempting to say they should stay closer to home. However, she found it impossible to say no to the three hopeful faces staring up at her. "It's okay with me. Before we go, I'll text Shay where we'll be in case he gets done at the fire station earlier than expected."

She kept the message short. *Taking Luca and company to the park. We'll walk the dogs and then eat a snack before coming home. Leaving in about fifteen minutes.*

After sending the message, she fixed bottles of water for her and Luca as well as one for Shay in case he joined them at some point. Then she filled two more for the dogs and added plastic bowls for them to drink from. After putting all of that in a small pack she'd found hanging in the utility room, she added apples, granola bars and a handful of doggy treats.

Luca was already waiting for her in the front yard while Bruno and Beau hunted for any sign that varmints had invaded their territory. "Okay, everybody, let's go."

It almost took longer to load Luca and the dogs in the car than it did to drive the short distance to the park. Carli double-checked the dogs' leashes were securely attached to their harnesses before letting them out of the car. Luca took control of Bruno's leash while she held on to Beau's and slung the pack with their water and snacks over her shoulder.

Once they finally got going, she was really glad they'd come to the park. It was a beautiful fall day, crisp and cool, and the air carried the spicy scent of the huge Douglas firs and cedars that accounted for most of the trees in the park. They started down the trail that circled the perimeter of the park. She made no effort to keep them moving along at a brisk pace, preferring to let Luca and the dogs have plenty of time to explore as they walked.

They weren't the only ones who'd decided to take advantage of the day off school and the nice weather. While she knew more of the people who called out greetings along the way, Luca had also shyly said hello to several of his classmates who stopped to talk to both of them. Carli always got a kick out of how many kids seemed surprised that she existed outside of the school. Did they really think all of the staff lived in the building 24/7?

Luca got way more animated around the other kids as he introduced them to Beau and Bruno. The dogs were both on their best behavior, sitting quietly as their admirers stroked their fur. When the children and their parents moved on down the trail in the opposite direction, Carli and Luca resumed their walk. At one point, the trail skirted the edge of the playground located in the center of the park where she asked Luca, "Would you like to play on the climber for a little while? If so, the dogs can keep me company while I sit on that bench over there."

Then she pointed toward a pair of boys approaching the climber from the other side of the playground. "Aren't they in your class?"

When Luca nodded, she decided to encourage him to join them. "Why don't you go say hi? I'm sure they'd be glad to have you to hang out with them for a little while."

After a brief hesitation, he surrendered Bruno's leash to her and trotted across the grass to join his classmates. She didn't know what he said to the boys, but they both turned in her direction and waved before the three of them charged up the steps that led to the spiral slide on the climber. They slid back down to the ground and immediately headed right back up to the top, laughing and chatting away as they did.

Shay would be happy to learn that Luca might have made some friends. If so, it would be another step toward normal for the boy. As she watched them play, she nibbled on a granola bar and slipped each of the dogs a treat before filling their water bowls for them. It felt good to relax and enjoy some time out in the sun without feeling the least bit guilty about it.

At work, she would've spent the day on the seemingly endless piles of paperwork running a school generated. Granted, most of it was actually done via computer these days, but that did nothing to staunch the flow of forms, information, reports and memos that had to be dealt with on a daily basis. At home, she would've had chores to do. Even if she'd spent the time outdoors, it would've meant mowing the lawn or weeding the flower beds. Anything besides simply enjoying some unexpected downtime.

She'd only been sitting there for a few minutes when footsteps warned her that she was no longer alone. Looking up, she was surprised to find Titus and his buddy Ned heading straight toward her and the dogs. It was impossible to predict how Bruno and Beau would interact with the much bigger dog, so she tightened her hold on their leashes.

Probably sensing her concern, Titus slowed his approach and murmured something to Ned before continuing toward her. The three dogs stood facing each other, tails wagging slowly as they considered whether they wanted to be friends. Finally, all three of them plopped down in the scrap of shade in front of the bench. Once they got settled, Titus sat down next to her.

It didn't take him long to spot Luca, who was about to cross the suspension bridge that connected two different sections of the climber. His friends followed right behind him until they reached a vertical pole they used to slide back down to the ground.

"Looks like the kid is having fun."

"He is. We lucked out and ran into two of his classmates. I know Shay has been hoping he'd start making friends soon."

"I'm sure none of this has been easy for either him or Luca, but Shay knows he's got a lot of people in his corner to help him when things get rough."

He paused to give her a quick glance. "Speaking of which, how did it go last night?"

"You already know that we ate dinner with Shay at the station, which was fun. After we got back to the house, Luca and I spent the evening watching movies and coloring."

She offered Titus a superior look. "Just so you know, Luca said I did a great job staying in the lines."

Titus's mouth quirked up in a small smile. "Keeping things all neat and tidy is hard work. You must be really proud."

"I am. First graders can be tough critics when it comes to artwork."

They both went back to watching the kids. After a bit, Titus asked, "I heard there was a fire out by the highway last night. Have you talked to Shay since then?"

"Yeah, he let me know he was tired but okay."

Titus shifted a bit as if trying without success to get comfortable. "It's not always easy to be the one waiting at home when someone you care about has a dangerous job."

She'd like to think Titus was talking only about himself, but she suspected that might not be the case. Rather than ask for clarification, she went with the assumption he was referring to Moira being a police officer. "I would guess you worry a little less about Moira working here in Dunbar than you would have if she was still working in Seattle."

"That's true enough, but fighting fires is no picnic, either."

He was right about that. "Funny, I grew up knowing about our volunteer fire department here in Dunbar. However, it never really sank in that some of my friends and neighbors routinely put themselves in such danger. I can't imagine putting myself at risk like that. That takes a certain kind of courage, something I seem to lack.

"So does serving in the marines, especially the specialized unit that Shay was in. From what I've heard about them, they're a pretty tough bunch."

Something else she hadn't known about Shay's time in the service. "He said that he missed being part of a team and that volunteering with the fire department filled that need."

She'd never spoken to Titus about his previous profession before going to culinary school, but that didn't stop her from asking a question now. "Did you have that same problem when you left law enforcement?"

His expression took on a harder edge, one that had been far more scarce since Moira had come back into his life. "No, but then I mostly worked undercover, which meant I was usually on my own. I was technically part of a team, but I didn't spend much time with them."

He glanced past her. "Speaking of Shay, he's headed in this direction. That's my cue to get going. Enjoy the rest of your day."

But before walking off, he evidently had one more thing to say. "Personally, I've always found it more satisfying to color outside the lines. It's not as tidy or safe, but it's a lot more rewarding. You might try it sometime."

Then he and Ned left, stopping only long enough to say something to Shay before continuing down the trail. She watched until he disappeared around a bend in the trail, still trying to figure out exactly what he'd been trying to tell her.

Meanwhile, Shay was now headed straight for her. She remained seated and waited for him to join her. As soon as Bruno and Beau spotted him, they lurched to their feet and vibrated with excitement. She kept a firm hold on their leashes until he crouched down in front of them and accepted their greetings. About that time, Luca saw him and called his name.

"Shay, come watch!"

He smiled at her. "I'll go touch base with Luca and be right back."

"We'll be here."

She tried not to stare as he strode over to the climber, but she couldn't seem to help herself. There was just something about the way Shay moved that captivated her, and she wasn't the only one whom he affected that way. At least three other women stopped to watch as he crossed the short distance to where Luca stood waiting on the platform near the same pole he'd been sliding down over and over.

Shay positioned himself where he could admire his young charge's prowess as he slid down the pole. Luca motioned for the other two boys to go ahead of him before following them down. As soon as he touched ground, Shay swept him up in the air and spun around three times before setting him back down as both man and boy laughed. It warmed Carli's heart to see the two of them enjoying a special moment together.

After a brief conversation, Luca went back to playing while Shay headed back in her direction. It wasn't until he sat down that she could see the dark circles under his eyes that showed the past twenty-four hours had taken their toll on him. "Rough night?"

He settled his arm on the back of the bench and let out a slow breath. "It had its moments. I did manage to get a solid six hours of sleep after we got back from the fire. The only call I got this morning was to respond to what was supposed to be a car fire on the far side of town. Turned out to be a blown radiator, so steam, not fire. There wasn't much to do except let the engine cool down and wait for the tow truck to come."

"That's good, but I thought you might be on duty for another few hours."

"I should've been, but Ryder showed up early to take over. He swears he's over whatever bug he had. He said he'd cover until the guy who is really scheduled for tonight shows up. There was no use in both of us sitting there doing nothing, so I left. I figured you might like a reprieve right about now. How has it been going?"

"Both Luca and the dogs have been great, and I'm really glad we came to the park. Those two boys he's talking to are in his class at school. They've been playing together for quite a while now."

"I'll have to get their names and numbers. I'd like Luca to invite friends over to play, maybe even spend the night sometime."

"I bet they'd like that."

By that point, the boys had left the climber behind to take turns crawling through a series of big concrete pipes. When they reached the far end, a woman was waiting for the other two boys. Evidently it was time for them to leave, and they waved goodbye as Luca headed back toward where Carli and Shay were seated. Shay tugged on Carli's ponytail and said, "It was really nice of you to help out like this."

"I've had a great time hanging out with Luca.

In fact, I was just thinking how nice it was sitting out here in the sunshine. It was the perfect excuse to relax and do nothing."

He laughed. "Yeah, I get that."

Luca flopped down on the ground by the dogs. "I'm hungry."

Carli reached for the pack she'd brought. "Well, lucky for you, I brought snacks."

She passed out water bottles, apples and granola bars. Shay seemed surprised that she'd brought enough for him as well. "I wanted to be prepared if by some chance you got off earlier than expected."

"Something else I owe you for."

For some reason, that hit her wrong. "You don't owe me anything, Shay. Friends help friends. No debts incurred."

He looked as if he wanted to argue the point, but he finally nodded. "Can I at least thank you?"

"Yes, of course."

Then deciding that she might have come across as a bit angry when that wasn't how she felt at all, she deliberately lightened her tone and added, "But I'm still expecting that steak dinner you promised me."

He tugged her hair again, a definite twinkle in his blue eyes. "I haven't forgotten, and I'll even spring for one of Titus's pies for dessert."

She rubbed her hands together with a greedy grin. "I can't wait."

"Since I'm off earlier than expected, why don't Luca and I grill those steaks tonight? That is, unless you've had enough of the two of us for one day."

"Tonight would be perfect."

CHAPTER SIXTEEN

SHAY WAS RELIEVED that it hadn't taken a lot of effort to convince Carli to hang out with him and Luca for the remainder of the afternoon. That made more sense than her going home only to have to turn around to come back later for dinner. After leaving the park, she drove Luca and the dogs back to Shay's place while he detoured to the grocery store to pick up everything they'd need for dinner. From there, he made a quick stop at the diner to buy a pie for dessert. Although he'd given the order to Rita, one of Titus's employees, it was the man himself who delivered the pie to Shay at the front counter.

"That's a lot of pie for you and Luca."

Shay handed Titus his debit card. "Actually, Carli is joining us. I promised her a steak dinner for staying with Luca last night."

It was difficult to interpret the odd look Titus gave him. Rather than wonder about it, Shay asked, "What's wrong with that?"

"Does she know this dinner is a thank-you gift and not anything like a date?"

Although Titus spoke softly, his words seemed to carry more weight than they should. Where was he going with this? Confused by what was going on, Shay frowned at his friend. "Yeah, she does. Like I said, that was the deal we made. Do you have a problem with that?"

"No problem. But she's a nice woman, and I don't want to see her hurt."

Shay's temper flared hot. "We're having dinner. That's all."

"Right."

"What's that supposed to mean?" When the other man didn't immediately respond, Shay leaned in closer. "If you have a problem with me being friends with Carli, spit it out."

For a brief second, Shay saw past the guy who baked pies for a living to the hard-edged cop Titus used to be. The facade disappeared as quickly as it had appeared. A second later, he took a deliberate step back to lean against the back counter, his legs crossed at the ankle. He might look calmer, but Shay wasn't buying it. "I'm waiting."

"I don't have a problem with you, Shay, but I do get tired of seeing my friends make stupid mistakes when it comes to how they treat the women they care about." Titus held up his right hand and began counting off examples on his fingers. "Cade Peters thought it was okay to lie and tell Shelby they were going on a date when that wasn't what was happening at all. You can only imagine how she reacted to learning he'd lured her up on the mountain for a picnic only to deliver news that turned her world upside down. The icing on the cake was when he tossed her in a jail cell for something he knew full well she didn't do. It's amazing that woman is still speaking to him, much less that she married him."

After letting that much sink in, he moved on. "Then there's Max Volkov. His bright idea was to set up an entire police sting operation at Rikki's bed-and-breakfast without telling her. He thought he would be protecting her delicate sensibilities when what he was actually doing was making life-altering decisions for her and her son without including her in the process. If he'd gone ahead with that plan, she would never have forgiven him. And before you go thinking I'm pointing fingers at everyone but me, what happened between me and Moira was worse. My stupidity cost us ten years that we could've spent together."

Still not particularly happy with the tone of this conversation, Shay grumbled, "What does any of that have to do with me? I'm not making any decisions for Carli. We're having dinner.

Like I said, it's a simple thank-you for her helping out with Luca."

When Titus still didn't look convinced, Shay prayed for patience. His voice was little better than a growl when he laid it all out for his friend. "The fact is that I'm not a good bet for any woman, especially one like Carli. Even if that weren't true, she's made it clear that she's not ready to date anybody at all. The bottom line is that we're friends, mainly because that's all we can be. For her sake and mine."

Titus's expression softened. "If that's true, fine. But I have to tell you, Shay. You don't look at Carli like she's 'just' a friend. And I doubt I'm the only one who has noticed."

He tossed Shay's debit card back to him. "The pie is on me."

Then Titus walked away, leaving Shay staring after him. It was tempting to leave the pie sitting on the counter or, better yet, toss it at Titus's head. However, his gut instinct said that would be a bad idea. He might not like anyone poking their nose in his business, but it was obvious the man was trying to prevent Shay from making the same kind of mistakes he'd made himself.

Besides, Titus was right. Carli wasn't simply a friend. Shay might not want to put any other label on how he felt about her, but it was far more intense and deeper than he was comfortable with. Jody was a friend, too, but his feelings for her were far different than those he had for Carli. Maybe it was because he was also Jody's employer, but he didn't think so. For one thing, his attention didn't become laser focused on every move she made when they were together. Heck, there were nights at work where they barely spoke.

By way of contrast, when Carli had walked into the bar the other night, everyone else in the place pretty much disappeared off Shay's radar. If she'd been anyone else, he would've made sure she made it to her car safely and then gone back inside the bar. Instead, like he'd told her, his inner caveman had insisted on following her all the way home. It was his way of making restitution for failing his sister all those years ago. Protecting those in his care was a compulsion he couldn't fight and wasn't sure he wanted to.

The real question was what Shay should do about it. Unfortunately, he had no idea, but he'd have to figure it out eventually. Right now, he needed to get back home. There were steaks to grill, side dishes to make and a pie to slice. For the duration of the evening, he would do his best to keep things light and uncomplicated between him and Carli.

Maybe he should start by focusing more of his attention on Luca, who had to come first in

Shay's life. Trying to be a good substitute father to the boy was sucking up every bit of emotional energy that Shay had. They'd made some progress in building a relationship, but it would take more time for the two of them to settle into a new normal that worked for both of them. Until that happened, neither of them could afford any more complications in their lives.

But come tomorrow, Shay needed to figure out what to do about how much better it felt when Carli was there with them, too.

CARLI DIDN'T KNOW what had happened while Shay was out picking up everything he needed to fix dinner for the three of them, but something had certainly taken the shine off of his good mood. He was making a valiant effort to behave as if nothing was wrong, but he was trying a little too hard to be the perfect host, leaping to his feet anytime she made a move. She'd cut him some slack the other night at the bar when he'd insisted on following her home because of the remote possibility that Dustin was still lingering in the area. But surely Shay knew an escort was unnecessary when she only went inside the house to pour herself another cup of coffee.

Settling back into her chair on the patio, she watched Luca as he played various games with Bruno and Beau. Aiming for a neutral topic of conversation, she said, "I could watch the three of them playing all day long. The dogs obviously love it, and Luca never stops smiling when he's with them."

Shay flipped the ears of corn on the grill. "It's nice someone makes him happy."

Then he glanced at her, his expression bordering on stark. "He's like that with you, too, in case you haven't noticed."

What was she supposed to say to that? Would he be happier if Luca didn't like spending time with her? That was ridiculous, but she was starting to doubt the wisdom of staying for dinner. Why had Shay even invited her if he didn't want her there?

"I'm sure the two of you have fun together, too."

"He seems to be getting used to living here with me." Shay jabbed a meat thermometer into one of the strip steaks he was grilling. "But then he doesn't have much choice, does he?"

She sat up straighter. "Are things not going well?"

After setting the thermometer back on the small table next to the grill, Shay shrugged. "It's still pretty hit-and-miss. Some days are better than others, and nights get pretty rough sometimes. Hopefully things will calm down a bit now that I've changed my hours at work."

"I bet that will help. Kids seem to do a lot better with a regular schedule." She offered him a small smile. "Grown-ups do, too."

"I hope so. I've been running on fumes for weeks now."

He checked the corn again and reached for one of the platters he'd set out on the round patio table. "Hey, Luca. Time to wash your hands. Dinner is ready."

The boy had been running toward the far side of the yard, but he immediately circled back around with his constant companions right on his heels. "I'm coming."

He charged past where Carli was sitting to let himself inside while the dogs plopped down on the patio at her feet, panting and happy. "Is there anything I can do to help?"

"Nope, I've got it."

Once Shay had the steaks off the grill, he set that platter on the table. "I'll be right back out with the salad."

She'd feel better helping out, but it wasn't worth arguing about it. She carefully stepped around the dogs as she moved her chair over to the table and sat down. By that point, Luca was back. As soon as he joined her at the table, the furry members of the family assumed their usual positions flanking Luca.

Deciding she could still do something useful, she picked up the pitcher of lemonade Shay had brought out on one of his previous trips inside. "If you'll pass me your glass, I'll pour the drinks."

She'd just set the pitcher back down when Shay joined them. "I hope you like spinach salad."

"I do. It's actually one of my favorites."

After taking some for herself, she offered the bowl to Luca. He hesitated before taking it from her. She did her best not to laugh as he barely took any of the spinach but carefully picked out a few bits of carrot, cheese and hardboiled eggs to put on his plate. When he was done, he looked to Shay for approval before passing the bowl to him.

Carli couldn't help but grin at the look of relief on Luca's face when Shay didn't order him to take more. Shay offered her a rueful smile. "I'm learning to pick my battles."

"Smart man."

The steaks were done perfectly, and the roasted corn was a nice addition to the meal. Once they'd filled their plates, no one seemed inclined to talk much, but at least the silence felt comfortable. Finally, Luca pushed his plate back. "I'm full."

Carli feigned shock. "Really? You're too full for dessert? That would be a real shame. Well, except for the fact that leaves that much more for me and Shay."

Luca looked horrified by Carli's comment. "No, I left room for pie."

"Ah, that makes more sense. Mr. Titus wouldn't be happy to find out that we'd rather eat spinach salad than a piece of his pie." She turned to Shay. "Speaking of which, you didn't mention what kind you got."

Shay set down his fork and leaned back in his chair. "Actually, I don't know. Considering the short notice, I asked for whatever whole pie was available."

Then he stood and started gathering up the dishes on the table. "I'll get this mess cleaned up, and then we can decide if we still want dessert. If not, I'll pack some up for you to take home for later."

Okay, what was going on? He was the one who invited her for dinner, but now it sounded as if he couldn't wait for her to leave. Never let it be said that she couldn't take a hint. "Maybe you should do that."

"But why do you have to leave, Carli?"

Luca wasn't the only one wondering that, but she had no idea how to answer the question. Shay looked even more ill at ease as he met her gaze briefly before answering the boy. "I didn't mean she *has* to leave, Luca. I was only offering to send pie home with her in case she wants to get back home. You know, to do stuff."

Now there was a lot of confusion in Luca's dark eyes as he stared at her. "Is something wrong, Carli? Don't you want to have pie with us?"

How was she supposed to answer that? The problem wasn't the pie. It was that even if Luca wanted her to stay, she was pretty sure Shay's feelings on the subject were more mixed. Rather than hurt the one innocent in all of this, she picked up her own dishes and offered a compromise. "If we can make it quick, I'll stay for pie. After that, I do need to get home and do all that important stuff Shay was talking about. Will that work?"

She'd directed the question to Luca, but it was Shay who answered. "Sounds like a good plan."

At least Luca seemed happier as he carried his dishes inside and then returned to help with everything else. Shay praised him for his hard work while Carli quietly loaded the dishwasher. Working together, they quickly put the kitchen back in good order. When they were done, Shay picked up the box containing the pie and set it in the middle of the kitchen table. "I think it's time to find out what kind of pie we're about to devour."

He looked at Luca. "Drumrolls, please."

When the boy only looked confused, Carli beat out a sample rhythm on the table with her hands. Luca laughed and joined right in. When they reached a crescendo, Shay opened the box with a flourish. "Just as I hoped—Dutch apple!"

Carli leaned forward to breathe in the rich scents of cinnamon, nutmeg and baked apples. "Titus isn't capable of making a bad pie, but that's definitely one of his best."

Lifting the pie out of the box, Shay studied it for a second. "I guess the only question left to answer is whether we want our pie plain or with vanilla ice cream."

Carli raised her hand. "I vote for a scoop on the side."

Following her lead, Luca did the same. "Me, too."

"Guess that makes it unanimous. I'll get the plates."

NONE OF THEM dawdled over their pie. By the time they finished, Shay seemed to have shaken off whatever had been bothering him earlier. Carli still had no idea what had been wrong, and she wasn't about to bring it up now. Far better to head home while the two of them seemed to be back on solid footing.

She gave Luca a goodbye hug and patted the dogs on their heads inside the house. It was no surprise that Shay followed her out to her car. "Thanks again for staying with Luca for me. I really appreciated it."

"We had a lot of fun together, and anytime that I don't have to cook is a good day in my book. Thanks to you, I haven't had to make dinner since Wednesday."

Although she meant it as sort of a joke, she wasn't exaggerating. Cooking for one wasn't much fun. She suspected Shay had had his own experience with that before Luca had moved in with him. He stood close by, his hands in his hip pockets. "Just so you know, Luca has decided he wants to try riding the bus in the mornings starting Monday. If that works out, I probably won't see you as often."

Carli had mixed feelings about that but tried to focus on the positive part of that announcement. "Good for him. Maybe that means he's feeling more comfortable at school."

"I hope so."

That's when it occurred to her that she'd likely be seeing Shay sooner than he thought. Unless something happened to change their plans, tomorrow evening was the night that she, Moira and Titus were supposed to stop in at Barnaby's for burgers and maybe a little dancing. Ordinarily, she would warn Shay that they were coming, but she was starting to think it would be wiser to beg off and stay home. Moira might not like it, but Carli would cross that bridge when she came to it.

She was about to get into her car when Luca opened the front door and yelled, "Aunt Meg is on the phone and wants to talk to you."

Shay called back, "Tell her I'll be there in a second."

As soon as Luca closed the door, Shay opened the car door for her. "Tonight was fun."

She thought so, but she wasn't convinced that was really true for him. "Dinner was great."

He nodded but didn't say anything else. Finally, she got in the car and set her purse and the container of pie that Shay had insisted she take home with her on the passenger seat. "You probably shouldn't keep your aunt waiting."

Shay finally stepped back after he shut her door. "Drive safe."

Then he walked back toward the house. As she backed out of his driveway and drove off, it dawned on her that for once he hadn't insisted on her texting him when she got home. Maybe he'd forgotten in his hurry to get back inside to return his aunt's call. It was also possible that he'd finally accepted that Carli was perfectly capable of driving across town safely, and he didn't need to worry about her. If so, it was about time.

She should be happy about that, but for some reason she wasn't.

CHAPTER SEVENTEEN

SHAY DREW ANOTHER glass of beer and called out, "Order up."

Tiffany swung by the bar to pick up the tray. "Thanks, boss."

As she walked away, she called back over her shoulder, "Don't look now, but it seems your lady friend is back."

What lady friend was Tiffany talking about? The only woman he'd paid any special attention to recently was Carli, and she had better things to do on a Saturday night than come in here again. If she'd had plans to stop by, surely she would've mentioned it last night at dinner.

He scanned the people milling around over near the entrance. Thanks to Titus's height, it wasn't hard to pick him out of the crowd. If he'd been alone, Shay would have invited him to sit at the bar and keep him company while he worked. Unfortunately, the man wasn't going solo tonight. No, he'd not only brought Moira with him but Carli as well. What was he thinking? Just yesterday he'd all but warned Shay off from spending any more time with Carli, and yet he still brought her to the one place he knew Shay would be.

It was tempting to pretend he hadn't seen them and go hide out in his office. That would be the smart—if cowardly—thing to do. Sadly, it was already too late. Titus looked directly at him and then shrugged his shoulders before leading the two women toward an empty table located at the edge of the dance floor on the other side of the bar. As near as Shay could figure, the gesture wasn't an apology but more likely an admission that this wasn't his doing. That meant it had been Moira's idea, and there wasn't much Titus would refuse his wife.

Before Shay could decide how to proceed, Jody tossed three menus and the new wine list down on the counter in front of him. "We're caught up. Go have fun with your friends."

He arched an eyebrow and did his best to intimidate the petite blonde. "Remind me again. Which one of us is the owner of this place?"

As usual, Jody stood her ground, a big grin on her face. "That would be you, boss, but we both know you're going to be totally useless working behind the bar as long as that woman is here. Instead of clogging up the works, why not just surrender to the inevitable and hang out with them?"

"What if they're waiting for someone else to join them?"

Jody frowned as if that possibility hadn't even occurred to her. She studied the trio for several seconds before responding. "Nope, that's not what's going on. If it was, at least one of them would be watching the door for him to arrive."

Shay had noticed the same thing but wasn't ready to give up the fight quite yet. Evidently neither was Jody. "Look," she said, "Carli has to be feeling like a fifth wheel…well, technically a third wheel right now. You'll provide symmetry. I bet she'd really appreciate that."

Okay, that was funny. "Right, everyone who comes into this place worries a lot about things like symmetry."

She gave him a not-so-gentle shove. "Scoot. I don't have time to stand here and argue with you. I've got orders to fill, and you know what my boss is like when he thinks I'm not doing my job."

At that moment, Titus stood and offered his hand to his wife. The two of them walked out onto the dance floor. Shay didn't blame them for wanting to lose themselves in the rhythm of the song playing on the jukebox, just the two of them alone in the crowd. What he didn't like was the look of envy on Carli's face, maybe because it was thc sccond time in a week that she was sitting in his bar watching other people have fun.

Finally, he picked up the menus. "Don't think this means you'll win every argument we have, Jody."

She patted him on the arm. "I'll settle for only winning the important ones. If things get too busy, I'll send up a signal."

"Fair enough."

As he made his way through the crowd, Shay wished he was wearing one of his newer T-shirts or at least jeans that didn't have frayed hems and a small hole in the right knee. Also, he really should've shaved for a second time before leaving for work. Some guys could pull off the slightly scruffy look, but he wasn't sure that was a talent he possessed. Regardless, it was too late to worry about appearances now. If he ever showed up in a suit and tie, Carli probably wouldn't recognize him anyway.

She glanced in his direction right before he arrived, her smile a little tentative, as if she was unsure of her welcome. Shay dropped the menus on the table and gave Titus and Moira a pointed look. "Want to show them how it should be done?"

"Aren't you supposed to be working?"

"One of the benefits of owning the place is knocking off early to spend time with friends."

He offered her one of his best bad boy grins, hoping that might tempt her into accepting his invitation. "Come on, what do you say?"

From the way she bit her lower lip, he knew she was at least tempted. He'd give her another few seconds to make up her mind before trying to dust off more of his decidedly rusty dating skills. He was feeling a little desperate when she finally put her hand in his. It was tempting to do a little victory dance on their way out onto the floor.

On the way, he stopped to feed quarters into the jukebox. "What kind of dance music do you like?"

She studied the list of possibilities and punched in the numbers for three songs, two country and one golden oldie rock 'n' roll. He'd put in enough money for a fourth song and chose a favorite of his that was perfect for a slow dance. A man could always dream.

They cut through the crowd to a spot on the opposite side of the floor from the space that Titus and Moira had staked out as their own. The last thing he wanted was to have the pair watching every move he and Carli made.

By thirty seconds in, they found the same easy rhythm together they'd had that night at the wedding reception. He loved the way she grinned as he spun her out and then back in. Then they held hands as she followed him effortlessly across the dance floor. At thc start of the second song, Carli started singing along, her voice a nice contralto.

She stopped long enough to lean in close to say, "Come on, don't make me sing alone."

"What if I can't carry a tune in a bucket?"

"Too bad. Sing or maybe I'll find someone who will."

Shay hoped that wasn't true. He'd hate to have to toss one of his customers out for the high crime of belting out lyrics on the dance floor with her. Surrendering to the inevitable, he joined in on the next verse. Her happy laughter was reward enough for making a fool of himself in public.

By that point, Titus and Moira had managed to dance their way over next to them. Titus stopped long enough to snap a picture of Shay and Carli. When he turned his phone around to show it to them, it was actually a short video complete with sound. He'd even managed to catch Shay being totally off-key on the high parts. From his friend's wicked grin, it was a sure bet that the traitor would be forwarding it to both Cade and Ryder the moment they returned to the table.

The good news was he seriously doubted Titus was into broadcasting everything on social media. He'd limit the distribution to people who would take great pleasure in giving Shay a bunch of grief. Oh, well. That's what friends were for.

When the last notes of their impromptu sing-along faded away, they briefly paused to see what song the jukebox cued up next. He smiled when he heard the opening strains of the ballad he'd picked. He was even happier when Carli didn't hesitate to let him wrap her in his arms. His good mood was only slightly dimmed by the questioning look Titus aimed in his direction just before he pulled his wife in close to his chest and started swaying to a song full of love and heartbreak.

What was up with that? After all, if Titus wanted to keep Shay from dancing with Carli, he shouldn't have brought her to the bar in the first place. Now wasn't the time for that discussion. He gradually put some distance between them and the other couple, wanting to concentrate on enjoying every second that he had Carli in his arms.

A few seconds later, Carli murmured, "This is nice."

"It is, and a pleasant surprise, too."

When his unexpected comment threw off their rhythm, she stepped back just far enough to be able to meet his gaze directly. "I probably should've told you yesterday that this was a possibility."

Glancing over his shoulder toward Moira and Titus, she continued. "A few days ago, Moira mentioned it would be fun to come listen to music and have burgers, but I wasn't sure it was quite a done deal."

Ordinarily, Shay would have accepted Carli at her word, but for some reason he suspected she was being less than truthful with him right now. "Did you think you wouldn't be welcome back after the last time you were here? For future reference, I don't make a habit of kicking even my most rowdy customers to the curb on their first offense. Most of the time, not even for their second or third."

She laughed. "Good to know. I'll hold you to that."

"Wait—are you planning to stage another kerfuffle?"

"With Moira's help and enough wine, it's a definite possibility."

Figuring she was only kidding, he waggled his eyebrows and offered her another of his bad boy grins. "In that case, Ms. Walsh, I'll tell Jody to send over a whole bottle of that new vintage so we can get the party started."

"I dare you."

"Be sure you want to go there, lady."

Too bad the song was ending, but at least Carli held his hand on their way back to the table.

Tiffany appeared only seconds after the four of them sat back down. "Can I get you drinks while you study the menu?"

Titus answered first. "I'll have that new IPA you have on tap."

Moira handed Tiffany the drink menu. "I'll have the same."

Despite their conversation on the dance floor, Shay decided to err on the side of caution and not order for Carli. As if sensing his reluctance to speak on her behalf, she gave him a wide-eyed innocent look and said, "Mr. Barnaby, what would you suggest for me this time?"

Fine. If she wanted a kerfuffle, he'd give her one. "Two glasses and a bottle of wine. Jody will know which one. Tell her we may need a second one later on."

Fighting to contain a grin, Tiffany looked first at Carli and then at him before writing anything down. "Got it. I'll be right back with the drinks."

He watched as she made a beeline over to Jody. It wasn't hard to imagine the conversation that ensued, but there wasn't much he could do about that. To his surprise, Jody looked straight at him and gave him a thumbs-up as if approving of how his evening was proceeding. She made quick work of their order and sent Tiffany hustling right back to their table.

After giving Titus and Moira their drinks,

she set wineglasses in front of Shay and then handed him the bottle. Jody had even sent along a corkscrew. He put it to good use and poured the two of them each a glass of wine. While he did that, Tiffany wrote down everyone's food orders. Once she was gone, he asked, "So what brought you all here tonight?"

Moira sipped her beer and set it back down. "Titus and I haven't had a night out since we got back from our honeymoon, and I had a hankering for good bar food and some dancing. I asked Carli to come with us."

Carli shook her head in clear denial. "As I recall, there wasn't much in the way of asking. I was told this was what was happening."

Moira shot her a smug look. "You didn't put up much of a fight, though, did you?"

Her cheeks flushed a bit pink. "No, I guess I didn't."

That was a relief. Shay would hate to learn that Carli was truly there against her will. He topped off both of their glasses. "After we eat, I'll give you two ladies more quarters for the jukebox."

Titus pulled out a handful of change and sorted through it for quarters. He pushed them across the table toward Carli. "Use these to pick out a few more songs on that thing for Shay to spoil forever by singing along with them."

"Hey!"

Carli snatched up the quarters before Shay could grab them. "You have to sing, too, Titus."

He started to protest, but his wife put an end to that. "We're here to have fun, big guy. And tonight that means you and Shay need to serenade us."

Titus groaned. "This will ruin our tough-guy reputations."

His wife reached over to pat his cheek. "Maybe, but it will still be fun."

Shay thought Titus was probably right. But then again, Moira wasn't wrong.

THREE HOURS AND an empty wine bottle later, Shay walked Carli out to the parking lot. Since Titus was driving, he'd limited the amount of alcohol he consumed. Shay had also erred on the side of caution since he was still at work. That had left both women free to get delightfully tipsy. All four of them had spent most of the evening on the dance floor, even switching off partners for a couple of songs. Carli and Moira had even coaxed others in the bar to join in singing several of the catchier songs over the course of the evening.

To his surprise, a couple of his other customers had even approached him about hosting a karaoke night sometime in the near future.

Titus seemed skeptical, but both Moira and Carli thought it was a good idea. If it would bring them back to his fine establishment more often, Shay would be only too glad to rent the necessary equipment. If the event proved successful, he might even look into buying his own.

As soon as they stepped out into the cool night air, he looped his arm around Carli's shoulders, feeling content with his lot in life. Shay couldn't remember the last time he'd had such a good time blowing off steam with friends. He let Carli set the pace as they strolled through the parking lot, but it seemed as if he wasn't the only one in no hurry for the evening to end. After he eventually tucked Carli into the back seat of Moira's SUV, he'd have to think about heading home himself. That didn't mean he'd give up one minute of the time he could spend with Carli.

She stopped to look up at him. "I think earlier I might have given you the impression that I wasn't all that happy to be coming here, but that was because I didn't want you to feel obligated to spend time with me again so soon. That said, I had a great time tonight."

"So did I."

He studied her pretty face, his gaze lasering in on her mouth. "If we were alone, I'd be trying to kiss you right now."

Her eyes flared wide. "Would you, now? As I

recall, that last time you decided to do that you thought it was a mistake."

Shay shuffled his feet and shoved his hands in his pockets. "Maybe I was wrong about that."

"Only maybe?"

"You know it would only complicate things for both of us."

Carli edged closer and pressed her hands against his chest. "What if I like complicated?"

Shay glanced around, taking note of several people also heading for their cars. "You do realize we're not alone out here."

Carli leaned in closer to him. "And if I don't care about that?"

His pulse kicked up into a higher gear even as his conscience wondered if that was the wine talking. "Are you sure? Because I feel obligated to remind you that our names will likely make the early edition of Bea's gossip report at the bakery in the morning."

Somehow his warning only seemed to encourage her. She offered him a siren's smile as she slid her hands upward to encircle his neck. "It's now or never, Shay. Titus won't wait around all night."

Oh, yeah. He'd almost forgotten about their companions. When he finally located them in the parking lot, he grinned. "He's too busy kissing his wife to care."

Carli spared their friends a brief glance. "Like you said earlier, let's show them how it's done."

Okay, then. Even a former marine knew marching orders when he heard them and would follow them without hesitation. Slowly, gently, he kissed her with great care. On second thought, maybe she kissed him.

Either way, it was the perfect end to the evening.

CHAPTER EIGHTEEN

CARLI HAD GONE to bed worried that she'd wake up Sunday morning with a headache thanks to the amount of wine she'd consumed at Shay's place. Even so, she'd set her alarm. She'd missed church last weekend and didn't want to do so again. Much to her surprise, she'd woken up feeling energized and ready to face the day. She even made it to the early service on time.

Now she was on her way back home with the rest of the day hers to spend any way she wanted. The trouble was, she had no idea what that would look like. Yeah, there were always plenty of chores to do, but she wasn't in the mood. She also had several books that had sounded good when she bought them, but so far none of them had managed to hold her attention for more than a chapter or two.

Back before Moira had married Titus, Carli would've given her a call to see if she wanted to go shopping or to a movie or anything else that sounded fun. However, they'd already included her on their date night last evening. She couldn't very well expect to lay claim to more of her friend's time so soon.

She pulled into her driveway still racking her brain for something to occupy her time. Well, something other than thinking about Shay Barnaby and the time they'd spent together last night. She wasn't sure what she'd been expecting when they'd walked into his bar. Maybe that he'd stop by the table to say hello. She'd certainly been hoping he would ask her to dance at least once. Her worst fear had been that he'd just wave from the bar as he went about his business serving drinks and calling out greetings to his regular customers.

But the evening had turned out to be so much more than that. She'd had a good time from start to finish. Especially at the finish. That kiss had been one for the record books. She'd been worried that Moira would say something on the way home to take the shine off the night, but thankfully that hadn't happened. Instead, when a favorite song had come on the radio, Moira had cranked up the volume and ordered both Titus and Carli to join her in one last silly sing-along before the night was over.

They'd literally ended the evening on a high note. The memory had her smiling as she let herself into the house and kicked off the heels she'd worn to church. After changing into her favorite yoga pants and an oversize fleece tunic, she put together a light snack before settling into the upholstered chair in front of the living room window. To occupy her mind, she decided to give one of the books another chance to capture her interest.

It failed miserably. Fifteen minutes in, she closed the book and tossed it back on the pile. The author was one of her favorite romance authors, so it wasn't the quality of the writing that was the problem. Instead, it was because the plot happened to hit a little too close to home. The hero was a single father struggling to raise his daughter alone. The heroine was a helpful neighbor who had always dreamed of having a husband and child of her own. Whenever she spent time with the hero and the little girl, she was reminded of everything she was missing in her life.

And that was exactly what Carli found herself thinking about after spending so much time with Luca and Shay over the past few days. It had felt so right to hang out with Luca by himself and to tuck him into bed on Thursday night. Their time at the park had been fun, too. Then there was dinner with both him and Shay on Friday. It had felt so normal spending the evening with them. There were periods of time where she'd almost forgotten that she was there as a guest, not as an official part of the life Shay was building with Luca and the dogs.

Last night had been fun at the bar, but it wasn't as if it had been a real date. She'd been there at Moira's invitation not Shay's. Granted, he hadn't hesitated to join them, and dancing with him had been a high point of the evening. In fact, if she was going to be honest about it, it had been the high point of far more time than that. Too bad he hadn't at least dropped a hint that he'd like to see her again sometime soon…or at all. That man definitely ran hot and cold, which was a huge disappointment.

Maybe Moira was right, and it was time for her to give dating apps another try. Before she could talk herself into checking out the possibilities, the phone rang. It was tempting to let it go to voicemail, but she made herself get up and at least check to see who was calling. What if it was Shay?

No such luck. She tried not to sound disappointed when she greeted Moira. "Hey, lady, what's up?"

"I wondered if you'd like to hang out with me this afternoon. It would be just the two of us. Ryder called earlier and said he needed Titus's help at one of the local animal shelters. I didn't get the particulars, but I think they are going to be doing some unexpected repairs or some such thing. Definitely nothing they needed me for."

Carli didn't hesitate. "Good timing. I was just trying to think of something more interesting to do than read a book that I'm not really loving."

"Do you want to go shopping at the outlet mall, or would you rather watch movies and stuff our faces with popcorn?"

"Do I get to pick the movie?"

That was important to get straight from the beginning. Although there were movies they both liked, Moira preferred to watch ones with lots of car chases and shoot-outs while Carli's tastes ran to animated films intended for kids and rom-coms.

"To keep it fair, I think we should each pick one."

"Fine with me. I baked cookies yesterday afternoon. Should I bring some?"

"That's a foolish question. Bring them all."

"I'll be there in twenty minutes."

AS THE FINAL credits for the first movie scrolled across the screen, Carli scooped up a handful of popcorn and tossed a few kernels at Moira. "You've behaved yourself this long, but I'm afraid your brain is going to explode if you don't get the inquisition over with. Might as well get it out of your system so we can relax and enjoy the next movie."

Moira picked up the last cookie on the plate and took a bite before responding. "You know I do my best to keep my nose out of your personal business—"

Carli almost choked on her popcorn. When she could breathe again, she gave Moira an incredulous look. "You need to warn me when you're going tell a whopper like that. You haven't kept your nose out of my business since the day we met. If you stopped grilling me over every detail in my life, I'd think you didn't care anymore or, worse yet, some alien pod-person had replaced my best friend."

At least Moira didn't try to deny the truth of Carli's assertion. "Fine, but give me some credit. I was trying to ease into the conversation."

"So not your style." Carli set the empty popcorn bowl aside. "Just go with your strength and jump in with both feet. I'm used to it after all these years."

"Okay, I will."

Still, she sat fiddling with a throw pillow. Finally, she tossed it on the floor and angled herself on the couch to face Carli directly but still not making eye contact. That only served to ratchet up the tension in the room.

"Come on, Moira. You're scaring me."

A deep sigh was her friend's only response. After a second one, she finally spoke. "Okay, here it is. I'm really worried about you. I know Peter's betrayal hurt you very badly. It was understandable that you went into defense mode after all of that, but I think you're stuck there."

When Carli started to protest, Moira held up her hand. "Let me finish. You know I'm speaking from personal experience when I say I've been there myself and understand the temptation to play it safe. No one wants to risk being hurt that badly again. I might have blamed my own lack of a social life on my job, but that was only an excuse. I'm not sure if I would have ever started dating again if Titus hadn't come back into my life."

Where was she going with this? Rather than demand an explanation, Carli waited impatiently for Moira to continue. By that point, her friend was picking at a loose thread on her sweater, another indication of how frazzled she was.

"I'm fine, Moira. Really."

"That's just it, Carli. You haven't been, but I think things are changing for you. Seeing you last night with Shay made it clear that you're finally willing to take risks again. I'm not sure what's going on between the two of you, but I haven't seen you kick back and have that much fun in way too long."

She reached over to take Carli's hand. "Six months ago, I would have said Shay isn't the kind of man I ever envisioned making you happy, but I certainly don't have any room to talk on that score. I'm in love with a man who describes himself as a glorified, tattooed short-order cook. But here's the thing—what he and Shay do for a living doesn't matter. It's the kind of men they are deep inside that counts."

Moira blinked a few times as if fighting some pretty powerful emotions. Finally, she said, "I just wanted to tell you that if you and he have something going on, you have my approval. You know, if my opinion means anything."

Carli squeezed her friend's hand but then let go. "Of course your opinion matters. It always has. However, your radar is way off track this time. I know I've said this before, but I'm going to say it again. Shay and I are friends. Nothing more."

"It sure doesn't look that way from the outside."

How to explain? That was the question—one with no easy answer.

"Keep in mind that he's never once asked me out on a date, and I'm old-fashioned enough to want him to do the asking. Yes, he fixed dinner for me the other night, but technically that was a thank-you for me staying with Luca so Shay could cover Ryder's shift at the fire station."

"That's true, but remember he promised to call you after the reception. I think he meant to do exactly that and would have if the whole thing with Luca hadn't happened."

"Maybe, but we'll never know for sure. Besides, he insists he needs to focus on Luca. I understand that."

Moira only looked confused. "But I got the impression the three of you get along really well. I know you like Luca."

"I do."

"So why wouldn't being happy with both Shay and Luca not be a possibility? You've always wanted a husband and children."

"See, that's just it. I have to wonder if that's not a big part of the appeal. You're right about Shay being a lot different than the men I've dated in the past. Say by some miracle that Shay and I did manage to work things out. Would it really be because we were meant to be together? Or would it be because I would suddenly have what I've always wanted—that husband and child you mentioned. Would Shay be settling for me because Luca likes me and having another adult in the house would make his life easier? How would I ever know for sure?"

That had Moira up and pacing the floor. "That's

ridiculous, Carli. Shay has had to make a lot of changes in his life to accommodate Luca's needs, but he's done it without hesitation. Even if there are some rough patches along the way, he'll get it figured out. That's the kind of man he is. Do you honestly think that he'd stoop to marrying someone for the sole purpose of saving on day care costs? You know him better than I do, but I think you're shortchanging both of you."

Then she dropped back down on the sofa next to Carli. "Learning how to trust again after someone has betrayed you isn't easy. Again, I know how hard it is. But don't let Peter's poor choices have that kind of power over you. Don't hide from life because you might end up with a few bruises along the way. You deserve to be happy."

Carli wished she believed that would ever happen. Maybe she was hiding, but she wasn't sure if she had the courage to take those kinds of risks again. She wasn't as brave as Moira—never had been. Before she could confess that shameful truth, the front door opened. Titus was back, saving her from having to continue this painful discussion.

Jumping to her feet, she picked up her purse. "I should be going."

He frowned big-time. "Don't feel like you have to leave on my account."

"I don't, but I have lots of stuff I need to do at home to get ready for the week ahead."

Stubborn man that he was, he blocked her way. "Seriously, are you okay, Carli? You look upset."

"I'm fine. We watched a sad movie."

His wife pointed the remote toward the television and hit Replay. "No, we didn't. It was a comedy. I'm the one who upset her even though I didn't mean to."

Titus made no effort to move, but his voice softened. "Is there anything I can do to help?"

His kindness only made matters worse. "No, but I appreciate the offer. Right now, I just need to go home."

He finally stepped aside. "Call us if you need anything. And the offer to have a talk with Shay still stands."

She managed a small laugh. "Not everything is about him."

"If you say so."

Then he finally let her escape. Right before she walked out, she stopped long enough to say, "I'll think about what you said, Moira."

"Do that."

It wouldn't be a hard promise to keep. She'd already been spending a lot of time lately thinking about her future and what she wanted it to look like. Maybe she'd even log into that dating app when she got back home. Or not.

"WHY CAN'T WE call her?"

Shay stared down at Luca and wondered how one small boy could be so stubborn. Once he got an idea in his head, there was no budging him without a fight. "Because we can't spend every day with Carli. She has other friends besides us."

Luca stood toe-to-toe with him, his arms crossed over his chest and his chin jutted out in anger. "But it's not fair. You got to see her last night."

That hadn't been Shay's doing. If Titus and Moira hadn't brought Carli to the bar with them, Shay wouldn't have seen her, either. Not that he was complaining about how his evening had played out. He'd enjoyed every minute he'd spent with her. His only regret was Aunt Meg letting it slip in front of Luca that she'd heard about the events of last night while picking up doughnuts at Bea's bakery for her Sunday school class. That was fast turnaround even for Bea's well-honed gossip network.

Shay really wished Aunt Meg hadn't told him what she'd heard, especially since there wasn't much he could do to put a stop to it. He didn't particularly like having his personal life discussed and dissected by others, but he had a pretty thick hide. It was Carli who deserved better than to be fodder for the local gossip mill. He also didn't need Luca fussing at him for daring to spend time with her without him.

He pointed out the obvious. "You'll see her at school tomorrow."

Luca stomped his foot. "But I want to see her today. Beau and Bruno have a new trick to show her, and I miss her."

So did Shay.

Time to change the subject. "We haven't taken the dogs for a walk. We should go do that."

"I don't want to go for a walk. Not unless it's at the park with Carli. I had fun when she took me there."

What had she done that Shay couldn't do? "I can take you and the dogs to the park if that's what you want. After that, we have to get back home to finish your reading time."

"I don't want to read today."

Obviously there was a lot that Luca didn't want to do today. Shay prayed for patience, trying to get past the negativity. "I've explained before that reading and your homework is your job just like running my business is mine. I don't like doing all the paperwork I have to do, but it still has to get done."

That argument didn't win Shay any points with Luca. The boy wasn't only stubborn, he had a temper, too. Stamping his foot again, Luca argued, "Kids don't have jobs. Just grown-ups do. I bet my mom and dad wouldn't make me read if I didn't want to."

Shay didn't believe that for a moment. "Yes, they would, Luca."

Still trying to deescalate the situation, Shay crouched down to look at Luca eye to eye. "Your parents loved you, Luca, and part of that love was making sure you learned the skills you need to succeed in school. All skills take practice, and that includes reading."

The boy's chin quivered. "You're not my parents."

No, he wasn't, and they both knew it. Shay took a deep breath and tried again. "That's true, Luca. They're not here, but you know what? They trusted me to do what was right by you. That means doing all kinds of important things, not all of which are necessarily fun or easy for either one of us. If I don't make sure you succeed in school, then I'm not honoring the trust your parents had that I would take good care of you."

When Luca didn't say anything, Shay tried again. "I know dealing with all of this new stuff in your life is hard, and you may not always like how things are going. But I hope at least you'll believe me when I say that I'm doing my best. I've never been lucky enough to have a son of my own, so I'm learning how all of this stuff works right alongside of you."

Should he also admit that sometimes the responsibility he'd taken on scared the stuffing out of him? No, that probably wouldn't convince Luca to trust him.

"So, let's get the dogs loaded up and head for the park. We can walk the trail and even stop at the playground if you want to hang out on the climber for a while. What do you say?"

The boy's surrender was anything but gracious as he trudged over to the cabinet where they kept the dogs' leashes and portable water dishes. "I'll get the stuff we need for Beau and Bruno, but I'd still rather go to the park with Carli."

So would Shay, but he kept that to himself.

CHAPTER NINETEEN

MONDAY WAS A pretty normal day at school. Mrs. Case had shown up again demanding to see the principal immediately, just as angry as she'd been on her last visit. The good news was this time Mrs. Britt was not only in the building, but she walked out of her office and intercepted the woman before she'd managed to work up a full head of steam. While Carli felt bad for her boss, it was a relief to not have to deal with that woman again.

A few minutes later, the counselor walked into the office to join the discussion. On his way past Carli, he whispered, "Wish us luck."

"You'll need it."

He shot her a quick grin before walking into Mrs. Britt's office without knocking. Maybe between the two of them, they'd be able to calm the woman down and come up with some satisfactory solutions. Carli really hoped so. The entire staff at the school worked very hard to help all of their students succeed.

Meanwhile, Carli got a visitor of her own. "Hey, Carli!"

She walked over to the counter and lowered her voice as she said, "Hi, Luca. It's nice to see you, but remember it's Ms. Walsh when we're here at school."

He slapped his hand over his mouth and looked around. "Sorry, I forgot."

"It's not a problem. How was your weekend?"

"Fine, except Shay got to see you on Saturday, and I didn't."

Judging by his frown, he wasn't happy about that. "Actually, it was Moira and Titus who invited me to go out for dinner with them. They wanted to have burgers at Barnaby's. That's the only reason I saw Shay. He didn't know we were coming."

"I know. He told me. But when I wanted to see you yesterday, Shay said we couldn't bother you. We wouldn't have been a bother, would we?"

This conversation suddenly felt as if she were trying to tiptoe through land mines without setting off any explosions. "Well, I wasn't actually home yesterday. I went to church, and then Moira asked me to come over to her house."

She checked the time. "Oops, you'd better hustle to class. The bell is about to ring."

"Okay." He started toward the door. "Did you know I have to stay here at the after-school day care now? Shay picks me up when he gets done at work."

"That's great, Luca. I know the kids have fun in the program. They get extra time out on the playground and then have snacks. It's also a good chance to get their homework done before they get picked up."

Luca didn't look excited by the situation, but then it was yet another new thing he had to get used to. "I'd rather wait here in the office with you."

She wrinkled her nose at him. "Sorry, but that's against the rules. Besides, I go home not long after school is out."

He brightened right up. "Then you could take me home and stay with me until Shay gets home. We could have dinner together again. That was fun."

"Yes, it was, but that was a special occasion, Luca, not something we can do every day." She pointed to the clock this time. "You really need to go now. Ms. Varne will be wondering where you are."

"Okay." He wasn't quite done, though. "If you were my new mom, I could come home with you instead of Shay."

Her breath caught in her chest. What was she supposed to say to that? Shay would be devastated to hear Luca say he would prefer to live with Carli. She had to nip this in the bud immediately. She leaned over the counter to speak, hoping to reduce the chance that someone passing by might overhear their conversation.

"Luca, anyone would be lucky to have a son like you, but I can't be your mom. That doesn't mean we can't be friends, but your parents wanted you to live with Shay for a reason. He and your father served together in the Marine Corps. I've heard Shay say that the two of them were as close as brothers. That means they thought of Shay as part of your family. Don't ever forget that he's the one who dropped everything to come running the minute he found out that you needed him. I can't emphasize enough how special that was. And you know he's doing everything he can to give you a good home. It might take time for the two of you to get everything worked out between you, but you have to know he's doing his best."

"But…"

The bell rang, causing him to jump. She reached for a pad of tardy slips and filled one out and handed it to him. "Luca, now isn't the time for this conversation. Take this note and give it to your teacher."

Still not happy, he stuck the note in his pocket. When he started to speak again, she pointed toward the door behind him. "Now, Luca."

He finally did as he was told and disappeared down the hall while Carli rcluctantly returned to her desk. Her hand shook as she picked up her water bottle and took a drink. It was hard to swallow thanks to the lump of regret in her throat. At least she and Luca had been alone in the office during that conversation. The last thing either of them needed was for people to start talking about how involved she was in Luca's life outside of work. While it wasn't against any rule she knew of, it could prove awkward.

That wasn't the only problem, though. Luca's comment only further reinforced her own concerns about letting herself get drawn ever deeper into the boy's life—not to mention his guardian's. Once again, it wasn't as if Shay had mentioned the two of them seeing each other again despite the good time they'd had on Saturday night. Yes, he'd kissed her good-night and made her feel as if it mattered. But he'd also done the same thing the night of Moira's wedding reception. She even understood why he hadn't called right away.

But she couldn't help but wonder why he couldn't have found a minute to at least text her about what had happened. When he'd shown up to register Luca for first grade, Shay clearly hadn't been expecting to run into her in the office. He'd seemed relieved to be dealing with someone he knew, but the truth was anyone there could have helped him.

She was probably overreacting or at least overthinking the situation. The problem was that they both knew there was an innocent third party whose needs had to come first. She couldn't let Luca become so attached to her that he thought of her not just as a friend but a replacement for the parents he'd lost.

Somehow she was going to have to gently put some distance between them without hurting his feelings. The only question was whether she should tell Shay about their conversation. Before she could decide, the phone rang. It was time to concentrate on her job. She wasn't being paid to sit there and stew about her personal problems. No, that would have to wait until she got off work.

Once she was back home and behind closed doors, there would be time enough to give in to the urge to cry.

SOMETHING WAS DEFINITELY going on with Luca. The past several days, the boy had barely spoken after Shay picked him up at school. Once they got home, Luca spent most of the time shut up in his room with the dogs. It was almost impossible to pry him out of there even long enough to eat dinner and walk Bruno and Beau.

While Shay didn't want to interrogate him, he couldn't fix the problem without knowing what it was. He'd tried asking him how things were going at the day care but had only gotten monosyllabic answers that told Shay next to nothing. It wasn't surprising that it might take a while for Luca to get comfortable with his new after-school routine, but Shay hadn't expected it to be this bad. Failing all else, he'd called Sean McKay, the coordinator at the day care, to get his take on the situation.

The news hadn't been good. According to Sean, it was hard to get Luca to join his age group out on the playground. He also turned his nose up at the snacks he was offered and showed no interest in joining his classmates in playing board games or coloring. Sean had planned to call about the situation, but Shay had beaten him to the punch.

Things couldn't go on like this, but Shay was running out of options. When he got to the gym where the day care operated, it didn't take him long to spot Luca. That was because he was sitting by himself in the back corner, his backpack next to him. He looked angry, glaring at anyone who came too close.

Shay needed to know what had happened before he approached Luca. He spotted Sean shooting baskets with some of the older kids and headed across the gym to see if he could interrupt him for a minute.

Sean saw him coming and tossed the basketball to one of the other players. “Kids, I’ll be back in a few minutes.”

He motioned for Shay to follow him out into the hallway. “I was hoping I’d see you today, Mr. Barnaby. We had a bit of an incident earlier, and I thought you’d want to know what happened.”

A feeling of impending doom washed over Shay. The few times he’d spoken with Sean, the man had always been upbeat and positive. Now he looked as if he were about to deliver the worst kind of news. “I appreciate that. What happened?”

“The kids know to check off their names as soon as they enter the gym. The teachers also do additional head counts periodically to make sure everyone is accounted for. Near as we can figure, Luca checked off his name but didn’t stay in the gym. When his teacher couldn’t find him, we had to do an all-call in the building to ask the staff to look for him. We finally found him hiding in the conference room in the school office down the hall.”

Shay could only imagine the panic the day care staff must have been feeling until they’d finally found Luca. “This is all still pretty new to him. Do you think he got confused about where he was supposed to be?”

Sean shrugged. “I have no idea. For sure, he’s

never done anything like that before, and he did come to the gym long enough to check off his name. When he was spotted, I sat down at the table with him and asked what was going on. It took a lot of work to get him to finally tell me why he was not where he belonged."

"Which was?"

"This is where it gets weird. He said that he was missing his friend, and he was waiting to talk to her." Sean looked hesitant about whatever he was about to say next. "I assumed he was talking about another student. As it turned out, that wasn't the case."

By that point, Shay could guess right where this was headed. "He was looking for Carli Walsh, wasn't he?"

Sean nodded. "Yeah. Evidently the kid considers her a good friend."

That last part sounded more like a question than a statement. Shay wasn't particularly thrilled with having to share his personal life with a virtual stranger, but Sean needed to know what was going on. "Carli is a friend of the family, and Luca has spent time with her outside of school."

If anything, Sean looked even more concerned. "That's not all. He also insisted that he was really supposed to go home with her instead of staying at the day care."

"He knows better than that, but I'll talk to him

to see where he got that idea. The lights are off in the office, so I'm sure Ms. Walsh has already left for the day. I'll try to call her over the weekend to find out if she knows anything. Failing that, I'll stop by and talk to her Monday morning."

"Good enough. Now, I'd better get back inside."

"Thanks for your patience with Luca. He's been through a lot, and we're still running into a few bumps in the road."

"Let me know if there is anything I can do to help. We do our best to make sure the kids are safe and happy while they are with us."

"I'll talk to him."

Shay struggled to maintain some semblance of control until Sean disappeared back into the gym. As soon as he was alone in the hall, he actively considered punching the wall or kicking a nearby trash can as hard as he could. Neither of those things would solve his problems, and he couldn't risk anyone seeing him pitching a fit in public. No, that would have to wait until later, after Luca was in bed asleep. Or maybe he'd drop the kid off with Aunt Meg long enough to go for a long run to burn off his frustration.

For now, he had one angry little boy to take home. Once there, they'd be having a long conversation about what was going on between Luca and Carli. If all else failed, he'd call her to get her take on the situation. Maybe something had happened to convince Luca that she was willing to watch him until Shay got off work. That didn't seem likely, but their relationship had definitely gone off the rails.

He put on his best game face and headed back into the gym. Luca was still sitting in the corner, looking so lost and alone. The boy watched Shay's approach with not even a hint of welcome in his expression. At least he stood up without protest and picked up his backpack. Shay didn't know what to say that would make the boy feel better, so the two of them walked out without speaking a single word.

That awful silence lasted all the way home. If there was ever a moment when Shay felt like a failure in his new role as Luca's guardian, this was it.

CHAPTER TWENTY

MAYBE FISH STICKS with a side of macaroni and cheese wasn't the healthiest of dinner choices, but that didn't matter right now. It was one of Luca's favorite meals, and Shay was willing to do whatever it took to keep the peace. After they'd eaten, they took the dogs for an extra-long walk, something else that Luca usually enjoyed.

Shay was well aware he was only delaying the inevitable. Things were bound to go sideways the second he asked Luca why he'd hidden from the day care and then claimed he was supposed to go home with Carli. While Shay didn't appreciate Luca fibbing about stuff, there had to be something behind his claims.

Shay considered calling Carli first, but this really was his problem to solve. Bracing himself for whatever was to come, he sat down on the floor next to Luca and the dogs. He stroked Beau's soft fur and then gave equal time to Bruno. "So, we need to talk about what happened after school today."

Luca barely glanced up from the picture he was coloring, but there was no missing the white-knuckled grip he had on the marker in his hand. Keeping his voice low, his expression neutral, Shay launched the opening salvo. "Mr. Sean said you went to the gym and put a check by your name on the list to let them know you were there. I take it that's what you're supposed to do when you leave your classroom at the end of the day. Do I have that right?"

That netted him the barest of nods.

"Well, that's good. It's really important that Mr. Sean and the other day care teachers know where everyone is at all times. It's their job to make sure all the kids stay safe so their parents don't have to worry about them."

"You're not my parent."

Okay, that hurt, but Luca wasn't wrong. "No, but I *am* responsible for you now, so it's my job to know you're safe. That's why you have to follow the rules at school and at the day care. But that's not what happened today. Instead, you didn't stay in the gym after you signed in. They had to search the building and found you hiding in the office. I need to know why."

"I wanted to go home with Carli."

No surprise there. "Was she even there?"

"I was waiting for her to come back, but she didn't."

After a second, he whispered, "I think she's mad at me."

That didn't sound right. If Luca had done something she didn't like, surely she would have given Shay a heads-up. "Why would Carli be mad at you?"

"Because I told her I wanted her to be my new mom. She said she couldn't be because you're my new parent. Then she made me go to class and doesn't let me visit her in the office anymore. And if she sees me, she won't let me stop to talk to her."

Luca finally turned to face Shay, a huge frown on his young face. "That's not fair. I miss my mom, and Carli hugs me like she did."

Shay's heart almost broke. It was tempting to gather Luca into his arms and hug him himself, but he was pretty sure that wouldn't satisfy Luca's hunger for his mother's touch. Having had his own experience with Carli's warmth, he also understood why Luca might prefer her hugs to Shay's.

Heck, right now Luca wasn't the only one who wished she was there with them. That didn't mean Shay was particularly happy to only now be finding out about the problematic conversation between her and Luca. Even if she'd thought she'd dealt with it satisfactorily, why would she be distancing herself from Luca at this late date?

There had to be more to this than what Luca was telling him.

"I'm sorry if something she's done has hurt your feelings, Luca. And I'm sure she'd feel bad if she knew that's what happened. I will talk to her about it as soon as I get a chance. But that aside, I'm going to need your promise that you won't sneak out of the day care again. That's not fair to the adults at the day care who are responsible for you."

Luca hung his head but remained silent.

"I need to hear it, Luca. I have to know you're going to do your part to be safe."

"But—"

"No buts, kiddo. Tell me you understand what I'm asking of you. I can't work or do other things I need to do if I'm constantly worrying about where you are. You wouldn't have wanted to upset your mom and dad like this, and I need you to treat me like you would have them."

Then he held up his hand to stave off another protest that Shay wasn't really his father. "I know I'm only a substitute for your parents, but that doesn't mean I don't care about you. You're mine now, Luca. I love you like you were my own son. I hope someday you'll come to love me, too. Regardless of how long that takes, I still need to keep you safe. I owe that to your parents."

He held out his hand. "So do we have an agreement? You'll do your part and follow the rules?"

After another hesitation, Luca accepted the handshake, but there was no missing the tears trickling down his cheeks. "I promise to follow the rules, but I still miss Carli."

So did Shay, but that was a whole different problem. "I'll see what I can do about that, but it will be up to her."

When Luca started to sob as if his young heart was broken, Shay reached out to hug him, pulling him close. At first, the boy remained as stiff as a board, but then he relaxed against Shay's chest as the tears flowed. The poor little guy had dealt with so much since the night his folks died, it was no surprise that he occasionally needed to shed a few tears. "It's okay, Luca. I've got you. Just let it all out."

He rubbed Luca's back and murmured reassurances, hoping to take the edge off his distress. When the tears slowly trailed off, the two of them sat there for several minutes longer while the dogs watched them. With that uncanny way of animals, they sensed the seriousness of the moment and stood guard on either side of Shay's legs. As soon as Luca sat up straighter, they both crept close enough to lick his face, doing a pretty thorough job of it. That had their buddy giggling as he tried to ward off any more of their slurpy affection.

At least the discussion ended on a happier note. Time to change the subject. "If you're going to want a bedtime snack, now's the time. What sounds good?"

"Can we have ice cream?"

Considering the evening they'd had, why not? "Vanilla or chocolate?"

Luca dried his face with the hem of his T-shirt. "Can I have both?"

"Sure thing."

Hopefully the ice cream might finish the job Shay's hug had started.

CARLI PACED THE circumference of her living room. She'd lost track of how many trips she'd made around the small distance. It was a total waste of energy and had done nothing to soothe her jangled nerves. What was worse was that she still had another ten minutes or so to wait before she'd find out why Shay had texted her to say that they needed to talk this morning. He'd set ten o'clock as the time he would arrive, without giving her any hint of what was on the agenda for the discussion.

But she could guess. It had to be about Luca. After all, he was the one real connection she and Shay had. The only question was what had happened that had Shay insisting on coming to her house so they could talk in private.

Her phone rang halfway through her next circuit around the room, startling her out of her reverie. Maybe Shay had changed his mind about coming over or had decided they could handle the problem over the phone. She felt a strange sense of relief mixed with a certain amount of disappointment. But when she picked up her phone, it was Moira's name on the screen. She was tempted to let it go to voicemail, especially since Shay had just pulled into her driveway, but that wouldn't be fair to her friend.

"Hey, Moira, what's up?"

"Nothing special. I haven't heard from you since last weekend and wondered how things were going."

Terrible, horrible, and likely about to get worse, but that discussion would have to wait until another time. "Look, I'd love to chat, but I'll have to call you back. Shay's here."

Moira didn't immediately respond, but then she said, "I'm guessing from the tone in your voice that's not a good thing."

"Not sure, actually. He texted earlier to say he wanted to talk. He didn't say why."

The doorbell chimed. "Sorry, but I've really got to go."

"Okay, but call me after he leaves."

Carli wasn't sure that would be a good idea, especially if Shay managed to upset her. Loyal friend that she was, Moira was likely to hunt the man down, and that wouldn't end well for anyone. "I'm sure it's nothing to get all worked up about."

"Then you can tell me that's the case. Regardless, it's not a suggestion. Call me or you'll find me on your doorstep before you know it."

Stubborn woman. "Fine."

She disconnected the call and opened the front door. One look at Shay's face and she knew she'd been right. There was no way this was going to be a fun conversation. "Come on in."

He followed her inside, stopping to look around. It hadn't occurred to her that this would be his first time inside her home. Whenever they'd spent time together, they'd usually been at school, the bar or his place.

"Would you rather sit in here or the kitchen? I made coffee, and I have chocolate chip cookies."

He hovered near the door. "Wherever you'd be more comfortable."

"Okay, the kitchen is this way."

While he took a seat at the table, she poured the coffee and piled a plate high with cookies. Having delayed as much as she could, she finally sat down across from him. As he reached for a cookie, he said, "I like your house. It fits you."

The comment pleased her. "Thank you. It's a far cry from the modern monstrosity my ex-husband liked so much, but I fell in love with this place as soon as I walked in the door. The place isn't much larger than most apartments, but it's plenty big enough for me."

Shay's mouth quirked up briefly in a small smile. "This is a completely different style, but somehow it reminds me of the cabin my uncle and I built for me to live in when I first moved here from Georgia. It's even smaller, but it was all mine. That's where I stayed right after I moved back here while my current place was being built." He sipped his coffee and smiled a little. "Who knows, maybe Luca will want to claim it as his when he gets older."

His smile disappeared completely as he set his mug back down. "Speaking of Luca, he's the reason I'm here."

That didn't come as much of a surprise. "Is he okay?"

Shay leaned forward, elbows on the table, his blue eyes worried. "No, actually, he's not. There was an incident at the day care yesterday."

That was alarming. "What happened? Was he hurt?"

"Not physically. At some point after he checked in at the gym, Luca snuck out and hid in the main office."

She tried to get her head around what he was telling her. "Why would he go there? Surely he knows the rules and routine at the day care by now."

"You see, that's where it gets interesting. I was hoping that maybe you could help me figure that out."

His grumbling comment made it clear that he didn't think it was "interesting" at all. No, *irritating* or maybe even *infuriating* would be closer to the mark. Knowing she would sound pretty defensive, she asked, "How on earth would I know why he did that? It had to have happened after I left for the day, or I would have taken him right back to the gym."

"His story varies a bit. Either he thought he was supposed to go home with you, or maybe that's just what he wanted to do. When I pressed him for more details, he also said you were mad at him for some reason."

Just what was Shay accusing her of? "I'm not mad at Luca."

Shay spoke slowly as if fighting to remain calm. "Well, he seems to think you've been avoiding him, but he doesn't know why. He also said you won't let him stop by the office to say hi in the mornings anymore. According to him, if you happen to see him during the day, you don't talk to him like you used to. If any of that's true, it would help me explain the situation to him if you told me what's going on."

She wanted to deny those accusations, but it was true. In part, she was trying to protect Luca from getting any more attached to her, but the truth was she was really protecting herself. "One reason that I won't let him stop in the office is that the last time he did, he wouldn't leave and ended up being late to class."

"Did you tell him that was why?"

"No, and that's on me."

To give herself something else to focus on, she chose a cookie at random and slowly broke it into ever smaller pieces and dropped them onto her napkin. "When he came in that day, he said something that knocked me a bit sideways."

"How so?"

"He wants me to be his new mom. I tried explaining that we could be friends, but that's all. I reminded him that his parents chose you to be his new family. They did that because you and his father were like brothers. I'm not part of that."

Shay got up to pour them each more coffee and maybe put a little distance between them. When he sat back down, he asked, "So why didn't you call me to let me know what he'd said? It would've been nice if you let me know you were going to distance yourself from him. Or maybe I should say both of us?"

Her eyes burned as if tears would start flowing any second now. "Because I'm a coward. I was thinking…no, I wasn't thinking at all." She wadded up the napkin with the cookie crumbs inside and set it aside. "But you're right. I should've called."

His voice was softer when he finally spoke. "I'm here now, Carli. Talk to me."

As full-on panic tore through her, the walls of her small kitchen closed in on her. She needed more space, more room to breathe. "Would you mind if we moved to the living room?"

Without giving Shay a chance to respond, she was already up and moving. Once in the living room, she couldn't seem to figure out what to do next. As she stood there dithering, Shay put his hands on her shoulders from behind and gently guided her over to sit on one end of the couch. He took the other end and patiently waited for her to get her thoughts in some sort of order.

Finally drawing a deep breath, she simply started talking. "This isn't Luca's fault, at least not entirely. I understand he simply wants his life to go back to the way it used to be—with his mom and his dad there to love him and watch him grow up. My best guess is that he's slowly coming to terms with the fact that they are gone for good. So to make up for their loss, he wants the next best thing. In his mind, that would be you as his father and someone as his mom. I'm guessing that I'm the only person he's met since he came here that comes close to filling the bill."

She forced herself to look directly at Shay. "I understand exactly how he's feeling. I have a good life here in Dunbar, but it's not the one I imagined for myself. I apologize if this sounds like I'm indulging in a major pity party. I'm trying to explain where my own head was when Luca asked me to be his mom. By this point in my life, I always pictured myself married with a couple of kids and that my parents would be around to spoil them rotten. But here I am, alone, single and childless."

She temporarily ran out of words, but a few seconds later she found the strength to continue. "I really had a great time with you at the wedding reception and frankly thought maybe the two of us had found something special that night. I can't speak for you, but it was the first time in ages that I had such a great time with someone. I won't deny that it hurt when you didn't call, but at least I found out it was for a very good reason. When you came back, I loved seeing how hard you were trying with Luca under such difficult circumstances. You could've turned your back on the situation and let someone else take care of Luca, but instead you focused every bit of your attention on him."

Shay tipped his head to the side as he watched her. "Those first days back were a bit of a blur, but one thing that really stuck out was how patient you were with Luca and me at the school that first morning. It felt like the first step back to normal for both of us."

"I'm glad I managed to help even that much."

Now for the hard part. "Back to the matter at hand. Every time our paths have crossed, hanging out with you and Luca has seemed so easy, so right. I can't remember the last time I laughed as much as I did the night we had pizza. Then there was the Friday I stayed with Luca, and the three of us had dinner together at the fire station. I also loved when you cooked for the three of us, and hanging out last Saturday night at the bar with you, Moira and Titus was amazing."

"I think it was pretty clear that I enjoyed those times, too."

"That's just it, Shay. We do have fun, but the only time we get together is either by accident or when you need my help with Luca. I want more out of life than that. It's not fair to me, especially because each time it happens, I find myself imagining what it would be like to be part of Luca's life all of the time. But, Shay, I can't be a placeholder until you find the right woman to share your life with. When that happens—and I'm sure it will—she's the one who Luca needs to complete his new family. Having me around would only complicate things for him…and me."

Her analysis of the situation didn't go over well with Shay. His voice was a harsh growl when he finally responded. "And avoiding us will free up your time to get back into the dating game."

That was not what she wanted to do at all, but she didn't argue. It wasn't as if Shay was interested in offering her any options. It was past time to put an end to this disaster. She pushed herself up off the couch and walked over to open the door. "I'm sorry I hurt his feelings, but I really believe it's best for the three of us to keep our distance for the foreseeable future."

Evidently Shay didn't want to take the hint and leave. "I've listened to everything you've said, Carli. I'd appreciate it if you allow me a turn to speak before you kick me and Luca to the curb."

She winced at the barely concealed anger in his voice. Knowing there was no way to make him budge if he was determined to have his say, she closed the door and returned to her spot on the sofa. "I'm listening."

"You're not the only one who has made mistakes. I knew that Luca was getting attached to you, but I didn't realize that was putting you in such an awkward position. I apologize for that. However, other than the dogs, very little makes him truly happy these days. You're one of the few exceptions to that. Actually, that was true for both of us."

He finally stood up. "I'll find some way to explain to him that you have your own life to live."

Before opening the door, he had one more thing to say. "Do me a favor. Take a break from hanging out at my bar."

When he was gone, Carli could barely breathe knowing she might have just made the biggest mistake of her life.

CHAPTER TWENTY-ONE

AFTER HE GOT HOME, Shay did his best to act like nothing bad had happened. Considering the way even the dogs had done their best to avoid him, he'd failed miserably. Finally, he had changed into gym shorts and a ratty T-shirt and set off for a long hard run. He couldn't remember the last time he'd been this angry, twisted up inside and so darned confused. Rather than subject his aunt or Luca to his bad mood, he had to get away for a while.

Half an hour into his run, his lungs were struggling to draw in enough air, and his legs and feet were killing him. A smarter man would slow down, cool off and walk back home. But that would give him too much time to think. That was the last thing he wanted right now.

Besides, if he kept on the move, perhaps he could eventually outrun his regrets and second thoughts.

There wasn't a shoulder along this stretch of country road, and there was a fairly deep ditch only a foot or so off the side of the pavement. Rather than risk a misstep that would send him tumbling down the slope, he ran on the edge of the road and kept an ear out for any approaching vehicles. Hearing the rumble of an engine coming toward him, Shay slowed down and moved closer to the shoulder, planning to pick up speed again once the vehicle passed.

But instead of disappearing into the distance, the all-too-familiar pickup truck circled back around and came up even with him. Shay resumed running full speed while the driver maintained pace with him. What on earth was Titus doing out here in the middle of nowhere when Shay knew full well the man should be back at his café dishing up food for the locals?

Finally, Titus drove ahead and backed into the next driveway up the road. By the time Shay got there, Titus was out of the truck and watching his approach. It was tempting to pass on by, but that would only postpone the inevitable. Shay should've guessed that Carli would immediately tell Moira everything—and that Moira, in turn, would fill her husband in on all the gory details before siccing him on Shay's trail.

He trotted up to where Titus stood, but kept jogging in place. He didn't want his muscles to stiffen up when he needed them to hold up long enough to get him back home. The look of disgust on Titus's face only made him feel more defensive and guilty than he already did. Deciding a good offense was the best defense, he glared at his friend. "I know you didn't just happen to be out cruising around in the middle of your workday. No doubt your wife sent you out here to find me. So deliver whatever threats you want to deliver on her behalf so I can finish my run."

After that little speech, his energy level bottomed out. Rather than worrying about maintaining any appearance of strength, he gave in and sagged against the side of the truck. At least that was slightly more dignified than collapsing in the dirt. Titus muttered something under his breath as he reached inside the cab of the truck and pulled out two bottles of water. Shoving one into Shay's hand, he snarled, "Drink that before you pass out."

Shay poured half the bottle over his head and then drank the rest. By the time Titus handed him the second bottle, he could breathe well enough to thank him. It didn't go over well.

"Don't bother thanking me. Your aunt asked me to deliver them. She was worried because you left without taking any water with you. She said to tell you that she would stay with Luca until your regular babysitter arrives. I take that to mean that you're supposed to work this evening."

Smacking his forehead, Shay winced. "I've lost track of time. I have to be at the bar by five."

"You've got a little time. It's not quite four o'clock. I'll drive you back home when we're done talking."

Shay took another swig of the water. "I'd appreciate it. My only question is whether I'll be in any condition to work when you get done talking to me."

Titus huffed a small laugh. "I'm not usually given to kicking a friend when he's down. Although seeing how upset my wife was after talking to Carli, I admit to having been tempted this time."

He gave Shay a long look. "But considering right now you couldn't put up a good fight against a stiff breeze, knocking some sense into you wouldn't be any fun at all. I'll settle for pointing out that you've messed up big-time. Again."

There was probably no benefit to defending his actions, but Shay tried anyway. "Carli told me to leave and stay away. Partly because she feels it's unfair to Luca to think she can be an important part of his life. Something about saving that role for my wife, whoever that might be. Lord knows I have no idea."

He picked up a rock and threw it as far as he could send it. "My best guess is she wants to start a quest to find the perfect date. Spending time with us…me, anyway, is interfering with that."

And didn't he just sound pathetic? At least when Titus responded, he kept his gaze pinned on some spot in the distance so Shay didn't have to see the pity in his expression. "I know. Moira shared the abridged version of what Carli told her."

He paused to get two soft drinks out of the truck. After popping the tops, he handed one to Shay. "Here's a question for you. Do you think she really meant any of that?"

"Sure sounded like it."

Titus snorted. "So at least you weren't the only one in your discussion whose brain was misfiring today."

Even if that were true, somehow it didn't make Shay feel any better about the situation. He felt like he'd been kicked in the gut, but he hated the thought of Carli hurting, too. "Why do you say that?"

"From a few things Moira has said, Carli has some serious trust issues, all thanks to the way her ex treated her. That selfish jerk was too much of a coward to tell her that he was unhappy. Instead, he snuck around behind Carli's back and started a new life without ever including her in the discussion. Who knows? Maybe if he had given her some warning, the gutless wonder's decision to end their marriage would've still hurt Carli, but at least she wouldn't have been blind-sided. From what I understand, despite putting off starting a family with Carli, he got his girl-friend pregnant."

Titus gave Shay another long look. "Betray-als like that have long-term effects on peo-ple. For example, if by some chance a woman found someone she thought might be Mr. Right, she's still bound to react badly if he's not smart enough to tell her what's really going on inside his thick skull."

Shay took a long drink of his beer. "I'm hardly anyone's Mr. Right. I'm not like you."

That earned him one of Titus's rusty laughs. "Do you really think that's how I saw myself when it came to asking Moira for a second chance? Because I'm telling you right here and now, I screwed up unbelievably bad back in the day. Then I compounded the problem by stay-ing away from Moira for ten years, telling my-self the whole time I was protecting her. The truth was she has always been the strong one, not me. Surprisingly, that didn't keep her from loving me. I count myself lucky every day that she doesn't expect me to be perfect, just that I own up to it when I screw up, and I try to make things right again. That's all any of us can do."

Shay decided it was time for some honesty.

After sharing the events of the night Shay's sister had followed him to a party, he explained the fallout it had on him and his family. "I live in mortal fear of not being able to protect the people I care about, that I'll fail them like I did Julie, and they'll get hurt in the process. For all practical purposes, I lost my immediate family that night. I've barely spoken to my mother and sister since. My father, either, but I count that as a blessing. At the moment, it's all I can do to take care of Luca."

Titus rolled his eyes. "Sure sounds like an excuse to me. Stop and think back, Shay. You were a kid yourself when all of that went down. Your parents were the grown-ups in the situation. If they'd handled things better, you wouldn't still be carrying around a bucketload of guilt after all these years."

After letting that much sink in, Titus continued. "I agree you need to take good care of the kid. But from where I stand, you've done everything you can think of to do just that. I also get why you had to focus all of your attention on him when you first brought him home, but you're entitled to have a personal life, too. Luca's parents wanted you to give their son a good life, but they didn't expect you to give up everything else that makes your own life worth living. It won't be easy, but somehow you need to find some balance."

Shay offered up one more token protest. "There aren't enough hours in the day."

"Now you're scraping the bottom of the barrel for excuses. Single parents find ways to date all the time. Married couples find time for each other. I'm not saying it's easy, but it's possible. Especially when you've found someone worth the time and effort."

He abruptly changed directions. "So tell me this. If you hadn't had to rush off to help Luca right after our reception, would you have really called Carli?"

"Yeah, I had every intention of calling her the next day."

"So you were interested in her from the get-go."

"Yeah, I was." Might as well lay it all out there. "In fact, remember the first time you brought Carli and Moira to my bar? Back before you and Moira got things figured out?"

Titus smiled. "You mean the night I wanted to punch you for daring to dance with my woman?"

"Yeah, that night. Well, I actually thought about asking Carli out right then, but Moira warned me off. She said Carli needed someone who would treat her gently and give her time to heal from an ugly divorce."

His friend winced. "I'm sorry she did that. I'm pretty sure she is, too."

"She wasn't necessarily wrong. I'm guessing Carli's husband was about as different from me as you can get."

"Different doesn't mean he was a good man, Shay. He certainly didn't make her happy. By way of contrast, she obviously enjoys the time she spends with you."

Titus held up his hand when Shay tried to speak. "No, listen to me. I know she likes hanging out with Luca, but the kid wasn't with the two of you at the bar the other night. She enjoyed having dinner with you and arguing over which is the best dipping sauce for fries. Besides me, you were the only one she danced with even though a couple of other guys asked her when you had to help Jody at the bar. In fact, I'm pretty sure she was the one who picked out four slow dance songs in a row."

Then his grin turned wicked. "And I saw how she kissed you out in the parking lot. That wasn't an innocent peck on the cheek to thank you for walking her out to the car. That was the kind of a kiss a woman like Carli only gives to a man who matters."

His words hit Shay like a sledgehammer. "You're right. I've been a coward, but that stops now. Luca and I both need Carli in our lives."

"It's about time you figured that out."

Then Titus nodded and checked the time again. "If we don't leave now, you're going to be really late. Get in the truck and then, for Pete's sake, get your head in the game."

Shay didn't much like taking orders from anyone—he'd had enough of that while he was in the marines. But he'd make an exception in this case. While Titus tore down the road, Shay made a mental list of what he needed to do.

First up, he should definitely take a shower before showing up at the bar. At work, he would put his personal problems on hold and focus on the job at hand. His employees and customers deserved more from him than a token effort.

Later, when he finally got home, he'd try to get a good night's sleep because he had plans to make and would need his wits about him. He'd learned a lot about planning missions in the military. Come tomorrow, he'd put those skills to good use and come up with a campaign that would achieve the desired goal: convincing Carli to give him another chance. Because there was nothing he wanted more than to build a family and a future with her.

CARLI HAD BARELY gotten home when the doorbell rang. Sighing, she quickly finished exchanging her church clothes for a red turtleneck sweater and jeans. Taking her shoes and socks with her, she padded barefoot to the front door. While she loved Moira like a sister, she really hoped her friend wasn't dropping by for another pity-and-pastry party. The emotional support was appreciated, but the long-term effects on her waistline weren't.

The doorbell rang again, which had her calling out, "I'm coming. I'm coming."

When she yanked the door open, she expected to find an adult on the other side. Instead, it was Luca standing there with a huge grin on his face. He held up an envelope that had her name on it in distinctly masculine handwriting. She guessed that it was Luca who had surrounded her name with stickers of cars, spaceships and stars.

"This is for you. It's an invitation from Shay and me. I decorated the outside envelope, but he wrote the message inside."

Even if she still believed it would be better if the three of them spent less time together, it would've taken a far harder heart than hers to deny anything to that hopeful little face. "Thank you, Luca. I can tell how hard you worked on it."

Before handing over the envelope, Luca gave her a serious look. "Shay said not to open it until after we leave. You're supposed to think about it and then text him your answer."

When the man in question pulled up in front of her house, Luca surrendered the envelope and then laughed like a loon as he took off running. As soon as he hopped up into the truck, both he and Shay waved and drove off down the street.

Even more confused than she was before, Carli watched until the truck disappeared from sight before going back inside the house. Rather than tear into the envelope immediately, she carried it down the hall to the kitchen to make herself a cup of chamomile tea, hoping it would soothe her jitters. As it steeped, she took a seat at the table and tried to work up the courage to read the message from Shay.

The envelope was a soft blue, which reminded her of the color of his eyes. Still in no hurry to read its contents, she traced her name with a fingertip. She liked Shay's handwriting, finding it bold and strong like the man himself. By that point, her hands were shaking slightly, making it more difficult to unseal the envelope without damaging it. She suspected whatever was inside would be something she'd want to add to the box of mementos she kept on her dresser.

Finally, with her pulse racing, she opened the envelope, withdrew the card from inside and started reading.

Dear Carli,
I know we didn't part on the best terms yesterday, and that just didn't sit well with me. I also know we still have some issues to deal with, but I'm hoping we can set those aside for an evening. Would you do me and Luca the honor of having dinner with the two of us tonight? We'd really like to take you to a nice restaurant and see how it goes. If you want to talk afterward about what comes next for us, we can do that, too. Luca says to tell you he's crossing his fingers you'll say yes. So am I.
Shay

She skimmed through the note twice more before reaching for her phone and typing, I'd love to. What time should I be ready?

After only a second's hesitation, she hit Send.

CHAPTER TWENTY-TWO

BEFORE KNOCKING ON Carli's door, Shay tugged on his tie one last time, wishing it didn't feel as if it were cutting off his access to oxygen. Millions of people wore the darn things every day, but he wasn't a fan. The only reason he even owned one was that he'd bought it to wear to Titus and Moira's wedding. The same was true of the sports coat and slacks he was wearing. He might not be comfortable, but at least Carli would know he'd made an effort to look presentable.

Luca mimicked Shay's action, tugging on his own tie. "Will she like our outfits?"

Shay smiled down at Luca. "Yeah, she will. You look great in your new suit, and ladies like a well-dressed guy."

The door swung open only seconds after he knocked. When Carli stepped into sight, he almost swallowed his tongue as he held out a bouquet of pink flowers. "You look beautiful."

Her look of pleased surprise hit him hard.

Why had he never told her that before? What was wrong with him?

She blushed as she took the flowers. "I love alstroemeria."

"Pretty fancy name."

"They're also called Peruvian lilies. I think that's where they originated." She smiled at him. "They're my favorite, especially this particular color. Thank you."

"I'm glad you like them."

He was even more glad that Moira had clued him in on what kind of flowers Carli preferred. It was only pure luck that he'd been able to find some on such short notice. He'd had a long list of things he had to get done to pull off this date besides buying the bouquet. He'd had to take Luca shopping for a suit, come home and iron his dress shirt, and then make reservations at the restaurant. His stomach had been a knot of nerves as he'd waited to hear if she accepted the invitation. He wasn't sure what he would've done if she'd refused, but he'd be eternally grateful she hadn't.

"Come inside, you two, while I put these in water, and then we can go."

After she put the flowers in a vase, she picked up a lacy shawl. Shay took it from her and settled it over her shoulders. "Thank you."

With that, he had something he wanted to say.

"I should have asked you out on a date long before this."

"You've had a lot going on, Shay."

It felt so right when she slipped her hand into his as they walked out of the house toward his freshly washed truck. It gave him hope that maybe they hadn't burned all the bridges between them. As he opened her door for her, he said, "I made reservations at a restaurant that Ryder recommended. It's right in the heart of that alpine-style village up in Leavenworth. The weather is supposed to be mild this evening, so we can browse some of the shops afterward if you want. But if there's somewhere else you'd rather go, just say the word."

"No, that sounds great."

SHAY DEFINITELY OWED Ryder big-time. The restaurant had turned out to be perfect, the tables arranged far enough apart to afford the diners some privacy and the lighting dim enough to be cozy without being too dark. As the waiter led the three of them to a table in a small alcove by the windows, Shay realized he couldn't remember the last time he'd gone out on a real date. What if he'd forgotten how to behave in polite society?

As things turned out, it wasn't a problem at all, mainly because Carli had a way about her that made everything easy. She kept the conversation flowing smoothly between the three of them. She'd started off by sharing details about what it had been like for her and Moira growing up in Dunbar. She'd listened intently as Luca described his latest attempts to teach Beau and Bruno a new set of tricks, assuring him that she couldn't wait to see them perform in person.

Eventually, she'd coaxed him into sharing some funny stories from his time in the Marine Corps. Shay loved her laughter when he talked about a few of the scrapes that he and Luca's father had gotten into during their various deployments together. It was as if she knew remembering the happy times with Kevin would soothe the pain Shay had been carrying around inside ever since the night he'd gotten the call.

But by the time the three of them finished dessert, his earlier case of nerves was back in full force. He'd made a promise that they could talk, and he meant to keep it. That didn't mean he was looking forward to it. After all, she and Shay had just come to a painful agreement to part ways. She had to be wondering what had changed in the interim. The fact that she was now seated across from him gave him some hope that he wasn't the only one with some major regrets about how that conversation had played out.

After he paid the check, he asked, "Would

you like to walk through town for a little while before we head back to Dunbar?"

She bit her lower lip and frowned. "Normally, I would love that, but I think we need somewhere more private to talk. How about we go back to my place?"

Turning to Luca, she asked, "Would you like to watch a movie in the living room while Shay and I have coffee in the kitchen?"

Luca nodded. "That sounds good. Can I choose?"

Shay ruffled the boy's hair. "Sure thing, kiddo."

Then he helped Carli with her shawl again and took her hand as they left the restaurant. They'd had to park a few blocks away and take a shuttle to the restaurant. The distance wasn't all that far. "We can wait for a shuttle or walk."

She gave his hand a soft squeeze. "Let's walk. That way we can still do some window-shopping along the way."

AN HOUR LATER, Carli led her two companions into her living room. She tossed her shawl on a nearby chair and kicked off her heels. "Luca, why don't you make yourself comfortable while I put on a movie for you."

He'd dozed off in the truck, and it was no surprise that he yawned sleepily as he curled up on the sofa. She was willing to bet that he'd fall back asleep within minutes of the movie starting. She hoped he did, because that would give her and Shay a little needed privacy for their discussion.

Shay must have been thinking along those same lines because he covered Luca up with the quilt she kept on the back of the sofa. Then he squatted down to talk to Luca. "Remember how I told you earlier that I had something I needed to discuss with Carli?"

"Yeah, you said it was grown-up stuff."

"That's true. It might take a little while, so sleep if you want to. I'll wake you when it's time to go home."

"Okay."

When Shay finally joined her in the kitchen, she smiled at him while she made coffee. "I meant to tell you earlier how handsome you both looked all dressed up in your suits tonight, but you can take off your tie and jacket if that would make you more comfortable."

When he immediately reached for the knot on his tie, she changed her mind. "But can I get one more picture first?"

She'd already snapped a couple of him and Luca earlier. They'd also asked their waiter to take one of the three of them at the restaurant. Now, though, she thought he might be blushing, but he didn't protest. A minute later, his jacket and tie landed on the kitchen counter. Then he took her hands in his, his mouth quirked up in a cautious smile.

"So about tonight. I want it to be the first of many."

Her pulse kicked into high gear. "But I thought you needed to focus on Luca."

"I did say that, but it was my fear talking. Remember when I told you about the night my little sister almost got hurt because of me?"

Carli nodded, hating that he still carried so much pain and guilt from that night. "You weren't that much older that she was, Shay. Your father was the one who really blew off his responsibilities that night. That your mom let her teenage son shoulder all the blame like that is inexcusable. I probably shouldn't say this, but they were both pretty poor excuses for parents. I'd love a chance to tell them that."

"Down, tiger." Shay pulled her closer to him as he continued, "But you're not wrong. There was plenty of blame to go around that night."

He pressed a kiss to her temple. "But the thing is that I've realized I've been using that whole mess as an excuse not to get seriously involved with anyone. You know, like a shield so I can't get hurt that badly again. Saying I only have room in my life to watch over Luca was just one more excuse. I've been running scared for too long, and I'm sorry I hurt you in the process."

She understood all too well how events of the past could cast shadows over the present. "You're not the only one living with emotional baggage, Shay. I have some serious trust issues even though I know not all men are like my ex-husband. Don't be so hard on yourself. Besides, you did have to find a new normal with Luca in your life."

Shay's smile turned a bit rueful. "Yeah, I have a lot on my plate these days, but so does everyone else. Just recently, a wise man pointed out to me that single parents find time to date, and married couples make time for each other. It might not always be easy, but it is possible and really important."

"And does this wise man happen to have a lot of tattoos and make great Dutch apple pie?"

"As a matter of fact he does."

"Did he have anything else to say?"

He captured her hand with his and held on tight. "Yeah, that he'd screwed up big-time about ten years ago. Evidently, he's tired of seeing his friends make their own huge mistakes when it comes to how they treat the women they love."

Wait—was he saying what she thought he was saying? The possibility had her pulse racing and made it difficult to draw a full breath. When he didn't continue, she whispered, "Shay?"

His breathing was a bit ragged when he finally continued. "There's so much I should have told you before now. You're beautiful, warm, kind and caring, and it's obvious that Luca already loves you. The thing is, he's not the only one. I love all of those things about you, too, and so many more."

Shay had been staring at their hands, but lifted his gaze to meet hers, his smile a bit crooked. "I'm hoping you'll find it in you to give me a chance to prove to you that you can trust me with your heart. That you, me and the kid can be a family. I won't try to rush you into anything or ask you for promises you're not ready to make. What do you say?"

This was terrifying, as if she were about to step off a cliff. But as she stared into Shay's eyes, a strange sense of calm washed over her, banishing her fear. Her heart somehow knew if she did take that leap of faith, Shay would be there to catch her. That was the kind of man he was and always would be.

She tugged her hands free of his and reached up to cup his face, loving the warmth of his skin against her palm. "You're strong, caring and everything I've ever wanted in a man. I love you, Shay Barnaby, and I want to build a life and a family with you and Luca. I will trust you with my heart if you will trust me with yours."

His answer was everything she could have hoped for. "It's already yours, babe."

Then he kissed her, stealing her breath and healing her wounded heart. When they finally came up for air, she asked, "What should we tell Luca?"

"That he's going to be my best man when I can convince you to set the date."

He offered her a crooked smile. "That is if you're willing to marry me. How about it?"

"I'd love to."

In fact, she couldn't wait to see the two men in her life waiting for her at the front of the church, dressed in matching tuxedoes. "I'll call the pastor in the morning."

"Perfect. Tell him the sooner the better."

She arched an eyebrow. "In a hurry, are you?"

"Heck, yeah. I want our future together to start as soon as possible."

"Me, too."

Then Shay enfolded her within the gentle strength of his arms, holding her close as they kissed to seal the deal.

* * * * *

Be sure to look for The Firefighter Next Door,
the next book in the
Heroes of Dunbar Mountain series
by Alexis Morgan, available April 1, 2025!